Unanimous Raves for Peter

L'Assassin

"A talented writer . . . Steiner keeps us fully engaged [and] guessing. A wonderfully vivid book about the solitary, sometimes bitter landscape of spycraft. It's a slam dunk!" —*The Washington Times*

"Unusual . . . generates the building tension associated with such classic international thrillers as *The Day of the Jackal*. Add to that a handful of richly drawn characters, and you have a novel with appeal for both political-thriller fans and anyone who enjoys international fiction." —*Booklist*

"A fresh perspective on the international thriller. Louis Morgan, his retired-agent protagonist, is a marvel, mixing a fierce intelligence with moral complexity. Cool writing, political machinations, exotic locales, and a plot that keeps you guessing until the end make *L'Assassin* a wonderful read. I look forward to more from Peter Steiner."
—Olen Steinhauer, bestselling author of *The Tourist*

"A pacy, engrossing thriller that is also a touching examination of the impact of terrorism and counterterrorism on the lives of those involved." —Robert Goddard, author of *Into the Blue*

"Packed with quirky surprises. Think of the twisty plot as a MacGuffin for a series of sublimely observed scenes." —*Kirkus Reviews*

Le Crime
(formerly titled *A French Country Murder*)

"Unforgettable . . . combines elements of Agatha Christie and Robert Ludlum." —*Bookreporter.com*

"A fantastic novel, at once a gripping political thriller and a complex mystery tale. A wise and penetrating look at ambition, duty, and lost illusions. Peter Steiner superbly evokes France, Washington, and international relations. It's rewarding on every level."

—David Brooks, author of *Bobos in Paradise*

"Le Carré and Deighton fans will welcome Steiner's engaging first novel. The scenes in small-town France capture the atmosphere and pace of life there wonderfully." —*Publishers Weekly*

"A page-turner—like a good Alan Furst or Graham Greene novel."

—*The Washingtonian*

"A rare phenomenon, a beautiful crime novel. When I realized what it was, I read it more slowly to make it last."

—Thomas Perry, *New York Times* bestselling author of *Nightlife*

"A riveting murder mystery." —*France Today*

"Morgon is a fascinating character . . . Steiner sketches such a rich life for his tiny town that he makes you want to forgive Jacques Chirac all his sins and get on the next plane." —*Chicago Tribune*

"Captivating . . . This is a novel for anyone who enjoys good writing, not just those who love a good mystery. Readers will find it difficult to concentrate on anything but finishing it. Then the tale will linger long after the last page is turned." —*The Tampa Tribune-Times*

"*Le Crime* est superbe." —Jim Fusilli, author of *Hard, Hard City*

L'ASSASSIN

Also by Peter Steiner

A French Country Murder
(available in trade paperback as *Le Crime*)

L'ASSASSIN

Peter Steiner

Minotaur Books  New York

This is a work of fiction. All of the characters, organizations, and events portrayed in this novel are either products of the author's imagination or are used fictitiously.

A THOMAS DUNNE BOOK FOR MINOTAUR BOOKS.
An imprint of St. Martin's Publishing Group.

www.thomasdunnebooks.com
www.minotaurbooks.com

The Library of Congress has catalogued the hardcover edition as follows:

Steiner, Peter, 1940–
L'assassin / Peter Steiner.—1st ed.
p. cm.
ISBN-13: 978-0-312-37342-9
ISBN-10: 0-312-37342-2
1. Americans—France—Fiction. 2. Police—France—Fiction. 3. Country life—Fiction. 4. France—Fiction. I. Title.

PS3619.T4763 A93 2008
813'.6—dc22

2008012475

ISBN-13: 978-0-312-37343-6 (pbk.)
ISBN-10: 0-312-37343-0 (pbk.)

First Minotaur Books Paperback Edition: July 2009

10 9 8 7 6 5 4 3 2 1

For Jane

1

It looked like a simple burglary at first. In fact, as crimes go, the robbery of Louis Morgon's house in the village of Saint Leon sur Dême seemed noteworthy only for its ineptitude. The burglar, a small-time criminal known to French police as Pierre Lefort, came to the house in broad daylight and broke a window to let himself in. He poked around the house for a while, and then he cut the lock on the barn, where Louis had his painting studio, and went in.

A short while later he loaded up his loot and left. The old car backfired as Lefort drove down the steep driveway and turned onto the lane. Solesme Lefourier was pruning her roses, and she paused to look as he passed. The handle of Louis's lawnmower bobbed and waved from Lefort's open trunk like a semaphore.

Solesme's eyes were failing because of her illness, so she could not read the license plate, but she got a good look at the car and the driver. She went inside and called the police, which in Saint Leon meant Jean Renard. He was wrestling with some overdue reports and was relieved to hear the phone ring. "Renard, you better come," said Solesme. "I think Louis's house has just been robbed."

Louis had returned home by the time Renard got there, and Solesme had flagged him down and told him what had happened. Louis was going through the house to see what might have been stolen, while Solesme sat outside at the table under the linden tree. Renard joined Louis inside. He wrote an inventory of what was missing, but as far as Louis could tell, nothing much had been taken.

Louis seemed disappointed, as though he had mainly been robbed of a bit of excitement. "It was a pathetic effort on the thief's part," he said. "Besides the lawnmower, which would barely start, the guy took some screwdrivers, an electric drill, and a couple of sweaters. I'm always glad to see you, Jean," he said to the policeman, "but I'm sorry you had to come out for *this*."

"Worst of all," said the policeman, "it means writing another report."

Renard went back outside and pulled two chairs up beside Solesme while Louis heated water. The air was heavy with the perfume of linden blossoms, and the three friends sat sipping tea and listening to the bees at work just above their heads in the sullen afternoon air.

When Solesme saw Louis looking at her in that way he sometimes had now, she waved her hand as though a bee had flown too close to her face.

Renard pushed his chair away from the table. "I have to get back," he said, and stood to drink his last sip.

Once the policeman was gone, Louis said, "So, what did he say?"

"Who?" said Solesme.

"Who. Bertrand, of course."

"Bertrand! He's just guessing. What does he know? They're all just guessing."

"He's your doctor," said Louis. "So tell me: what did he say?"

"He said it has spread," said Solesme. "It is in my bones. But still, even with all his tests, what does he really know?"

"He's your doctor," said Louis, sounding helpless this time.

Louis had expected this news, but he was not ready for it. He stood, but he did not come around the table to her, as she feared he might. The last thing she wanted right now was his comfort.

"I'm just going to look at the garden," he said, and took a few steps in that direction. Solesme stood up to go with him. Her spine was deformed—it had been since birth—which caused her to shift her body oddly as she rose, projecting her right shoulder forward and rising under it. She had the same slight twisting motion in her walk. To Louis she always seemed to be dancing. It was a subtle and odd dance, but he still found it mesmerizing, as he had from the first time they had met.

Thirty years ago he had just arrived in Saint Leon for the first time. It was the summer solstice, the night of music. All over France cities and towns stationed orchestras and bands and choirs in their streets, and music filled the night. The town square in Saint Leon had been decorated with colored lights and cleared of cars. A small stage had been erected.

Louis had not planned to stay the night, but the Chalfonts, who ran the hotel, had insisted he be their guest. Chalfont leaned close to him and spoke in a conspiratorial whisper. "This night is not to be missed, monsieur," he said. Then the music began to play and the entire village rose to dance. The spectacle swept over Louis and somehow, in a way he did not understand that seemed—though he certainly did not believe in magic—to be magical, transported him out of his unhappiness.

As it happened, later in the evening Louis was seated next to Solesme, and, though it was not something he would normally have done, he invited her, a complete stranger, to dance. He had always found dancing to be dangerous somehow—its sexuality was so public, but he invited her nonetheless.

Solesme stood up in that peculiar way of hers. "Oh, madame, I am sorry," Louis said in his awkward French. "I did not know. Please forgive me."

"But I love to dance," said Solesme with raised eyebrows and a charming smile, and held out her hand to him. The gypsy musicians played and sang plaintive waltzes, and Louis and Solesme danced around and around the square, caught up in the swirling throng.

The next day Louis continued on his journey, but afterwards he was drawn back to Saint Leon, and not only because of that evening. The town was small, and out of the way, and ordinary. It suited him—someone who wanted to disappear and begin life anew—perfectly. He bought the house and the barn at the top of the hill. He cleaned out the barn and made it into a painting studio, although he had never painted before. He planted a large vegetable garden and flowers and shrubs, although the only gardening he had ever done had been to push a lawnmower back and forth around his yard in Virginia.

Louis and Solesme had now been lovers for most of those thirty years. It was not surprising, therefore, that he did not give the burglary as much thought as he might have. Her illness terrified him. However, the burglar, Pierre Lefort, seemed determined that Louis should not forget his handiwork. The day after the burglary, while Louis was in the market picking out a fish for supper, he saw a man—Pierre Lefort—walking across the square wearing his sweater.

"You won't believe it," he said as he burst through the door of Renard's office. "I just saw the thief."

"What?!" said Renard.

"The burglar," said Louis, "the man who robbed my house. I just saw him. He fits Solesme's description, and he's wearing my sweater."

By the time Louis and Renard rushed outside, the man was no longer in the square. They walked through the side streets. "How do you know it's your sweater?" said Renard. They found Lefort behind the post office wearing a vivid, blue and yellow striped sweater, too short in the body and too long in the arms. He was getting into the car Solesme had described. Renard confronted him and placed him under arrest.

Pierre Lefort appeared before a judge in Tours. He was convicted of burglary and was sentenced to serve a year in the Granville prison. Louis repaired the broken window, replaced the padlock on the barn door with a new, sturdier one, and forgot about the robbery.

Dr. Mauricio Bertrand, the oncologist, had been unsparing in describing for Solesme the likely course of her cancer, how it had moved from her bones to her organs, and how it would eventually spread into her brain. "There is nothing more we can do," he said finally. "We can, however, keep you comfortable until the end."

"And when is the end?" Solesme wanted to know.

"It is only a guess," said Dr. Bertrand, shrugging, "but judging from the scans, I would say two months, three at the most."

Solesme was resigned to her illness and to her death, but Louis was not. "It is something we all have to do," she said. "Even you." But the thought of having only three months weighed heavily on him. Ninety days. "It is only a number," said Solesme, "and it is only Bertrand's number. It will come when it comes."

Louis dredged the fish in cornmeal and rosemary and put it on the fire. The air grew fragrant with burning rosemary. After eating, they watched a movie together, a funny thing called *Les Visiteurs.* They had both seen it before, but they laughed and laughed all over again. Then they sat down together to read.

"I'm going," said Louis suddenly. He stood and went to the door. Solesme did not try to stop him. He left without looking at her and trudged up the steep driveway to his house. The smell of rosemary hung in the air, like a promise, or a memory. He wanted to weep. How could Bertrand be correct? Solesme seemed fine. She still accompanied him on long walks across the valley. And just last week they had spent the entire afternoon visiting museums and galleries in Tours. They had even returned to several galleries because she had insisted on buying him a small pencil drawing that he had admired, and he could not remember which gallery it had been in.

But now a number had been named. And the limit on their time had become specific and severe. It forced its way into his consciousness again and again, and sometimes—like now—it became all but unbearable. Time was now unimaginably precious. And yet, at the same time, he felt as though he might suffocate in her presence. In his mind he could not separate Solesme from her death. How dare she be dying?

Louis lay in his bed listening to the church bell. Four o'clock. He had heard every hour and every half hour through the night. Louis thought about death, the utter absurdity and the complete power of it. He gave death a face in his half-awake mind, and it came up looking like Hugh Bowes: nearsighted, pallid, fat, and dangerous. Louis had not thought of Hugh for a long time, and suddenly there he was, looming in his mind's eye like the moon.

In his first life Louis had gone straight from graduate school to the United States Department of State and the CIA at Hugh Bowes's urging. And, thanks to Hugh's encouragement and support, he had risen rapidly through the ranks. He was married, had two small children, and everything was on track for a brilliant future. Then, one day, he was called before the secretary of state and accused of serious malfeasance. Carefully constructed evidence was produced, and, though the charges and evidence were false, Louis was summarily dismissed. As so often happens, one catastrophe led to the next. He was estranged from his wife and children, his marriage ended, and he found himself alone and lost.

It was a long time before Louis realized that it was Hugh, his mentor and patron, who had engineered his destruction. Louis tried to understand Hugh's hatred but could not. He wallowed in his own misery for a while, but eventually the entire episode mutated in his mind into a set of philosophical questions about truth, about justice, about the human soul, about evil. It was rich material, and he ruminated on it for years after his dismissal, but slowly these ruminations subsided too. Louis came to Saint Leon sur Dême and found a sort of peace.

Once, just a few years ago, Hugh Bowes had inexplicably tried to destroy Louis all over again. Hugh had become the secretary of state by then. Louis was shocked by Hugh's continued enmity even after all this time. But again, despite the lethal nature of Hugh's efforts, things had turned out well enough for Louis, and so he let this episode disappear into the recesses of his mind, as the earlier one had. For Louis, as long as it remained in his past where it belonged, it was of little concern or interest.

Louis was startled out of his reverie by the clock ringing five. It was still dark, with only the first light showing, but he got out of bed anyway. He dressed and stepped into his leather boots without turning on the light. He pulled the laces tight and tied double knots. The first band of light in the east broadened, and the sparrows began chattering and rattling about under the eaves.

In the kitchen he toasted two pieces of baguette and slathered them with butter and marmalade. He sat at one end of the long table, his elbows on the checkered oilcloth, and sipped from a bowl of *café au lait*. He watched his reflection in the window. The glass twisted his features in strange and alarming ways. But as the light rose outside, the linden tree and the barn came into view through the glass. His reflection disappeared and with it his uneasiness.

Louis got out his knapsack and stuffed it with a few clothes, a drawing pad, and a book. By the time he opened the barn door and pulled the old Peugeot to the top of the driveway, the sun had risen, and all that remained of the night was a lingering coolness. He stopped the car and looked out across the garden and into the fields beyond. The freshly turned soil went from black to purple to golden. The sun rose above the laurel hedge and cast the car's elongated shadow the entire length of the garden and into the plum trees. Louis saw his own shadow inside the car's shadow and raised his hand and watched his shadow wave back. *I'm still here,* he thought. The sun rose higher and found the roses, one by one, and the tomato plants with their tiny green fruits and the carefully tended beans and beets and lettuce.

Even as he was greedy to escape, he was reluctant to do so.

He got out of the car again and stood in the morning sun. *I am being stupid,* he thought. *I am afraid of shadows. I am frightened of death. Of hers and of mine.* He had said more or less the same thing to Renard a few days earlier, although he had left out the particulars. "I am frightened," he had said, "and I don't like being frightened. I am not used to being frightened." Renard was not used to hearing confessions of this sort from his friend and could not think of anything to say.

Louis released the hand brake, coasted down the drive, and turned onto the narrow lane. He coasted past Solesme's house so she would not hear the engine. He knew, though, that she would hear him anyway. He tried not to look, in case she might be watching from the window. He could not bear to think of life without her, and of course he could think of nothing else. He remembered their entire time together, all at once, in one long endless moment, as though he were drowning.

It had rained the night before, and puddles in the road reflected the brilliant morning sky. At the corner, Louis turned toward Marçon. The narrow road wound through fields of wheat and sunflowers, along pastures where Holstein cattle grazed, past the mill owned by the Belgians, past the small vineyard they had planted. In Marçon he carefully nosed the car out of the narrow lane and turned toward Flée. He got stuck behind a tractor, but eventually the farmer pulled as far off the road as he could manage and waved Louis by. Louis drove past farms and through forgotten villages as though he were alone in the world, away from death and inept burglaries. Only when he entered the city of Le Mans did he find himself caught up in the rush of morning traffic. Inexplicably he felt relieved to be among people.

He left the Peugeot in the car park, bought a ticket for Quimper, punched his ticket in the orange machine, and went to the platform to wait. The fast train from Paris to Quimper raced into the station, and Louis got on board and found his seat by the window. He pulled the book from his knapsack, but it remained on his lap while he watched the landscape fly past, like a sped-up movie, like a sped-up life. Wires swooped exuberantly above the fields, cows grazed for an instant, villages appeared and disappeared in a flash. The gray, granite city of Laval came and went in a matter of seconds. He wanted it all to slow down, to give him time to catch his breath and to understand what he was seeing, but it would not. Then the landscape flattened out, and before long the train slowed and they arrived in Quimper, the capital of that region of Brittany known as the Finistère.

The Finistère, le Finistère, is the westernmost part of France, a thick finger of land in the north just below the English Channel which reaches far into the ocean and toward the New World. Surrounded as it is by the cold waters of the Atlantic, it is a windswept and bitter landscape, buffeted by frequent storms. Its people have long been cut off from the rest of France by geography, by their culture, and by their language, and consequently they are tough and solitary and self-reliant. Their flag is black and white.

It struck Louis as fitting that the defiant Bretons would have a flag without color. During the time of Caesar, the Roman soldiers stationed in those far reaches had found life here to be utterly lonely and desolate. It was beautiful in its way, but it was a world too far from gentle Italy, so they called it *finis terrae*, which in Latin means the end of the earth.

Louis left the Quimper train station and boarded a waiting bus whose sign indicated it would be going to the Pointe du Raz, which was the westernmost point of the Finistère, in essence the *end* of the end of the earth. He wondered whether it was far enough. He paid the driver and took a seat by the front door. After a few minutes the driver tugged on a long handle and closed the door, and, with a gaseous groan, the bus backed up and lumbered out of the station and out of town.

They stopped at a crossroads, and a band of chattering children climbed on. The children showed the driver their passes and rushed past Louis, pushing and jostling to find seats. The bus followed a curving highway over small hills, stopping at various crossroads to take on more children, until it was rocked with shouts and laughter. Finally they stopped in front of a school, and all the children spilled out into the playground, as though someone had pulled the cork out of a bottle, and it was silent again.

By the time they reached the last stop, Louis was the only passenger. He got off and found himself standing at the edge of a gravel parking lot facing the black-and-white lighthouse at the Pointe du Raz. Beyond the light lay the vast gray ocean. Louis walked along a stony path until he could go no further. The rocky coast fell away in front of him, and the gray surf crashed against it, sending up clouds of spray. Gulls rose on the wind and darted about above him. The salt air stung his eyes. He squinted hard across the sea, as though he might actually be able to see the silhouette of the American continent on the horizon.

Then he turned and began walking southeast along the cliffs. Louis had a surprisingly long and confident stride for someone his age—he was sixty-seven—and he walked with great energy and purpose, as though he were on an urgent errand, which, in a sense, he was. It looked like he was being held back by an invisible hand and as if he might broaden his step even further and go even faster if only he were allowed to do so.

Farm fields and pastures came right up to the trail at the edge of the cliff, and cows raised their heads and gazed after him as he passed. They strained against their fences, as though they might like to join him. Larks fluttered up from the grass and hovered high above, calling out their lovely alarm. The ocean drove against the cliffs, and Louis puffed out his cheeks and then took deep breaths as he walked, in order to take in the briny smell. The churning water went from gray to blue and back to gray again as an endless procession of small clouds moved swiftly across the sun.

Thirty years earlier, the first time Louis came to France, it had been to cross the country on foot like a medieval penitent, even though he did not quite know the reason for his penitence. That was when he had spent that solstice night in Saint Leon. And since that time, walking had become his refuge. It was the best way he knew to manage things that could not actually be managed, like his disintegrating marriage and career back then, like Hugh Bowes's enmity, like Solesme's illness now. He had discovered that, in the course of putting one foot in front of the other day after day, he was able to sort things out and find their meaning. And if not their meaning, then their undeniable reality. Things—the difficult and even the impossible—settled into place and became part of life's landscape.

Louis followed the coastal trail past whitewashed cottages, along snug, walled fields, through villages, and around little harbors where boats bobbed and creaked, their loose rigging clattering against their masts. Gulls wheeled and dove above each harbor, their cries urgently announcing his arrival. After several hours he stopped and sat on a bluff above a horseshoe-shaped harbor. The tide was retreating and boats sat on the ground while gulls picked through great mounds of seaweed. Louis cut slices of Mimolette onto pieces of baguette. He took a bite of the bread and cheese and then a bite from a tart apple. He grew restless, and after a short time he set off again.

Toward the end of that first day of walking, the cliffs gave way to beaches. Louis took a front room at the Hôtel des Voyageurs, which sat directly on the beach facing a broad, sandy bay. After a hot bath he sat on the terrace and gazed at the sea, or rather at the sand flats where the sea had been. The sun dropped behind a bank of blue clouds, and the day ended with the light being sucked from the sky. The proprietor turned on the strings of little lights that hung every which way above the terrace. He brought a pitcher of cider and a platter of *galettes*—buckwheat crepes—still steaming and awash with tiny scallops and clams in garlic butter. Louis was hungry, and he ate until there was nothing left on his plate. Then he mopped up the last drops of sauce with a piece of bread.

The evening grew cooler, and Louis pulled his jacket more tightly around him. He took two wedges of cheese from the platter, and then ordered a *crème caramel,* which he pronounced delicious.

"*Merci, monsieur,*" said the proprietor, who was also the chef. "It is my speciality."

Louis left the window in his room wide open, and the chilly night air poured in, bringing with it the smell and sounds of the sea. The moon rose in front of him, climbed straight up the center of the window, and disappeared above him, leaving behind bright blocks of light on the floor. The curtains swayed and rustled. The surf grew quieter as the tide receded.

Louis lay with his hands behind his head. The cold air on his arms felt good. His book lay unopened beside him. He fell asleep to the mournful melody of the distant surf. He had a dream in which dark, massive heads with slit-eyes bobbed about in a murky ocean. He awoke with a start, but the world was dark and silent.

The next day, Wednesday, broke sunny and warm. The tide

was in, crashing noisily on the sand a hundred meters from the hotel terrace. Louis ate a quick breakfast and set out on his way. He was impatient. He walked all day, leaving one beach, climbing dunes and bluffs, descending to the next beach, crossing it, then climbing again, walking as though he had no choice, as though geography were destiny. He peered out at the sea, waiting for something to arrive, but nothing did. He sat in the shade of a tree and ate the last of the Mimolette and an apple. The day was hot, and he drank two bottles of water. He stopped for the night at another small hotel, this one a slight distance inland.

Celtic dance music was playing on the kitchen radio while Louis waited for dinner. A small three-legged dog hobbled in and out of the dining room, as if to check on him. The dog did not beg for food, but rather sat with his back to Louis and faced in the direction of the sea. "He used to go fishing with me," explained the proprietor. "He misses it." Louis patted the dog's head and the dog leaned his small body against him.

On Thursday morning Louis stepped onto the vast beach that runs in one continuous eighteen-kilometer swath all the way from Kerdor to Saint Guénache. He stood atop the tall, grassy dunes and looked out onto the great expanse spread before him like a gigantic amphitheater. The beach beckoned and then disappeared into the distant haze. The roar of the distant ocean was all but swallowed up by the huge openness of the place. The sky was clear and pale blue above him and went to white where it met the water. Puffy clouds receded into the distance.

During the Second World War the German high command had believed that the Allies would try to land on the broad, flat beaches of the Finistère, and most particularly on this beach by Saint Guénache. In anticipation of the invasion, the Germans had built great defensive fortresses along the shore. You could still see the ruins of their railroads and their sprawling concrete weapons depots and fortifications behind the dunes. And all along the beach, in front of the dunes at indeterminate intervals, there stood round concrete bunkers. The huge bunkers tilted this way and that, as a result of repeated efforts to dismantle them, and sixty years of buffeting by powerful tides and weather and shifting sand. But they remained in place, like gigantic old men, disquieting, slightly menacing even, the heads in Louis's dream, staring out to sea through their slits, and waiting for the invasion that would never come.

Far to the south Louis could see a solitary figure. The man—Louis thought it must be a man—appeared to be walking in his direction, although he was too far away for Louis to be sure. The tide was out; the beach sloped imperceptibly toward the distant water. If you wanted to swim here—and Louis was suddenly overtaken with the desire to do so—it would take a good while, even walking as briskly as Louis did, to reach the water's edge, then a while longer of wading to reach water that was deep enough to swim in.

Because of these distances and the extremes of the tides, these were dangerous waters. When the tide turned and started coming in, the ocean rushed across the flat beach, consuming it in great gulps, two, five, even ten meters at a time. The beach rose but then fell also as it approached shore, and when the water found one of these dips, a great, apparently flat expanse of beach could fill with surging water in just moments. If you were unfamiliar with the tides of this corner of the Finistère, as most visitors were, you might easily find yourself running toward the dunes with the entire ocean in full pursuit.

By the time the tide was at its highest point, ponds and inlets had formed, even behind the dunes, and the entire beach had disappeared beneath churning water. The ocean swirled and foamed, as though an enormous dam had given way.

Of course Louis had consulted the tide tables—they were posted in every hotel along with warning notices—and he had set out this morning in plenty of time so that he could safely pass the ponds and inlets and bogs while the tide was out. He checked his watch and found that there was time to spare. The tide was still on its way out. The beach was glorious, and the water sparkled in the distance.

It took a good fifteen minutes for Louis to walk to the water's edge. He took off his pack. His back was wet with sweat. He peeled off his clothes and walked into the cold water. He waded across the fine sand for a few hundred meters until the water was above his knees, deep enough, that is, for him to lie down on his back and float. Looking back toward the dunes, Louis could only just see the small bundle of clothes he had left behind. The dunes themselves were more than a thousand meters away.

Louis lowered himself into the shallow water and turned onto his back. The surf rocked him gently. His feet dragged lazily on the sand beneath him. "I could never float," he said aloud. His ears were beneath the surface of the water, so that he heard his own voice strangely distorted and resonating in his head. He heard the great whispering hum of the ocean and felt the light slap of the waves on his arms and thighs. And yet, in what he had hoped would be a moment of great tranquillity and sublime forgetfulness, fear rose inside him like a huge, dark sea creature. A premonition that had been gathering inside his brain struck him with near physical force. "My God!" he said. "Hugh Bowes means to kill me."

Louis dropped his feet to the sand and stood up so quickly that he almost fell over. *Hugh Bowes means to kill me.* The thought was preposterous and entirely unexpected, and yet it seemed to Louis to become more certain with each repetition. *How could I have been so foolish as to think otherwise? He has always meant to kill me.* This was true. Hugh's hatred of Louis was as profound and undeniable as it was unfathomable and absurd.

Louis hurried to his clothes. The solitary person he had seen earlier had disappeared. Where could he have gone? Louis dressed quickly, fearing his own nakedness, fearing the fact that he was entirely alone on this immense beach.

Louis leaned into the wind and hurried toward the dunes. Hugh Bowes had twice tried to destroy Louis's life. There had never been any apparent motive or reason. Bowes's enmity had been like a force of nature, like wind or tide or whatever other destructive force you could think of. *How,* Louis wondered, *could I have let myself believe it was over? Someone of Bowes's power and temperament, a driven man like him, doesn't give up. Why would he? Why should he? He's a malignant human being with almost limitless power. And the means—he has the means. And time is on his side.* Everything *is on his side.*

"My God," said Louis, stopping in his tracks. "It was the burglary! It was the burglary! Of course! How could I have missed it?" Hearing his own voice startled him, and yet its sound was lost in the vast emptiness around him.

Hugh's most recent effort, the episode of just a few years back, had happened this way. Hugh had murdered a man in France, or rather he had arranged for it to be done, and had then, as a sinister prank, arranged for the dead man's body to be deposited on Louis's doorstep. He had meant to intimidate Louis, then to toy with him, and then, perhaps, eventually to do away with him. But to Hugh's surprise and chagrin, Louis had, in defending himself, come perilously close to exposing him and had even managed to make a tape recording of Hugh—Secretary of State Hugh Bowes—incriminating himself. And so Hugh had been forced to withdraw from the battle, held in check, or so Louis had allowed himself to hope. *How could I have?* He walked even faster.

Louis found a pay telephone outside the post office in the first village he came to. Renard could hear seagulls in the background. "Hugh Bowes," said Louis. "I don't know how I could have missed it. The burglary was orchestrated by Hugh Bowes."

"Hugh Bowes? *What* burglary?" the policeman wanted to know. "*That* burglary? You said so yourself back then: it was a small thing and the thief was a moron."

"He was *too* inept," said Louis. "His ineptitude was on purpose. He was *supposed* to get caught. It was Hugh Bowes setting things up, setting things in motion. I don't know how I missed it."

"What a ridiculous idea," said Renard.

"I know," said Louis. "That is part of what makes it so beguiling."

"If you start to think that way . . . ," said Renard. But he sighed and left the thought unfinished. "We have Bowes on tape threatening you . . ."

"The tape. My God, *the tape*!" said Louis.

"What about the tape?" said Renard, but Louis had already hung up the phone.

11

Louis left the car in his driveway and ran straight to the bedroom. The tape was still at the back of the dresser drawer where he kept his sweaters. He put it in the cassette player and pressed the PLAY button, but he heard only the whirring sound of the machine. He pressed the FAST-FORWARD button, then STOP, then PLAY and again there was only the sound of the machine. The angry voice of Hugh Bowes was missing. The evidence of his malignant plot was gone. There was nothing recorded on this tape.

"The thief is not such a moron after all," said Louis. He was sitting with Renard on the terrace in front of the Hôtel de France. "I'm the moron. He even wore my sweater to taunt me, to flaunt what he had done. What's his name again?"

"To *taunt* you?" said Renard, looking amazed.

"It's where I hid the tape. With the sweaters. What's his name?"

Renard shook his head. He paused to decide how much he could tell Louis. Finally he said, "His name is Lefort, Pierre. He's a career criminal. Small stuff. Burglary, some drugs. He's been in and out of jail a lot. And you think this 'master criminal' was working for Bowes? That the burglary was a search for the tape?"

The sun shone brilliantly and Louis had pulled his straw hat down so far that his face was all but invisible to the policeman. A chilly wind rattled the colorful umbrella, rocking it back and forth on its stand. Louis cupped his hands so Renard could light his cigarette. "And why—I have to ask you this," Renard said, blowing out a cloud of smoke, "why did you keep the tape in your dresser drawer, when it was the *only* evidence you have against Bowes, where even a moron like Lefort would find it? You the 'master spy'?"

"*Former* master spy," said Louis without smiling.

"That was not brilliant. You have to admit that much."

Louis admitted nothing. "There are other copies," he said. "You have one. I have several."

"But now," said Renard, "he knows what's on the tape. Or rather he knows what's *not* on the tape. And, as I recall, there's not much on the tape."

"That is unfortunate," said Louis. "That he knows, I mean." Then: "Can I get in to speak to him? What's the procedure to do that? Can you help me get in to see him?" Louis took off his hat and ran his hand through his hair.

Renard stared at his friend. *Louis is an old man,* he thought. *Which means I will soon be an old man.* "To speak to . . . ?"

"Lefort," said Louis. "You know who I mean."

"No," said Renard. "You *cannot* get in to see him. And even if I could help you get in to see him, I wouldn't do it."

Louis shrugged and put his hat back on his head. "Fine," he said. "Then I'll have to manage on my own." *Now* he smiled.

"Are you sure you want to do that?" said Renard. "If you're right, which is . . ." Once again he did not finish the thought. In the world of espionage and intrigue that Louis had once inhabited, marvelous schemes were regularly hatched, fantastic crimes were routinely committed, and the preposterous—the word Renard had almost spoken—was thought to be entirely normal. As young men, Louis and Hugh Bowes had engaged in . . . who knew what? Louis had somehow mortally offended Bowes, and it had cost him his career and more. Renard could not imagine half of what went on in that world, and he had decided long ago it was better not to try.

"And yet," said Renard, "Hugh Bowes is the American secretary of state."

"Was," said Louis. In fact, Louis's unmasking of Hugh's murderous intentions had been instrumental in Hugh's decision to retire. "His high office means nothing, except that he feels above questions of right and wrong, and above the law."

Renard found Louis's cynicism frightening. But sometimes he tried to think like Louis did, stacking suspicion upon suspicion, and question upon question, until the entire hypothetical construction seemed in imminent danger of collapsing in on itself. "If you talk to the guy, to Lefort, then you would be telling Bowes that you know what he knows, wouldn't you?"

Louis smiled at Renard. "I'll be telling him what I know," he said. "But there's also the chance that I will be telling him that I know something which in fact I don't know. And besides," he added quickly, realizing that he was on thin hypothetical ice, "I might actually learn something from this Lefort."

"Such as?" said the policeman.

Instead of answering right away, Louis rose from the little table where they had been sitting. He closed his eyes and remembered how the entire business had begun the last time, with the body on his doorstep. "Do you remember?" he said finally. "At first we thought the dead man was African. We thought so because he had an African skullcap on his head. But he wasn't African, as it turned out; we were just supposed to *think* he was African. I wonder what I'm thinking now that isn't true. Something that I am just *supposed* to be thinking.

"Just imagine, Renard." Louis turned back to face the policeman. "We're looking for something that may not even exist within the realm of our perception, at least not yet. We may be searching for a crime that may not even have been committed yet, that may never be committed, but that could, in some sense, still exist." Louis was excited by the prospect. "We're like astronomers looking for something in outer space where there appears to be nothing at all. The radio waves are compressed, or light bends slightly in a suggestive way, but the telescopes reveal nothing. We need very fine instruments—exquisite instruments!—of detection to sort this out."

Renard said nothing.

"So let's see what we've got," said Louis, forging ahead. "Lefort took the tape and left a blank one. But there's more to it than just the tape, just like there was more than the sweater. There has to be. And more than the implied threat too. If it's Bowes at work here, and if he has set something in motion, the trick is to figure out what it is."

Renard remained seated and examined his cigarette. "I am not an astronomer," he growled with a great exhalation of smoke. "I am not like one of your astronomers. I am a village policeman." He did not like these philosophical disquisitions, and he was not fond of Louis's premonitions or speculations either. And yet, suddenly—he did not know why—Renard felt a great sadness come over him, as though there had been an imperceptible shift in fate's weather. He had the sense—entirely new for him—that something impossibly terrible was about to occur, and he had no way to prevent it.

He turned away, so that Louis would not see his face, and looked across the square at the townspeople talking, walking, carrying their groceries, stepping into and out of their cars. Denis Martel, in his fluorescent green vest, had swept a small pile of debris together and was carefully coaxing it onto the dustpan he would then empty into his cart. Renard envied Denis. If only it were that easy.

Renard looked at the hills above town, toward the cemetery, just where Louis had been looking a moment earlier. Fields of sunflowers nodded in vanishing rows. Last year there had been wheat planted there. He could not remember what had been there the year before last. The fields of sunflowers rose and disappeared over the hill in a shimmering golden haze that seemed to resemble nothing so much as oblivion. After a long time, Renard said, "It was sunflowers then too, wasn't it?" In the end, Renard gave Louis a letter of introduction on official stationery to send to the warden of the Granville prison along with his own.

The village of Granville is just off the Paris *autoroute,* some fifty kilometers northeast of Le Mans, about an hour by car from Saint Leon sur Dême. The prison stands just at the edge of town, surrounded by wheat fields. The wheat had already been cut this year, and its straw had been bound into square bales that stood in rows in the stubble, waiting to be loaded onto a wagon and taken away like so many prisoners.

The Granville prison had been built in the nineteenth century on the site of a medieval chateau that had burned many years earlier and had then been razed. The "new" building had tall, windowless walls of pink granite. Its proportions were so graceful that Louis was compelled to stand for a moment and admire it. Even its entry, where so many men had surrendered their freedom, was elegant and almost welcoming.

Louis knocked, as the paper notice tacked to the door instructed visitors to do. The door was opened immediately by a uniformed porter, a small, graying man who looked more like a schoolteacher than a prison guard. "Monsieur?" he said. Louis introduced himself and presented the letter he had received from the warden. The porter studied it for a moment, then escorted Louis through a narrow hallway to a brightly lit room. Louis was interviewed there by a second man in uniform.

"Pierre Lefort is . . . ?"

"The man who robbed my house," which is what Louis had written in his letter to the warden. "Certain keepsakes of mine are missing. They are precious to me. I was hoping I could persuade him to tell me where they are. I have some experience in such matters."

"Experience? In interrogation?"

"Yes," said Louis. "That is all I am permitted to say."

Louis's response was noted down by the guard. He wrote unhurriedly in a careful, round hand, his pointed tongue sliding about between his lips as he wrote. He read over what he had written, and only then did he pose the next question.

After the questions were finished Louis was made to stand with his legs spread and his arms raised. "I am sorry, monsieur, but it is part of the routine."

"Of course," said Louis. He was patted down by a third man while the porter and the guard who had interviewed him stood against the wall in a respectful pose of attention, their feet together and their arms at their sides. Even though they had witnessed this procedure many times, they were still made uncomfortable by it. It seemed particularly unseemly to them to show this kind of disrespect to a man of Louis's years.

Louis was required to sign several forms, including one that contained his responses to the questions he had been asked. Then he was instructed to sit down and was left alone in the room. After a short while the third guard returned. "Monsieur, follow me please," he said. "Are you a relation of Pierre Lefort?" The guard spoke casually as they walked, as though he were just making conversation. Everything seemed to change in prison, including the meaning of words.

"You could say that I am," said Louis. "In a manner of speaking."

The guard continued walking. He did not turn toward Louis or indicate in any way that Louis's answer had been impertinent or mysterious or otherwise noteworthy. "Have a seat, monsieur," he said, and Louis again found himself alone on a hard metal chair in a brightly lit room.

This room was small and there were no windows. Louis had the sense that they were deep within the prison. The green walls were clean, but you could tell they had not been painted for many years. The ceiling lamps were bare bulbs surrounded by steel cages. The chair on which Louis sat was bolted to the floor. It faced a similar chair across a heavy wooden table, which was also bolted to the floor. A vertical board ran lengthwise down the center of the table, put there, presumably, to prevent physical contact between visitors and prisoners, and to prevent the passing of anything between them. The room had an antiseptic smell, which Louis found strangely agreeable.

The metal door at the other end of the room opened. Pierre Lefort was escorted in by the guard who had brought Louis there. The guard gestured toward the chair and Lefort sat down. He looked across the table at Louis and smiled. His dark hair was unkempt and looked as though he had just been brought inside on a windy day. He studied Louis, his eyebrows raised, and smiled a pleasant, even friendly, smile. "Here's your cousin, Lefort," said the guard, without apparent irony, and stepped back.

Louis and Lefort looked at one another. After a few moments had passed, Lefort's eyebrows formed a question. "So?" he said.

"Do you know who I am?" said Louis.

"Yes," said Lefort. "Yes, I know who you are. You're the guy whose crap I took. They told me you were coming."

"It was not crap to me," said Louis.

"It was crap," said Lefort. His face remained friendly.

"And you took it because . . ."

"I took it because? Why does anybody take anything? I took it because I wanted it."

"You wanted a broken lawnmower and some old screwdrivers?" said Louis.

"That's right." Lefort smiled at Louis as though he had just made a joke. "I wanted *your* lawnmower."

"What did you do with it?"

"It didn't work," said Lefort. "It was a piece of shit. I threw it away."

"You know," said Louis, "there was money in the house—it wasn't even hidden. A television—a fairly new one."

"I didn't need money. I didn't need a television," said Lefort. "I only take what I need. Besides," he laughed, "there's nothing good on television anyway, is there?"

"No, there isn't," said Louis. "And you needed the sweaters too?"

"Is this going somewhere?" Lefort asked. He made a show of turning toward the guard. The guard shrugged and gestured with his head toward Louis, as if to say, "Talk to him, not to me."

"That depends on you," said Louis. "Whether it's going anywhere depends on you. Anyway, do you have some other pressing engagement?" Lefort leaned forward a bit and his smile widened. The guard shifted his weight from one foot to the other. "I just have to wonder," said Louis, "why someone would serve a year in jail for an old sweater and a broken lawnmower. That just doesn't make sense to me."

Lefort smiled even more broadly now. "No, it doesn't, does it? Maybe there's more to it than that, you know?"

"Like what?" said Louis.

"How should I know? You tell me," said Lefort. He shrugged and looked away as though he were bored. "You're the smart guy. I'm just a guy doing time."

"You took the tape too, didn't you?" said Louis.

Lefort turned to the guard. "It took him long enough, didn't it?"

Louis locked his eyes on his own hands, folded on the table in front of him. So he was right. His hands were wrinkled and spotted with age and had red paint on them. They looked old and helpless. He opened them and looked into the palms. Finally he looked up at Lefort again, and Lefort was studying him. His smile had vanished.

"There are other copies, you know," said Louis.

Lefort shrugged. He continued watching Louis but said nothing. Finally he said, "I don't know about any of that."

"So," said Louis, "you took the other stuff so that I would notice the tape had been switched. Is that it?"

Lefort seemed to consider whether he might be giving anything away. "It was in the drawer with the sweaters," he said finally.

"You know, I thought you were a moron for taking all that junk." Lefort shifted in his chair. "Well," said Louis, "it turns out I'm the moron. I mean, I didn't even notice. I didn't even know the tape was gone. All this time your elaborate message went undelivered."

"Really?" said Lefort. "Well, it's been delivered now, hasn't it?" With that, he shaped his hand like a pistol and pointed it at Louis. "Bang." He mouthed the word soundlessly, so that the guard standing behind him did not notice.

It was plainly a threat," said Louis, "or it was meant to *sound* like a threat. I wonder, though, was he supposed to deliver it or was he just improvising?"

"Is that important?" said Solesme. She and Louis were sitting in her garden. She had been clipping dead blossoms from the rosebush beside the front door when he arrived. He had been startled to find her on a ladder. "How else am I going to get up here?" she had said.

"It does sound like a threat," she said now. "In fact, so does the whole robbery. But why?" she wondered. "Why would he threaten you in such a peculiar and convoluted way? There must be something else to it. Maybe there is something, some other aspect of the robbery, that's still missing." He could tell she loved the mystery of it as much as he did.

"I think there is something missing," said Louis. "Something's still missing, but I don't know what it could be." His own voice struck him as soft and sad, as though he were reciting a love poem or an elegy:

Something is missing, but what could it be?
I think there is something that I can't see.

Solesme got a disapproving look on her face. She withdrew her hand from his and folded her arms across her chest. "No dog eyes, please," she said.

Louis smiled at the expression. "No dog eyes," he promised.

Solesme's skin had grown pale in recent weeks. Blue veins showed at her temples, and her eyes glistened with bright intensity. She was thinner now, and her chin was pointed and more defiant. Her hair, as unruly as ever, had gone almost completely white, and it wafted about her head like a cloud.

Then Solesme relented. "Is it very difficult for you?" she asked.

"Yes," he said. "I don't want . . . I don't know how . . ."

She smiled at him and touched his cheek. She stood up in that peculiar way she had. Louis could see the pulse throbbing at her throat. He stood up and followed her.

It was cool and dark inside the house. Solesme stepped out of her dress and lay down on the bed while Louis undressed. She held her head propped on one hand and watched him. Her other arm lay along her side and draped over her hip. She seemed oblivious to her own nakedness.

She laughed as Louis folded his clothes into a neat pile on the chair by the window. Louis got in bed next to her. They slid together and they wrapped their bodies as closely as they could around one another. Their breathing slowed down, and they synchronized it so that they were breathing in and out in unison. Their faces were pressed together side to side. Louis heard Solesme's soft breath and felt it on his cheek, like an object almost, like something he could take in his hand. *This is life,* he thought, without knowing quite what he meant.

Solesme felt Louis's breath against her cheek. His ear rested like a cool pillow beneath her eye where she could see its entire delicacy. With each breath they took, she felt his chest rise and fall and her own breasts sliding up and down against him. Each felt the other's stomach expand and contract. Their legs entwined, and they lost themselves in gentle, ardent motion.

It seemed to Louis to be a peculiar fact of his life that important things revealed themselves to him when he least expected that they would, like his sudden sense on the beach that Hugh Bowes was up to something. Louis had not been expecting that insight, he had not been ready for it, and so it came. The following weekend Louis cooked dinner for his friends, and, in the course of the dinner, the meaning of the robbery was suddenly, and unexpectedly, revealed to him.

Solesme had made a pear tart, and she arrived early to help Louis cook. Louis had also invited the new neighbors from up the road, Isabelle and Luc Martin, recently arrived from Paris. Luc was a painter, which pleased Louis. In fact, Luc had actually earned his living as a painter of portraits and landscapes. His work had been exhibited regularly in Paris and Berlin and had been favorably reviewed in some important newspapers. Louis looked forward to long conversations about art, but, as it turned out, Luc did not want to talk about art. "It's my job," he said. "I don't want to talk about my job. Would you enjoy talking about your job?"

"No," Louis admitted. But they became friends anyway and talked about other things.

Renard arrived with his wife, who was also named Isabelle, and their son, Jean Marie, who was visiting from Paris. Jean Marie worked for the customs service as an electronics expert, designing and installing electronic surveillance systems in France's airports, and he had been instrumental in obtaining the incriminating recording of Hugh Bowes.

Louis had bought some monkfish at the fish market and had made a stew with tomatoes from the garden, olives, capers, and fennel; he had served it with saffron rice and green beans. They had all been sitting around the long kitchen table for several hours now. Four wine bottles stood empty. They had finished the salad. Isabelle Martin asked for Louis's vinaigrette recipe. "Champagne vinegar is the secret," he said. The cheese plate had gone around twice. Renard lit a cigarette.

Louis was making coffee, and Solesme had just set her tart in the center of the table. The others cleared away bottles and plates and glasses to make room. Everyone was oohing and aahing over the tart. Jean Marie, the Renards' son, began rhapsodizing too, but he stopped in mid-sentence. "Excuse me," he said suddenly, and got up from the table and hurried outside. "Is he all right?" someone wondered.

"He's fine," said Renard, looking puzzled.

"I'll go see," said Isabelle Renard. She was still his mother. Isabelle went outside and Louis followed.

The night was cool and clear for July, and there was no moon. The stars were myriad and vivid in the vaulting sky, and Louis paused a moment to look at them. The enormity of a clear night sky always took him by surprise. Jean Marie was walking down the driveway away from the house, and Isabelle hurried after him. "Jean Marie," she called. "Jean Marie! What is it?"

Jean Marie stopped about a hundred meters from the house

and turned toward them. He waited silently while Isabelle and Louis caught up to him. "What is it, Jean Marie?"

Jean Marie took out a cigarette and lit it. The flame from his lighter seemed to illuminate the entire yard. The linden trees threw great dancing shadows against the barn. "Louis," said Jean Marie. He spoke softly. "Can I have a word with you?"

"Of course, Jean Marie. What is it?"

"Mother, excuse me, but I have to speak with Louis . . . alone. It's nothing for you to be worried about, I promise. But it's very important. Please, would you go back inside? Say that my stomach is upset and I just need a little air. Please."

"Jean Marie . . ."

"Please, Mother. I can't explain right now."

Isabelle did as Jean Marie asked. "Jean Marie doesn't feel well," she said. "It's nothing serious." She waved her hand. "He just needed a little fresh air. I'll get the coffee." Renard studied her face and then looked toward the door.

Jean Marie drew on his cigarette. "Louis," he said, "I don't know how to say this gently. Maybe you already . . . did you know that your house is under surveillance?" Louis did not seem to comprehend his words at first. "Your house is bugged, Louis," said Jean Marie. "I just spotted a camera, and there are probably more. Microphones too, undoubtedly. I don't know how many or where, but it's obviously a professional job. I only saw it by chance, and I deal with this stuff all the time," he added, sounding slightly embarrassed.

"There's at least one camera in the kitchen. There are sure to be others. I didn't look around and you shouldn't either. But after we go back inside, at some point check your watch against the clock. Then look at the ribbon holding the clock on the wall. Just at the top of the ribbon, where the hanger goes into the wall, is a camera no bigger than this." Jean Marie held the glowing end of his cigarette under Louis's nose.

"Aha," said Louis. "So that's it."

"What?" said Jean Marie. "Then you *did* know?"

"No, I didn't," said Louis. "But it may explain the robbery, or what I took to be a robbery. My house was robbed a while ago. It seemed inconsequential at the time. Not much damage, not much taken. But that might be a part of what the robbery was about. I was wondering, and now, thanks to you, Jean Marie, I have a good idea."

"What do you want to do?" asked Jean Marie. "I'll help you, of course."

"What do you mean?" said Louis.

"Do you want them removed? The bugs, I mean. I'd suggest leaving them alone for now." He thought about that for a moment. "I'm sure it's not us," he said. "Not the French, I mean. I'll help you find and get rid of them if you want."

"I know you will, Jean Marie. Thank you." Louis reached out and touched Jean Marie's shoulder. He had known him since he was a small boy. "For the moment, I think I'll do nothing."

"That's right," said Jean Marie. "And don't try to find the others. You should do that only when you are ready for them to know that you know. You know who's doing it, don't you?"

"I think I do."

"Is it Bowes again?"

"I'm guessing it is, but I don't know why. Once I figure out why, then I'll know what to do."

Louis went to Renard's office the next morning. He scanned the walls of the office as he walked in. Maybe the entire village of Saint Leon was bugged. Louis told Renard about the camera Jean Marie had found. Renard laid down the pencil he was holding. His eyes widened. "You don't mean it. Is that true? So that was it," he said. "Jean Marie found it? So that was it." He stood up. "Where is it? Show me."

Louis laughed. "I'll show it to you later. I don't want whoever it is to see us staring into their camera. First I need to figure out what they're after."

There was always the possibility that they simply meant to intimidate Louis. Even someone as familiar with espionage and eavesdropping as Louis was could be thrown off by having his life watched and listened to. He might even be driven to do something incriminating. It was not unknown for people who knew they were being observed to begin behaving as though they were actually guilty of something. "Knowing you are being watched changes everything," said Louis. "You become self-conscious and furtive. That might be of use to Bowes."

"If it *is* Bowes," said Renard. "You keep assuming it's Bowes. But you don't know. Besides, this is different from the burglary. The camera was cleverly placed. You weren't meant to find it. Maybe," suggested Renard after a minute's thought, "the correct answer is the most obvious one. Maybe someone just wants to know what you're up to."

"But I'm not up to anything. And surely anyone who would plant such devices would know that already. Maybe," said Louis, "they want my vinaigrette recipe."

As it happened, it was Solesme who figured out what they were after, whoever *they* were. Louis did not tell her at first that the camera was even there. But Solesme always knew when he was keeping something from her. "I keep things from you for your own good," he said. "For your safety," he added.

"For my *safety*?" she said. "Don't be ridiculous. I have a few months left. At best. What safety are you talking about?" Louis tried to protest. She raised her hand to his mouth to stop him. "Besides," she said. "I want to know *everything*. Everything about everything. While I can still know anything about anything."

Louis told her about the camera, and Solesme thought about it for a moment. She did not ask to see it. But then she wondered whether a hidden camera might not be used to show something going on that had in fact *not* necessarily actually gone on. "Maybe it is not there to inform the one who placed it there. Maybe it is there for *other* people. Don't you call it misinformation?"

"*Dis*information?" said Louis.

"Disinformation," she said. "After the American war in Afghanistan weren't Osama bin Laden's people using cameras to show he was still alive and well? But no one knew for quite a long time whether he was alive or not, and many believed he was not. And the Americans showed trucks in Iraq that were supposedly mobile biological laboratories or some such business, and they turned out not to be. And then there are those kidnappings and beheadings. The people in those tapes claim to be certain people doing certain things. But are they who they say they are? They quote holy verses, but isn't that for public consumption?

"Maybe someone, *he,* if it is him again"—Solesme did not like to even pronounce Hugh Bowes's name—"is staging something. Maybe he wants it to look like something is going on in your house that is not really going on, something that might somehow incriminate you."

"So," said Louis, "the camera could have been planted long before the robbery." He thought about it for a moment. "Maybe," he said, "they've been in and out of my house . . ."

"Think of it," said Solesme. She shuddered. "It is horrible."

"It is an unpleasant prospect," he said. "But now we know

something." Louis stared at Solesme for a moment and then took her by the arms and kissed her forehead enthusiastically. "You are right. *You are right*. I am *sure* you are right," he said.

"Of course I am right," she said.

And, in fact, she was right.

IV

Hugh Bowes gazed through the tinted glass as his car carried him along Pennsylvania Avenue. The reflected sunlight danced from one office building to the next as they drove, and Hugh raised his hand to shield his dazzled eyes. Seymour, his driver, slowed down as they approached the White House and threaded their way through the concrete barricades. Police wearing bulletproof vests and carrying automatic weapons stood along the way and watched them pass.

Seymour lowered the front and rear windows so the White House guards could peer inside. Once the guards recognized both the driver and his passenger, the heavy iron gates swung open. A guard waved them up the drive toward the White House while another guard phoned to announce their arrival.

They stopped under the portico, and Seymour got out and stepped to the back of the car. He lifted the wheelchair from the trunk, unfolded it, and rolled it forward. Hugh waited until Seymour opened the car door before he swung his legs out. He planted his feet and pulled himself upright. Seymour held him by one arm and Hugh lowered himself onto the chair.

Hugh had gotten fatter since his retirement. He had less hair too, although it was still black and still slicked back against his head. The thick lenses of his glasses made his eyes, which were actually rather large and soft, seem small and remote, as though he were looking at you from far inside his skull. The result was a look of utter indifference, which he had learned over the years to use to excellent effect.

Hugh took a variety of medications with every meal, and there was a growing list of things he could not eat or drink. He had never been particularly fit, but now his body appeared to consist almost entirely of unsupported flesh. He preferred not to know this about himself, so he dressed and undressed without looking in the mirror. He consulted mirrors only when he was fully clothed, to make certain that his collar was crisp and straight, his tie properly knotted, his jacket smooth across his breast, his hair in place.

Hugh had not reached this state of decrepitude because of illness or age. He could have been said to be decrepit out of conviction. He despised his physical self and found it to be a nuisance and an impediment to the success and fulfillment he continually pursued. Hugh rode when he could walk. He leaned on someone's arm when it was available. When the physicians who treated him dared to suggest he should try to take a short walk every day, he regarded them with contempt.

Hugh lived almost entirely in his mind, where he was quick and agile and could still maneuver with grace and intelligence and patience. His ambition was as enormous as it had ever been. It was true he lived on broiled fish and rice, but his appetite for power remained huge and all but insatiable.

Hugh had once been married to a beautiful and accomplished woman. He had hoped, when they married, that marriage to her would complete him, an astonishingly, almost touchingly, naïve hope for a man of his experience and position. But it had not worked out that way. How could it have done so? She had failed to recognize his needs or to engage his desires, principally because he had done his best to conceal his needs and desires from her.

When Hugh had courted her, she must have seen something in him besides his intelligence and success, a suggestion of warmth perhaps, or a certain tender fragility, for he had both. But these were qualities about himself that Hugh detested, and so, once they were married, he saw any effort by Ruth—that was her name—to connect with his warmth, or his fragility, or any of his other human qualities as insulting and contemptible. It was as though she were pointing out his essential insufficiencies to him. Her efforts were greeted on his part with chilly wariness at first, later with withdrawal from her, and eventually with hostility and rage.

Hugh had not proved to be at all skilled at love. After Ruth died, he had never tried romantic love again. Love did not suit him. Enmity was another matter altogether. Enmity was his métier. He had discovered varieties and manifestations of enmity that dazzled his opponents even as it left them defeated at his feet.

Hugh Bowes moved through life strategically. He had positioned himself well from the very beginning of his career and had climbed from one point to the next without ever yielding his desire for power and influence and, ultimately, for control. By the same token, Hugh could be kind and generous, but these actions were not the result of feelings of kindness or generosity. Hugh knew what kindness and generosity looked like, and he did his best to exhibit these traits when it suited his purpose. Along the way he dispatched personal rivals, enemies, and those who just happened to get in his way with cunning and skill, and with such artfulness that they usually did not know that it was Hugh who had done them in. People were charmed and amused by him, even as he was plotting their annihilation.

Hugh could not love those close to him, but he loved his enemies. Not as the Bible instructs that we should. He loved them once they had fallen, *because* they had fallen. He loved them for having been vanquished by him. He loved them for being weak or inept or vulnerable, and for revealing to him, yet again, his own power, or, put another way, for helping him conceal from himself his own terrible and unforgivable fragility.

Politics was the perfect medium for Hugh's temperament and ambitions. It required skill and cunning of the sort that came naturally to him. He saw politics, and especially high international politics, as the arena where champions met to do battle. Like Hugh, his rivals had few illusions beyond their own importance. They engaged in their wars, their treaties, their shifting alliances, their betrayals and realignments without concern for those who suffered. They operated without sentiment or, for that matter, acrimony. They saw themselves as *above* sentiment.

Louis Morgon was the fly in Hugh's ointment. Louis had a way of intruding into Hugh's thoughts at inopportune moments, like now, for instance, as Hugh waited to see the president. The trouble was that Hugh could not forget that he had suffered defeat and humiliation at Louis's hands. Hugh had the sense that Louis, more than anyone else, had seen into his soul. Of course, Louis would have found this idea preposterous. He knew some of Hugh's weaknesses, that was all.

A copy of Louis's tape recording of Hugh's threatening voice had recently come into Hugh's possession. There was no denying that it was Hugh's voice on the tape. And it was angry. *"Stop the son of a bitch. Stop him!"* Those were his words. But what did they mean? And who was he threatening? It would be easy to manufacture a plausible and harmless explanation for his outburst. One could not even tell from the tape where and in what context the recording had been made. If there were other copies of the tape, as Hugh was certain there were, it demonstrated nothing so much as the fevered imagination of the man who had made the recording in the first place. It would be easy to show that Louis Morgon was a deranged and confused man whose mind was awash in silly delusions and imaginary conspiracies.

"The president is ready for you, sir." The president's military aide, a pretty, young marine colonel, got behind the wheelchair and pushed Hugh across the carpet. Someone opened the door from inside, and the president rose from his chair. He walked around from behind the desk and extended his hand. "Hello, Hugh. I hope you're well."

"Very well, Mr. President. Thank you."

"Well, thanks for coming, Hugh. I appreciate it. We all do." The president nodded to indicate the people around him.

"I am glad to be of service, Mr. President," said Hugh, smiling and nodding toward the president.

The secretary of state, Hugh's successor; the director of Central Intelligence; and the chief national security advisor had risen from their places on opposite couches. The secretary nodded toward Hugh. Hugh peered through his spectacles and smiled at the secretary.

The two men did not like or trust each other. Each believed that the other had more influence with the president than he deserved. The present secretary of state thought that the discredited policies that Hugh's administration had authored were a large part of the reason they were now living in an age of terror. Hugh considered both the current secretary and the president amateurs. He thought their policies were based on superstition and half-baked history. They allowed domestic political considerations to guide foreign policy, which, to his way of thinking, could only be harmful to both domestic and foreign politics, and which he would have prevented were he still in office.

"I think you know my intelligence people, Hugh?" The president turned to indicate the three men standing behind him.

"Yes, Mr. President, we have met. Gentlemen."

"May I start, sir?" said one of the three after a brief pause. He was the president's chief national security advisor, a short, thin, eager man with glittering, rimless glasses, a strong jaw, and slicked-back hair.

"Go ahead, Phil," said the president. He returned to his chair behind the desk and folded his arms to listen.

"As you know, Secretary Bowes, from our previous communications with your shop, it appears that some of our efforts are paying dividends. However, we were wondering, sir—"

"Which efforts might those be?" Hugh interrupted.

"Sorry, sir. Intelligence efforts. Infiltration. Let me back up a bit." There was not a bit of irony in the man's voice. He stepped aside to reveal a chart propped up on an easel behind him. It purported to show the organizational connections of major terrorist groups around the world. Some of the groups represented by small circles were linked to each other by dotted lines, while others had question marks between them. There was a thicket of dotted lines going in every direction.

Phil looked at the chart and then laid out in scrupulous and, as far as Hugh was concerned, excessive detail what one quick look at the chart had already revealed: that, as far as anyone in the room knew, some terrorist groups were linked to others, and some were not. But no one knew for certain which were and which were not. It was almost always the case that the more explicitly and specifically intelligence was enumerated, the less likely it was to be known to be true. Specificity always seemed like a good substitute for certainty.

Phil went on about how some intelligence assets were beginning to yield useful information about the activities of militant Islamic organizations, and most particularly al Qaeda, "in Europe, Asia, Africa . . ." He proceeded to name nearly every continent. He began naming countries—"Russia, Pakistan, Turkey, Spain"—before Hugh cut him off.

"In short?" said Hugh, looking sharply at the man.

"I am afraid, sir, there is no 'in short,' " said Phil. The current secretary of state allowed the corners of his mouth to flicker into a brief smile. "We have always believed," Phil continued, "that these cells were not connected in any way. They were essentially independent units making independent plans to commit terroristic acts, or so we thought.

"And yet we are picking up indications lately, particularly from some of the valuable data you have sent our way"—he kept paying homage to Hugh—"but also from sources we have developed through Langley and elsewhere"—here Phil turned slightly to acknowledge the director of Central Intelligence—"indications that these are not all sleeper cells, as we had believed.

"There appears to be central direction, in fact, a command and control center, implied in much of the chatter we are hearing. If we could establish the connections between various cells and discover who is directing things, then we could take a large step toward preventing the next attack, which we all know will eventually come." He went on in this fashion for some time.

"I think I see where you are going," said Hugh, cutting Phil short again. "What have you got?"

"Sir?" Phil was momentarily confused.

"If you let me see what you have got."

"Transcripts, actual tapes?"

"Primary sources. Yes. Whatever you've got," said Hugh.

"Sir, we have reams, thousands of cartons, raw data, transcripts, tapes, video . . ."

"Send me the French transcripts and tapes then. I'll start there."

"Thanks, Hugh," said the president, rising from his chair and opening his arms to indicate that the meeting was over. Everyone else in the room rose. "We're grateful, as always, and sorry to take you away from your work. Frankly, we're just a little stymied, as you can see." Phil looked down at his shoes. The president continued, "The information has to be there somewhere, Hugh. Our people are just missing something. Give it a look, would you?"

"Whatever I can do, Mr. President. I am glad to be able to help."

Later that afternoon six cartons of documents and tapes were delivered to the offices at Bowes, Powell, and Clayton by Secret Service men wearing dark suits and sunglasses and pushing hand trucks. The office manager signed for the cartons and led the couriers to Hugh's office. The office manager watched from the door with his arms folded while they rolled the trucks across the deep pile carpet and stacked the cartons beside Hugh's desk.

Hugh arrived as evening was falling. The sun had set, and the sky was turning dark. He sent Seymour away. The office manager was the last one left in the office.

"Do you need anything else before I go, Mr. Secretary?"

"Would you lift those cartons down for me, Arthur? Just place them side by side. There. Thank you. That will be all. Now you go home to your family."

"Thank you, sir," said the office manager, and left the office.

Hugh settled into the great leather desk chair. He swiveled to the side and opened the cartons one by one. He sorted through them from front to back, pulling files halfway out, looking inside, and then letting them slide back, as though he were searching for something in particular.

In the fourth carton he found what he was looking for. He removed a disk from a bundle of disks and slid it into his computer. The machine whirred briefly. A grainy gray image appeared on the screen. Hugh tapped a few keys and the image became sharper.

Hugh saw a room with a long table surrounded by mismatched chairs. The date and time of the recording—18.2.2004, 14:14:36—was displayed across the bottom of the screen in yellow type. Hugh clicked on FAST-FORWARD and watched the minutes, then hours flash by. Suddenly a figure appeared and dashed across the screen.

Hugh stopped the disk and reversed it. He searched until he found the figure again. He clicked on PLAY. The figure—a man—carried dishes to the table. He disappeared and then reappeared with cutlery, then with a bottle of wine. He held the bottle up and studied the label. "Champalou," said the man. Hugh zoomed in on the figure's face and froze the image. He studied the look on the man's face.

"Hello, Louis," whispered Hugh, as though Louis might be able to hear him.

Hugh sped through the rest of the disk. He inserted another into the reader. He sped through that one too, through many days of Louis eating, walking past the camera, reading the newspaper, drinking coffee. On the next disk he heard Louis and Renard talking about cooking, about the weather, about Renard's wife, Isabelle, about Solesme's recently discovered cancer, about art. He saw Louis having dinner with his friends. He stopped now and then and listened to the conversation, as though he might want to jump in with his own contribution. He went through several more disks until there were suddenly four men on the screen.

Hugh stopped the disk and played it from that point. The four men sat at the table. One sat with his back to the camera. You could not see his face. The men were drinking tea. You could hear their voices clearly. They were speaking French. Hugh knew the language well enough to recognize that they spoke with foreign accents. Hugh followed the French transcript.

Man 1: When?
Man 2: You got this . . . ?
Man 1: From him.
Man 2: From him. He says millions should be involved.
Man 3: He is certain?
Man 1: It's big. Let's put it that way.
Man 3: Yes, but when?
Man 2: That's up to us. I'm just saying . . .
Man 3: How about Roland Garros? How about the French Open?
Man 4: Tennis? What's the point?

Man 2: Like I said. It's up to us. Just remember: the *flics* are onto us. The phones are tapped. I'm sure of it. Still, we're too far to turn back now.

Hugh fast-forwarded the disk and began playing it again.

Man 3: They're not that smart. I know them. I worked for them.
Man 2: We still have to stay loose. And careful.
Man 3: Meaning what?
Man 1: Did he say when?
Man 2: That's up to us too. It's all up to us.
Man 4: I mean, fifteen kilos.
Man 1: Marseille?
Man 3: He'll let us know.
Man 1: But where should we stash it?
Man 4: I've got the place in Paris. [Incomprehensible.]
Man 1: Got it.
Man 2: [Incomprehensible.]
Man 3 rises and leaves. He returns with a book, which he opens.
Man 3: Read this.
Man 1, 2, and 4 read the book.

Hugh sent the recording forward again.

Man 2: Allah be praised.
Man 1, 3, and 4: Allah be praised.

Hugh stopped the disk.

If Louis had been there watching with Hugh, he would have recognized himself and his friends coming and going in his own kitchen. He would not have recognized the four men, but he would have seen that the conversation among the four had taken place around his kitchen table. He could have deduced that Man 3, whose face remained out of sight, was supposed to be him, and he would have recognized that Man 2 was Pierre Lefort. As he had surmised, the bug had been planted and the drama with the four men had been staged well before the burglary had taken place. The actors in the elaborate charade had let themselves in and out of Louis's house without his ever noticing.

The page that covered the surveillance transcript Hugh was reading was gray with a red border. It was marked at the top and bottom in bold letters: **TOP SECRET. EYES ONLY.** In that regard, it was like all the other transcripts of all the other recordings Hugh had sorted through. At the bottom of this one, however, there was a small label—*Sécurité Nationale Algérienne*—indicating that the recording had been made by Algerian agents.

Hugh had forgotten how hard-pressed and ill-equipped American intelligence services were. They did not have time to carefully assess which reports were reliable and/or useful and which were not. Most likely the American intelligence officer who had received this set of recordings and transcripts from the Algerians was inundated with work and had, after brief consideration, written LOW PRIORITY on the routing slip (it was Algerian intelligence, after all), initialed it, and put it on a growing stack of similar papers.

The entire stack had been shipped to Washington in the next diplomatic pouch and had found its way into the CIA's voluminous French files, where it had quickly gotten buried. It had not surfaced on its own, as Hugh had hoped it would, but that did not matter. In fact, he had now been given the opportunity to "discover" the disks and reveal their significance to the astonished president and his embarrassed staff. Hugh read through the complete transcript and found it to be highly satisfactory.

V

A few days later Seymour drove Hugh onto the White House grounds once more. He helped Hugh out of the car and pushed the wheelchair up the ramp into the reception area. The pretty colonel wheeled Hugh into the Oval Office, where Hugh greeted the president and the other men gathered about him. With great effort, and some help from the colonel, he stood up from the wheelchair and lowered himself onto an overstuffed couch. He reached into his briefcase and withdrew a sheaf of papers, which he quickly put in order on the low glass table in front of him. He took the Algerian disk from the briefcase and slid it out of its acetate envelope. "Mr. President, you will forgive me, I hope, if I get right to the point. I have just made an important and, I fear, alarming discovery.

"On a hunch, really, I began my research with France," he said, "and it is fortunate that I did. This is what I found." He waved the disk in the air. "We know, of course, there are a number of terror cells operating in France. That is nothing new. That is why I started there. I know your people"—he nodded toward Phil—"have been keeping track of them, and I congratulate you for finding and tracking them.

"There is one cell, however, and I fear it is a most dangerous one, which seems to have escaped your notice. It is not in Paris, and that is perhaps why it eluded you. In fairness I should add that it might have escaped *my* notice too"—a smile flickered across his face—"but for the curious, even astonishing, fact that I actually recognized one of the terrorists involved. I know the man. Personally. Or rather, I knew him once." The president and his men looked back and forth at one another in amazement.

Hugh held up the disk once more. "Would you mind playing this for the president?" he said. One of the intelligence officers retrieved it and inserted it in the DVD player, which was stacked along with other electronic equipment on a tall metal stand beside the president's desk. He turned on the television and stepped aside. Louis's kitchen came into view. After a few seconds Louis appeared.

"Fast-forward, please. Does this tape seem familiar to you at all?" said Hugh, knowing full well that it would not. Louis dashed back and forth across the screen until the four men appeared, at which point Hugh instructed the officer with the player's controls to slow the disk to normal speed. The little drama played itself out while the president, his various military and security advisers, and his secretary of state stared at the television. They watched in silence for a full ten minutes before Hugh finally instructed the officer to stop the player. The image of the four men froze on the screen.

"I am certain you speak enough French," said Hugh, knowing that they did not, "to recognize that the men we have just watched are involved in what appears to be a drug smuggling operation." The president and his men looked at him blankly. "It's in the transcripts," said Hugh, brandishing a sheaf of papers in their direction.

"The fact is, however, that the references they make to kilos, which might seem to refer to drugs, is, I fear, a reference to something far more ominous. These conspirators are speaking of some deadly agent that they do not name, whether biological or chemical is not quite clear. Quite possibly it is sarin or some other nerve agent." Hugh paused to allow this terrible idea to sink in. The president scowled. He leaned forward slightly, as though he were uncertain that he had just heard what he thought he had just heard.

"And you *know* one of these guys?" the president said.

Hugh continued. "If you will allow me, Mr. President, I'll explain that in a moment. But first: the millions they speak of refers, not to money, but to the numbers of people who might be killed or sickened by the release of this agent. Roland Garros refers, of course, to the French Open tennis tournament, which begins shortly and which they consider and then, fortunately for us, dismiss as an occasion for the release of this agent. They have not agreed on a target, at least as far as I can tell from these surveillance tapes. I assume surveillance is ongoing.

"Now to your question, Mr. President. What makes a grave matter even graver is the man who appears to be the central figure in the enterprise, at least as far as we can tell. He is the man you see at the beginning of the tape and then in conversation with three other men. The tape was made in his home in . . ." Hugh looked at the papers in front of him. "Saint Leon sur Dême, a small town in the Loire Valley, southwest of Paris.

"As I said, this man is known to me, or rather he *was* known to me—was *well* known to me—some thirty years ago. I have not seen him since then, but he represents a painful episode in my early career and in the history of the State Department, and I would not forget him easily. He has changed a great deal, but I recognized him immediately. His name is Louis Morgon. I doubt that the name means anything to you. Did you know him, Mr. Secretary?"

The secretary of state shook his head.

"Louis Morgan?" said Phil, the man in the glittering glasses. He began writing in a small notebook.

"Louis Morg*ON*," said Hugh. "M-*O*-R-G-*O*-*N*. Louis Morgon."

"How do you know him?" asked Phil, sounding as though he were beginning a police inquiry.

Hugh turned to peer at him and waited until he had lowered his pen. "Louis Morgon is an American expatriate," he continued. "He was once an important adviser to me when I was an undersecretary of state under President Ford. He occupied a position . . . similar to yours.

"Morgon came to us from academe. He was smart—a young professor who had done some interesting work on the balance of power in the Middle East. He was a rising star in the State Department and pretty soon he moved to an important post at the CIA. Then it was discovered that he was undercutting our efforts in the Middle East.

"There was evidence that he was a foreign agent. Morgon was dismissed from service and investigated. But, while the evidence was strongly suggestive, they could never get enough on him to charge him with a crime. He was too smart for that.

"When he was fired, he became embittered and vengeful, so much so that he eventually left the country. And he has lived in

France—where they tolerate such people—ever since. That is a long story made short," said Hugh, gathering his papers together and forming them into a neat stack on the table in front of him. "I will leave all this information with you. You can find all the historical details you need in his State Department and CIA files."

The president and his men leaned forward in their seats and peppered Hugh with questions, which he patiently and frankly answered, even to the point of admitting his own failure to recognize Louis Morgon's dangerous tendencies those many years ago. There followed a brief discussion about how best to proceed with this startling new information. Hugh offered to help in any way he could, although he cautioned that his previous relationship with Morgon might suggest to some that he should not be too closely involved. "I know the limits of my objectivity," he said. "I am not impartial when it comes to this man."

"Nonsense, Hugh," said the president. "Impartiality isn't at issue here. Your knowledge of the man's character will be a big help as we decide how to proceed. We'll study the matter and keep you in the loop as we figure out our course of action. Whatever we do will obviously have to happen quickly. There is obviously not a moment to lose."

The president rose from his chair and so did everyone else in the room. "Thank you again, Hugh, for all your help. As always, it has been absolutely indispensable. I don't know what we would have done . . ." The president's voice trailed off as he thought about the dire possibilities.

Two days later Hugh was called back to the Oval Office. An intelligence officer who had not been at the earlier meetings reported that Louis Morgon's files at the CIA and at the State Department were sealed. "It looks as though someone has maintained a special interest in our man all these years. The files also appear to be incomplete."

"Which could mean any number of things," said Hugh with a wave of his hand.

"Of course," said the intelligence officer. He continued. Louis's current whereabouts had been easily discovered, since he had not moved and his address and phone number were listed. Apparently he did not know or care that he might be under suspicion. French security knew nothing about him either. However, they were dispatching agents at this very moment to the village of Saint Leon sur Dême to make their own appraisal of the situation.

"An extremely cautious appraisal, I would advise," said Hugh. "You should warn them to proceed carefully. Not to be too dramatic, but they are dealing with a highly experienced intelligence officer and a cunning man. He will spot anything the least bit suspicious, and the consequences of that could be deadly serious."

The officer continued. "The translation into English of the Algerian disk has borne out entirely Secretary Bowes's interpretation of the discussion among the four men. Nor can there be any doubt that Louis Morgon is the leader of the cell. We only saw four men, but it is safe to assume from their words that others are involved, in Paris and elsewhere, perhaps even in the United States.

"Morgon's bitterness against our country is well documented and obviously remains active, as do his treasonous ways. It is unclear just what he and his cell might be up to. The large terror event scenario is a distinct possibility, but the recorded language just isn't conclusive enough. Too much is missing. We are hoping the French agents will fill in the blanks until our own people can arrive on the scene."

"You are right to be cautious in your interpretation," said Hugh. "I am inclined to be cautious myself." He paused briefly and looked around the room at the men gathered in front of him. "Having said that, however, I feel compelled to add, Mr. President"—and here he turned to look the president in the eye—"I know the man. I know and have vivid firsthand experience with his venality. I know the full depth of his hatred for the United States. When his career ended, he lost his wife, his children, his country, and his entire significance. He lost everything.

"You have found evidence in his file, I am sure, of his desperation and rage. And while I have only circumstantial evidence for this—it is certainly possible that I am wrong—I believe Osama bin Laden and al Qaeda have provided him with the perfect channel for the expression of his hatred." Hugh paused. "That is only my opinion, sir, and it is, as I have already said, a biased one. But there you have it, Mr. President. Gentlemen."

There is a curious quality, more a failing, really, that all humans share, even the most intelligent and reasonable among us. It is this: fear and uncertainty can, and usually do, overwhelm even the most unassailable facts. Fear and uncertainty are stronger and more compelling than factual evidence can ever be, especially when the evidence is ambiguous, as evidence almost always is. And the weight of evidence has a peculiar way of turning in the direction in which fear directs it.

Each of the men in the Oval Office stood silently and considered in his own mind the catastrophic consequences of guessing wrong. If they underestimated Louis Morgon's desperation and dangerous intentions, the results could be too horrible for words. Phil was the first to speak. His voice was grave. "Mr. President, I believe, based on the surveillance tape, that Morgon and his cohorts have managed to acquire serious weapons. It is quite possible, likely even, that, besides being armed with personal weapons, they have biological or chemical weapons." He looked at Hugh. Heads nodded around the room.

"So where the hell are we then?" said the president.

"The cell in Saint Leon is most likely al Qaeda," said Phil. He had already organized his doubts and uncertainties into a coherent assessment. "The Algerians bugged the place for a reason, and they were correct to do so. I'm afraid, sir, that we, our intelligence services, dropped the ball. We're in touch with the Algerians now, sir, and we're asking for everything they've got. Everything they already sent us that might have gotten sidelined, but also all the preliminary stuff.

"It seems likely, sir, that the Morgon cell is planning something big. We should have people on the ground in Saint Leon ASAP, Mr. President, who should be able to determine whether that is so or not. We have requested surveillance types as well as a joint French-American assault team."

"Including snipers?" asked the president. "We don't want anything to go wrong. We've got to be sure we stop this guy."

"Including snipers, yes, sir," said Phil. "Also, the French national police and INTERPOL are aware of the situation. We are certain there are other al Qaeda involved, elsewhere in France, and maybe elsewhere in Europe, other cells. It is a potentially explosive situation, but if we are careful and play our cards right, this could be a tremendous opportunity. The Morgon group could very well lead us to some of the others before we have to take them out. This also lines up with our assessment, sir, that there is an operational nerve center, a central command, in play."

The president rubbed his hands together. "Then this could be a terrific break." The secretary of state was startled and swiveled his head to look at the president. "In the war on terror, Harold," said the president. "It's the war on terror I'm talking about." There were nods and glances around the room.

"Mr. President," said Phil, "you can be sure we will proceed expeditiously."

"And, Phil," said Hugh. Phil turned back to the couch where Hugh was sitting. "I cannot emphasize this enough: do not underestimate Morgon. He is cunning and he is angry. I know nothing about the others involved or about their devotion to their cause. But I know Louis Morgon."

Phil turned to look at the frozen image of Louis on the television monitor. Others followed his gaze and were startled to see Louis's face looking back at them, almost as though he could see them and hear what they were planning.

"Louis Morgon," said Hugh, "is a man whose life has been thwarted at every turn. That is worth remembering. Now he has a chance to avenge his perceived injustices and go out in a blaze of glory."

That afternoon four Secret Service men in dark suits arrived at Bowes, Powell, and Clayton to retrieve the six cartons of secret materials. Arthur, the office manager, signed the release forms, and the cartons were wheeled out of the safe and onto the elevator, and that was the last that Hugh ever saw of them.

That evening Hugh sat at the glass dining table in his Watergate penthouse apartment. The cook slid a plate of food in front of him, which he ate without hesitation or interest. He chewed and swallowed, chewed and swallowed without noticing what he was eating. He drank from a goblet of water with a slice of lemon in it. After a few minutes, the cook cleared the table.

Hugh remained seated there, gazing through the floor-to-ceiling windows and across the Potomac River. The lights outlining the tops of the tall buildings danced and shimmered in the hot night air. An airliner came whining across the sky, seeming dangerously close, its wheels down, heading for a landing at Reagan National Airport. And Hugh made a wish, as though the plane were a falling star. If only Louis would do something incriminating, something that would demonstrate conclusively, once and for all, how dangerous he was. It was too much to hope for, but if only . . .

Summer had come to Saint Leon sur Dême. Renard came out of his office and looked across the square at the hotel terrace with its bright blue and yellow umbrellas, unfurled and waiting for guests. He loved this time of year. The sun was high in the sky each morning when he got up, and sometimes it was still up when he went to bed. He loved how, in summer, everything came to life and yet slowed down. Life took on a delicious, measured pace.

He loved the feel of the sun on his arms and head. He always took the long way home for lunch, looking in the shop windows, smelling the chickens roasting on the rotisserie outside Charbin's Boucherie de Paris. He stopped and gazed lovingly at Charbin's window, at the stuffed eggs with their little dots of pimiento, at the tray of creamy potato salad. He studied the chalkboard propped there listing the day's offerings in a careful hand.

Renard and Isabelle ate a light lunch at the table in their garden. Afterwards he rinsed off the dishes and watched Isabelle through the window as she worked among the flowers. She looked like a flower herself, he thought. That was as poetic as Renard ever got.

He roused himself from his reverie and headed back to the office. He had paperwork to finish, and then there was Philippe

Géricault's assault on his girlfriend. Marie had showed up at Renard's office this morning with blood all over her. Renard had driven her to the hospital. "Keep your head back," he told her. "Keep some pressure on it." He showed her where to press the handkerchief.

Her nose was broken, and she had two black eyes. They stopped the bleeding and bandaged her nose. Géricault was a troublesome drunk, and Renard did not look forward to arresting him. Marie was out of harm's way, so he decided to give the man a few more hours alone with his thoughts. With any luck he would be in a remorseful frame of mind by the time Renard showed up at his door. That was usually the way it worked with Géricault. Rage followed by remorse.

Meanwhile, Louis had managed to examine the camera surreptitiously. And Jean Marie had stopped by to have a look at it too. They drank tea at the kitchen table and then wandered through the rest of the house while Louis pretended to show Jean Marie some recent paintings. "I can't be sure," said Jean Marie afterwards out in the garden, "but it looks like there's only the one camera and microphone in the kitchen. The mike is behind the stove. All of which is a little peculiar."

"Peculiar?" said Louis.

"It's unusual to put just one set of devices in a place. Once you're inside, you usually put them all over, backups, different angles, so you don't miss anything. So, what do you think it's all about?"

Louis had his speculations, but how could he have ever imagined the elaborate, and preposterous, scenario Hugh had concocted to demonstrate for the president of the United States that he was a terrorist, of all things? How could Louis have ever imagined the men in his own kitchen, the false Algerian intelligence, the White House discussions about how best to get rid of him and "terminate" his operation? It was all beyond his wildest dreams.

Neither, of course, did Louis know anything of Hugh's fervent wish that he somehow incriminate himself. Which made it all the more surprising that he set about fulfilling Hugh's wish as though he were bent on his own destruction.

VI

After working all morning in the garden, staking the small tomato plants, hilling earth around the new asparagus stalks, and walking up and down the rows with a watering can, Louis cut half a dozen thick asparagus shoots from the old bed, picked some lettuce, and headed for the house. It was a beautiful, hot day, and the front door and the windows were wide open. Whoever was listening at the other end of the microphone would hear only birds, and particularly one small sparrow sitting on top of the chimney. The sparrow's song came down the stovepipe and went right into the microphone.

Louis washed the lettuce and sliced a scallion, a radish, and a hard-boiled egg onto the lettuce. He splashed olive oil and squeezed lemon juice onto the salad, and when the asparagus were cooked, he put them on the plate too. He stuck a fork, knife, and napkin in his pocket, tucked half a baguette under one arm and a bottle under the other, and carried the salad and a glass to the table on the terrace. Just as he sat down to eat, the telephone rang. He closed his eyes and waited for it to stop.

In the field beyond the garden, the sunflowers nodded in the soft breeze. They disappeared in rows over the hillside and reappeared climbing the distant hill. The flower heads were still small, but soon they would fill out and bend over under the weight of the seed. The petals would dry and fall off, and the stalks would turn black and ugly.

A small airplane flew high overhead, its noise barely distinguishable from the insects and bees that buzzed around in the linden tree above his head. Louis watched the airplane as it turned in a wide circle and came back in his direction. *First the telephone and now this. Maybe someone is taking pictures,* he thought.

That afternoon Louis drove back to Granville for another conversation with Pierre Lefort.

"He is gone, monsieur," said the warden after checking his book.

"Gone?"

"Released."

"Had he finished his sentence?'

"He was given time off for good behavior."

"Can you give me his address?"

"I cannot," said the warden. He closed the book. "And even if I could, it is in Algeria."

"Pierre Lefort is from Algeria?"

The warden was an exacting man. "I do not know where he is from, monsieur. But he is now in Algeria. At least that is the information he left with us, as required. I am not permitted to tell you the address. He had completed the required term of his sentence, and he was free to leave."

The next morning Louis went to see Renard. "Lefort has been released. How can I get his address?"

Renard squinted at Louis as smoke from his cigarette curled into his eyes. Louis gave a disgusted wave of his hand. "I am quitting," said Renard, which is what he always said when Louis decided to make a point of his smoking. "You are chasing phantoms," said Renard. "And in Algeria of all places."

"Phantoms?" said Louis.

"Phantoms. You imagine that Lefort had something to do with the bug in your house."

"It was probably planted by Lefort."

"How do you know that? You don't know that."

"You are right. I don't know that. However, I strongly suspect it to be true."

"And on the basis of this suspicion, you want to go to Algeria, a place you are entirely unfamiliar with, in pursuit of a man you have only the slimmest possibility of finding."

"How many Pierre Leforts can there be in Algeria?"

Renard paused and gave Louis a long look. He shook his head and sighed an exaggerated sigh. He opened the center drawer of the desk and withdrew a slip of paper. He studied it for a moment, looked at Louis, and then studied the paper some more. "In Algeria he does not call himself Pierre Lefort," Renard said. "He calls himself Abu Khalil.

"Do not smile at me that way," said the policeman. "Do not look at me like that. I checked into Lefort knowing that, if I did not, you would go off without any information at all and would get yourself in a lot of trouble. A *lot* of trouble.

"Listen . . . ," said Renard. Louis continued smiling. "I'm serious," said Renard, sounding like a stern father. "Are you listening? You don't know Algeria. Algeria is not Washington. It is not Saint Leon. It is a strange and violent place. Islamic terrorists control vast sections of the country, including much of Algiers. There are kidnappings and killings on a regular basis. Some tourists were killed there a few months ago. Remember that? I can't stop you from going, but you don't know the Arabs. You're getting in way over your head this time."

"What you say is true," said Louis, and the smile vanished from his face. "You can't stop me from going."

Louis did not tell the policeman that he had been to Algeria. It had been more than thirty years, but Louis had gone there several times for lengthy stays on official assignments. He had met with Algerian nationalists in an effort to put together an endemic anti-revolutionary militia. It had been a thankless and ultimately hopeless job. The Algerians were suspicious of the Americans and particularly of the CIA. There was little support from the State Department for the project, and eventually none from the Agency itself. The money for his mission vanished, and Louis was called home.

Despite all that, Louis had liked Algeria, and he had liked the Algerian people. They were closed and suspicious at first, which Louis considered right and proper. Samad al Nhouri, the proprietor of the small Hôtel de Boufa where Louis had stayed, had watched him come and go for several days. Then one day, as Louis stood by the front desk looking through his mail, al Nhouri cleared his throat and spoke. "Excuse me, sir. You are from the United States? Forgive me for intruding on your thoughts." Samad al Nhouri had learned English from reading English novels and listening to the BBC, so his English was heavily accented and formal. He invited Louis to join him for a cup of tea.

Once they were seated at a small table in the hotel's courtyard and Samad al Nhouri had poured them both tea, he said, "Describe for me New York City, if you would be so kind. You see, sir, owning a hotel is a bit like traveling, but it is something less. People come and go from all over the world, and through them the hotelkeeper gets a glimpse of their part of the world. But never more than a glimpse.

"You are my first American guest. Forgive me for my curiosity." He pronounced the word so that it sounded like an entire sentence. "Cu-ri-o-si-taye." Louis answered all his questions patiently and truthfully. Only when Samad asked whether Louis was by any chance with the American government did Louis smile and say no.

Eventually Samad took Louis to a café next to the hotel and introduced him to his friends. They were literate men, conservative in their opinions, knowledgeable about world events, and well read in world literature. They met regularly at the café, where they drank tea and talked about ideas and books and politics. Louis joined their conversations in his broken French, and they responded in French or English. Samad al Nhouri's friends regarded Louis with curiosity at first, then with respect, and finally with affection.

When it was time for Louis to return to the United States after his final visit, Samad al Nhouri invited the circle of friends to the hotel for a farewell dinner. He roasted a lamb on a fire of rosemary logs in the hotel courtyard. The air was filled with fragrant smoke. There were bowls of couscous and yoghurt, pots of tea, and bottles of French and Italian wine. The men sat on the ground and ate and drank until their legs were so stiff they had to help one another to their feet. One by one, they each kissed Louis good-bye.

Algeria had been dangerous then too. Some of the meetings he had with the young nationalists could have ended badly. But what Louis remembered now, all these years later, was the café, the scent of lamb roasting on a rosemary fire, and Samad al Nhouri's friendship.

Louis had been uncertain about returning to Algeria. The

thought of leaving Solesme, even for a few days, troubled him. He had been uncertain about going, that is, until Renard had said, "I cannot stop you." Renard had certainly not meant it that way, but Louis decided to hear his words as a vote of confidence.

"Upon his release from prison, Pierre Lefort/Abu Khalil gave his mother's address," said Renard, stubbing out his cigarette. "Her name is Camille Lefort—a *pied noir* probably. Anyway, I would be very surprised if you find him there. But here is what I have. And this." He first handed Louis a slip of paper with Camille Lefort's address on it and then a recent United States State Department advisory on Algeria.

> August 8, 2003. The Department of State urges U.S. Citizens to defer nonessential travel to Algeria and to evaluate carefully their security and safety if they choose to travel there. Over the past several months, the city of Algiers and its immediate suburbs have recorded a drop in the number of terrorist-associated incidents. However, there are continued security concerns. Random attacks still occur in rural and remote areas, on public transportation outside the major cities, and in some parts of the country at night.
>
> In November 2002, ten European tourists were taken hostage by terrorists in the Sahara desert areas of southeastern Algeria, between the cities of Ouargla and Tamanrasset. Two died in captivity and the others have been released.
>
> The Department of State cautions Americans who reside or travel in Algeria despite this warning to take prudent security measures while in the country, including arranging for pre-determined local contacts to meet and accompany them upon arrival and departure at Algerian airports. Nighttime and overland travel outside the greater Algiers area should

> be avoided if at all possible. Visitors to Algeria are advised to stay only in the large, internationally recognized hotels where security is provided. Americans should arrange for a known Algerian companion to accompany them when moving about anywhere in Algeria.

It was with trepidation that Louis told Solesme of his plan to go.

"I will be here when you come back," she said.

"You can't know that," he said.

"I can't," she said, "but oddly enough, I do. Anyway, *of course* you must go. What can you do from here? It's important that you find out everything there is to find out."

"Maybe there's nothing to find out," said Louis.

"There is always something to find out," said Solesme. "And you will tell me everything when you get back." Her eyes glistened with excitement.

Louis took the train to Charles de Gaulle airport the next morning, where he caught a plane for Algiers. Before his plane had even landed in Algiers, his flight information had found its way onto desks at the United States State Department, the Central Intelligence Agency, the National Security Council at the White House, and, of course, onto Hugh Bowes's desk at Bowes, Powell, and Clayton.

The Hôtel de Boufa is not one of the large international hotels recommended in the State Department advisory. It is well kept and clean, but it has only six guest rooms which share three baths, and its clientele is almost entirely Algerian. Moreover, the Boufa is located on a narrow street in the old city where few foreigners ever venture. Women going to and from the nearby market carrying straw shopping bags, men stopping and visiting with one another, children racing about and playing tag, dogs and cats and cars all share the cobblestones and the state of general bedlam.

People stepped aside as Louis's battered taxi bounced and rattled up the hill, the driver peering up at house numbers whenever he could find them. The cab jolted to a sudden stop and the driver jumped out. "Monsieur," he said with an exaggerated flourish and opened the rear door for his passenger. Louis leaned forward and looked about. He did not recognize the street or the hotel. The building looked unfamiliar. Beside the open door, however, hung a small sign with faded Arabic characters on gray metal, and below that, in small letters, simply "boufa."

The lobby was dark and cool. The walls were painted maroon. The blue and white tile floor was cracked and had several tiles missing. Louis wondered whether the small reception desk might not have been on the other side of the room when he had stayed there before. He put down his bag and stepped into the narrow courtyard. It was draped in flowering vines, and sunlight filtered in here and there and made bright spots on the floor and wall. Unseen birds sang unfamiliar songs, and the scent of cooking hung in the air. "Cumin," said Louis.

"You want?" said a voice behind him. Louis turned to see a tall young man with curly black hair and a ferocious mustache standing in the doorway. "You want, mister?" he repeated.

"I made a reservation," said Louis, speaking English. "I called a few days ago." He repeated himself in French.

The man returned to the desk and ran his finger down the page in a large battered ledger. "Monsieur Morgon," said the man. "Yes. Room six. You asked for room six. You have been here before?"

"I have. It was many years ago. I stayed in room six then too. Tell me. I wonder. Is Monsieur Nhouri—he was the proprietor then—is he . . . still around?"

"Monsieur Nhouri?" said the young man. His face darkened. He reverted to English. "Why do you ask?"

"When I stayed here before—the last time it was for three months—he was very kind to me. I would like to see him again. If . . ." Louis could not bring himself to finish the sentence.

"Yes, of course," said the young man. "He is still the proprietor. Shall I tell him you are here?"

"Is he here?"

"No."

"At the café then?"

"You know it?"

"I will put my things in my room and go over and see him."

"Does he know you have come?'

"No," said Louis.

"But your reservation? He pays close attention to the reservations," said the young man.

"I will put my things away and go right over," said Louis.

Louis went up the stairs to room six. He opened the wooden shutters onto the courtyard. Light and sound and memories flooded in on him so suddenly and so intensely that he had to step back and sit down on the edge of the bed. He looked out into the tangle of vines and flowers for a while, then stood and went to the sink. He splashed cool water on his face and went downstairs.

After a brief confusion, Louis found the café. It was to the left of the hotel and not to the right, as he had remembered. As he threaded his way between the pedestrians and the parked cars, two young men in a doorway across the street stopped their conversation and watched him pass. Louis stepped aside for a small old woman. Her dark eyes studied him unashamedly. A small boy darted between the two of them. The old entryway to the café was blocked by an *étagère* piled high with plants. A pair of gray cats slept in the shade underneath. Flies buzzed about the plants, and a few butterflies drifted from blossom to blossom.

He entered the café through a side door on the narrow alley. The door was so low that even someone of Louis's modest stature had to bow his head to enter. This involuntary nod served as a greeting to the other patrons, some of whom inclined their heads slightly in return and then went back to their newspapers or conversations.

Louis looked around the room. There were about eight men seated at several of the small tables. The television above the bar was showing a soccer match, but the sound was turned off. An electric fan on the corner of the bar swung slowly back and forth, seeming to move the noise from the street as much as it moved the air. The sound of cars and voices rose and fell with the motion of the fan. Aside from the elaborate mosaic tile on the floor and the dense pyramid of plants in the front door blocking the sun and the heat, the only other decoration was an old calendar on the wall with a faded picture of a minaret in silhouette against an orange sky.

Samad had stood up with the help of a cane when Louis had entered, but Louis did not recognize him immediately. He was smaller than Louis remembered. After a moment's hesitation, Samad walked toward Louis. His once thick, black hair was white and thin, and his dark eyes seemed to have retreated further into his head. He smiled at Louis and said, "But I know you. Louis Coburn. Louis Coburn, if I am not mistaken."

"Yes," said Louis. "Samad al Nhouri. I know you too, and I am glad to see you." The two men embraced and kissed on both cheeks. Then, without further greeting or preliminary discussion, and without hesitation either, Louis said, "I told you a lie many years ago. Or rather, two lies. I told you I was not with the United States government, when I was. And I gave you a false name. My name is not Louis Coburn. It is Louis Morgon. I beg your pardon for that. I hope you can forgive me."

"I knew both these things," said Samad, and he smiled proudly. "Of course I did not know your real name—is Morgon your real name?—but when I saw Louis Morgon on the ledger, I hoped it might be you. I do not think Louis is such a common name in America. You were my first American guest, you know. And, believe it or not, you are now, after all these years, my second."

"I left the CIA soon after I was here . . ."

"It does not matter," said Samad with a wave. "It was too long ago to matter." He linked his arm through Louis's and took him back to his table.

"And I left the United States soon after that."

Samad waved his hand again as though the facts of Louis's history were but a few persistent gnats. "We were young and foolish. I had lies too. Now we know better. We have a saying here: there are no lies where there is no truth. I am glad to see you, Louis," said Samad. "And that is the truth." He took Louis's hand in his. The two held each other's hands like young lovers.

The two men drank cardamom tea and talked about their lives. Louis told Samad how he had lived in France for the last many years. He explained how his career had collapsed and how, in despair, he had left his wife and his children. Now he had reconciled with his children and, to some extent, with Sarah, his former wife. He knew he could not heal the terrible hurt he had inflicted on them earlier, but, fortunately for him, they all three had forgiving and generous spirits.

His daughter, Jennifer, had been married briefly and had already divorced. She had gone back to school and become a nurse. She had worked at Arlington Hospital in Virginia for a while and had then founded, and now ran, a community clinic for the indigent, the Arlington Nursing Clinic. She had raised money, gotten hospitals to sponsor the effort, and persuaded doctors and nurses to volunteer their time and energy. "She is a forceful and resolute young woman. I am very proud of her." Louis took a photo from his wallet.

"She is a beautiful young woman," said Samad.

"Michael, my son," said Louis, "and Rosita, his wife." He passed another photo across the table. "Michael is an artist, an illustrator. He does drawings for scientific journals mostly, and for textbooks. They are of animals, plants, insects, even microscopic things. He draws very meticulously and quite beautifully, I think. He uses India ink and watercolor and has an exquisite sense of color. I would like him to exhibit these drawings, but he doesn't yet see their artistic worth."

Samad had six children, all born after Louis had left Algiers. "My wife, Jasmine, whom you met, died giving birth to the last, Melina, who herself died two weeks later. That is already many years ago. You met my son, Moamar, at the desk." Louis must have looked surprised. "Forgive him," said Samad. "He is very protective of me. He is the youngest. My eldest son lives in Paris, where he is a doctor. I do not hear from him very often. The other three are here in Algiers.

"My life has been more or less as it was when you were last here. My hotel, my travel books. My children give me travel books on my birthday. Every year. I will show you my library. It has become quite extensive since you were here. I have quite a few books on travel in the United States. You will have to tell me which are the good ones. I went to Egypt fifteen years ago, but otherwise my travel has been entirely in my head.

"The trip to Egypt convinced me that I was ill suited for the rigors of travel. The unfamiliarity of a strange place bothered me, even when it was a beautiful unfamiliarity. I felt uprooted. I could not sleep in unfamiliar beds in unfamiliar rooms. The noise was wrong. The night air was wrong. It was too wet, or too cool, or it did not smell of the right spices.

"I decided that my destiny is not to travel but to encourage the travel of others, to read of their travel, to hear stories of their travel, which I still do enthusiastically and with great relish.

I will insist that you tell me about where you live in France and what life there is like. I want to know about the food, and the houses, and the countryside, and the people. I will live it all with you and through you and, who knows, maybe help you to savor its delights all over again as though you were arriving for the first time."

"I look forward to it," said Louis. "I have come to love the place. In fact, for me, every time I arrive is a little bit like the first time. One of the things I like best about traveling is coming home."

"Have you written about France?" said Samad. "I enjoy nothing more than falling asleep in my own bed with a good travel book open on my chest. Instead of traveling, I welcome those who travel. That has been my calling."

When Louis and Samad rose from the café table, the sun had moved to another part of the sky. "Moamar is an excellent cook," said Samad, "although I warn you: he favors the fiery recipes. It will not be fancy, but he and I would both be honored if you would join us for supper."

Moamar soaked sardines in vinegar and pepper then breaded them and grilled them on a charcoal fire. He slid four sardines onto each plate along with curried rice and peas and cold roasted peppers and tomatoes tossed in olive oil. The sun had set and the heat of the day had lifted. The sardines shimmered in the dim light. The three men sat at a small wooden table in the hotel courtyard and ate.

When they had finished, Louis said, "I have come back to Algiers in search of a man. I do not quite know what to say about this man. In fact, I know very little about him. In France his name is Pierre Lefort, but here he calls himself Abu Khalil. I believe he is Algerian but with a French mother.

"The most interesting thing I know to say about him is that

he robbed my house a while ago. He was caught and served several months in prison. I thought at first that it was just an innocent robbery, by which I mean I thought it was *only* a robbery and nothing more. But it was a strange robbery. He did not take much, and he allowed himself to be caught too easily. I believe now that the robbery was meant to hide a larger crime. I think it was meant to serve as the prelude and setup to my own murder."

Moamar and Samad stared at Louis in astonishment. Not quite knowing what to say, Moamar rose from the table. "I will make coffee," he said. He carried the dishes away and rattled them about in the sink. Samad looked at his friend of many years ago, trying to understand how such bizarre speculations could possibly be true. Or was Louis simply mad?

Moamar returned with a carafe of Turkish coffee. Louis took a sip from the tiny white cup Moamar set in front of him. Then Louis told the entire story from the beginning. He told them about his early relationship with Hugh Bowes and how Hugh had become the American secretary of state. They had both heard of him, of course. He told them about the dead African on his doorstep, who turned out not to be an African at all. And he told them about the plot that he believed had been set in motion with the robbery. "It is not a travel story like you are used to," he said to Samad. "I apologize for that."

Samad smiled. "Travel or not," he said, "it is an amazing story."

"The great Satan is devouring its own," said Moamar, scowling into the cup he cradled in his hands.

"It is an amazing story," said Samad again. "I hope, my friend, you will excuse some scepticism on our part. It is hard to comprehend what you have told us. At the same time, the picture you paint is, unfortunately, not entirely unbelievable.

In this part of the world, such behavior on the part of high American officials is not seen as out of character. You were once a part of that, so you know this to be true, better than Moamar or I do. And as the United States has become more unknowing and callous in its view of the rest of the world, as its official policies seem more and more based on a peculiar combination of ignorance and power, these policies have come to seem more and more misguided and desperate.

"Let us assume," Samad continued, "that it is as you have speculated. Then we have to believe that this Abu Khalil is not eager to be found by you. Which means, quite frankly, that you will not find him. He can go places you could never go; his mother will certainly not give him up to the man he was hired to rob and—who knows?—eventually murder. Why would she do that? She would not."

Louis thought for a moment before responding. "It strikes me," he said, "that he might be willing to meet with me if he can be made to understand that *his* life is in danger along with mine. First, he is in grave danger from the Americans. Once their objectives have been accomplished, those who hired him are not going to want to leave him behind as a witness. *And* he is in danger from his Arab friends who would be very unhappy to learn that Abu Khalil is an American agent."

Samad and Moamar sat silently and considered what Louis had said. "But how," said Samad finally, "do you find him to explain all this to him?"

"I do not need to find him," said Louis. "I only need to find his mother."

Camille Lefort lived alone in a modest white villa of recent construction on a bluff overlooking the city. From her terrace she had a marvelous view down to the busy harbor and the Mediterranean Sea beyond. Each morning, after returning from the market and putting away her purchases, she settled down there, under date palms and fig trees, to read her beloved French novels. She was cooled by sea breezes and lulled into vague reveries by the cry of circling gulls or the hoot of ships and other dim noises from the harbor below.

Camille looked up over her book when Louis pulled the thin chain that rang the bell hanging by her gate. She stood up, laid her book aside, and walked to the gate. Madame Lefort was a tall woman with a fair complexion and straight brown hair, which she wore pulled back behind her head. She had soft blue eyes and thin, straight lips. She raised her hand to shield her eyes as she stepped into the sunlight. "Yes?" she said. "What may I do for you, monsieur?"

"Madame," said Louis. He was wearing a straw hat against the sun. He lifted it with one hand and bowed slightly. It was as if this gesture were a signal, for Camille Lefort opened the gate and motioned for Louis to enter, which he did. Louis closed the gate carefully behind himself and stooped down to pet the black-and-white cat looking up at him.

Camille Lefort led the way to where she had been sitting and motioned in the direction of another chair that was folded and leaning against a low stone wall. Louis picked up the chair and unfolded it, and a pair of lizards scampered into a crack in the wall. Louis placed the chair on the stone walk facing her own.

"What can I do for you, monsieur?" Camille said again.

"I have come," said Louis, "because I have urgent business with your son, Abu Khalil."

"Pierre?" she said. "Oh dear. What has he done now? Are you from the police?"

"No, madame, I am not from the police. I am the man whose house he broke into in France. This robbery, as I am sure you know, landed him in jail in France." Shc began to rise from her chair. "Madame, please, I assure you, I mean him no harm. In fact, I have some information which I am certain will be of great interest and value to him. It could well concern his safety."

"I am sorry, monsieur," she said, standing now beside her chair, "but I do not know where he is. I am not in touch with him, and I am afraid I cannot help you." She motioned toward the gate.

"I understand, madame," said Louis, ignoring her gesture and remaining seated. "That is a shame. As a result of something he left behind in my house, he needs to know that his life is in jeopardy. Not from me. Not at all. But from the people who hired him.

"Yes, madame, I believe he was hired and handsomely paid to commit an inept robbery and then to spend time in jail. He may not have told you all the facts of the case. Like any son, he does not want you to worry needlessly.

"I cannot help but notice however, madame, that your villa is new. It is a handsome house of respectable size and with splendid views. It is the kind of house that does not come cheaply, I am quite sure of that. And it is the kind of house every son would gladly provide for his mother, if only he could."

Camille walked swiftly to the gate. "I think you had better leave, monsieur." She opened the gate and held it open. "Now."

"I understand, madame. I have children of my own. I would feel as you do if someone said to me about one of my children the things I have just said to you about your son. I apologize for my brutal frankness, madame. However, I assure you that you will thank me someday for what I have to say to Pierre, and he will thank me too. If only I can discover a way to deliver my message to him. But I see that you do not know where he is."

Louis had risen. "I understand that it is unlikely, but if you should hear from him, please tell him that I am staying at the Hôtel de Boufa." He gestured in the direction of the city below. "I mean him no harm. And what I have to tell him could save his life.

"Thank you for your hospitality and your patience, madame. I am sorry to have upset you. As I said: the Hôtel de Boufa." Louis reached down and scratched the cat behind the ears. He tipped his hat as he left the gate. He walked to the waiting taxi and got in, tipping his hat once again as he did. He could no longer see Camille Lefort, but he was quite certain that she was watching him.

The number seventeen bus left the Algiers railroad station and followed the Boulevard Hassiba Ben Bouali for a kilometer before turning off. It then wound through narrow, cobbled streets, wheezing and coughing whenever it stopped to take on or discharge passengers. Louis and Samad sat just behind the driver, and Moamar sat three seats back, next to an old woman wrapped entirely in black. She held a wicker basket on her lap, and every once in a while some living thing inside the basket made a rustling sound.

The bus climbed out of the city, past high-rise apartment buildings and along a string of broad boulevards joined, like a necklace, by a series of traffic circles. The streets were lined with ficus and palm trees, oaks and plane trees, as well as other trees Louis did not recognize. The bus stopped at a market where a jumble of stalls and stands was filled with shoppers. Some passengers got off the bus carrying empty shopping bags, and others got on, their canvas and straw bags bulging with groceries and clothes and even small appliances. The bus proceeded past factories and oil storage plants.

Soon they left the city behind. Occasional shacks and shanties had been cobbled together of scrap wood and cardboard and corrugated metal. What few trees they passed were sickly and coated with dust. The road straightened, the bus gathered speed, and soon they were crossing a vast desert interrupted only by grotesque stone formations rising out of the sand. Everything was red and orange with purple shadows. The colors were so vivid against the azure sky that the horizon shimmered. Louis tried to imprint the colors in his mind so that he could paint with them later.

They passed a stretch of olive orchards and then more desert. Every now and then they came upon solitary people riding donkeys or walking. *Where could they have come from,* Louis wondered. *Where could they be going?* A man in a dirty and tattered robe pushed a wooden handcart on wobbly wheels. On the cart was a white appliance—a stove or a washing machine—lying on its side and tied down with ropes, as though it might try to get away. The man leaned into the handle of the cart at a steep angle, and still the cart barely moved. Further along, a small barefoot girl pulled a reluctant goat on a rope. She flailed at the goat with a switch from time to time, and it scampered forward, only to stop in its tracks once again.

The bus windows were open against the building heat, and great clouds of dust swirled through the bus. Louis held a handkerchief over his nose and mouth, but it did little good. He could feel the grit between his teeth and under his eyelids.

Louis, Samad, and Moamar got off at the Al Harib crossroads, where they faced a rambling building, a store, made of concrete blocks and corrugated tin. Men milled about under the tin porch roof, smoking and talking. There were two bright yellow gasoline pumps out in front of the store, and a hand-painted, and highly improbable, sign—GOLF 16 KM—pointed along a small dirt track that disappeared into the desert.

Somebody had laid out a circle of stones between the gasoline pumps and the road and had placed a dilapidated fountain at its center. Cars could not approach the pumps without driving around this imaginary driveway. There was no water in the fountain, nor had there ever been. It sat cracked and ruined and lopsided on the dusty earth. Behind the building, arrayed in a long row, were dozens of cars in various stages of deterioration and demolition, and beyond the cars stood the forbidding peaks of the Atlas Mountains.

Louis and Samad walked to the building to wait, as Louis had been instructed to do in the letter he had gotten the evening before. Samad had been sitting in the lobby when it arrived, delivered by one of his friends from the café. "Someone dropped it off," said the friend. "He said it was important."

"Why didn't he deliver it himself?" Samad wondered.

"Why not indeed?" said his friend.

The envelope was addressed to Monsieur Louis Morgon, Hôtel de Boufa. "It is from Lefort," said Louis. "He tells me where to go. Someone will pick me up there by car and take me to him." He handed the letter to Samad. "It says I am to come alone."

Samad read the letter. "That is ridiculous," said Samad. "I will not let you go alone." And he actually took hold of Louis's arm, as though he meant to physically restrain him.

After some argument, Louis relented. "Perhaps Lefort will think two old men are twice as helpless as one," he said. Next Moamar insisted that he would go along to protect his father. He would remain apart, and once Louis and Samad were picked up by car, he would follow them as best he could. "Don't worry," Moamar said. "It's a store. I'll find someone to drive me. Someone will want to earn a little money."

Louis stood in the shade, his hat pulled far down over his face. Samad went into the shack and returned with two small bottles of pomegranate juice. The two men sucked the sweet nectar through plastic straws.

After a while, a battered panel truck swung into the drive, circled the fountain, and slid to a stop in front of where Samad and Louis stood. The driver leaned across the seat and peered at them with a mixture of curiosity and alarm in his eyes. He could not have been much older than thirteen. "Morgon?" he said in a high, scared voice. "Monsieur Morgon?"

Louis and Samad stepped toward the van. The boy recoiled and waved his hands. "No," he said. "No, no, no. Only Monsieur Morgon."

Samad said that he could not allow his friend, Monsieur Morgon, to come out here alone. "This is a dangerous country for a foreigner, my son. Besides, I am a harmless old man." He smiled and waved his stick to demonstrate his age. The boy looked this way and that before he motioned the two men into the van. Before Samad had even shut the door, the boy stepped on the gas and they sped away.

Moamar approached a man leaning against a battered Ford who agreed to take him wherever he wanted to go, for a price. "Follow that van," said Moamar, and gave the man several bills. The man did not hesitate or question Moamar. It was as though following strangers were a normal thing to do. The man tucked the money into his shirt pocket and Moamar climbed into the car. Rap music was playing softly on the radio. A red, black, and green tassel danced from the rearview mirror as they raced off. "Don't lose him, but don't get too close," said Moamar.

In the van the boy's thin legs barely reached the pedals, and the steering wheel was huge in his small hands. But he drove fast and with assurance. Louis held onto the door, and the boy turned and smiled broadly, as though he knew exactly what Louis was thinking. After a short while they turned off the main road and onto a stone track. There seemed to be nothing between them and the mountains, when they swung around a great boulder and dropped steeply over a ledge.

In front of them was a small house sitting in the center of a grove of fruit trees—oranges, lemons, figs, and a tall, somewhat weary-looking date palm. Beside the house was a small vegetable garden. Some chickens pecked about in the garden and under the trees. An improvised irrigation system of interconnected black rubber hoses wound around the property.

The van slid to a stop, and the young boy jumped out and ran toward Pierre Lefort, who stood in the doorway. He put his arm around the boy's shoulder as the boy explained how Louis had refused to come alone. "I am not surprised," said Lefort. "He is not an idiot.

"I cannot help you," Lefort said, turning toward the men. "You have come a long way for nothing."

"On the contrary. I have already learned something," said Louis.

"And what is that?" said Lefort.

"That you are a man who still listens to his mother."

Lefort laughed. He turned to the boy and instructed him to go inside.

"It is true," said Louis, "that there are things I could learn from you. About the camera you put in my house, for instance. But as to why it is there and who paid you to put it there, I am fairly certain I know more about that than you do."

"Well, in that case, my son can take you back to the bus stop," said Lefort.

"You know, of course, that someone intends to kill me. That is not news to you, and probably it doesn't concern you either. Why should it? But here's the part you haven't thought of. If you had, you wouldn't allow yourself to be found so easily. It is this: when they have finished with me, they will kill you too. They'll shoot you from those rocks." Louis turned and pointed. Lefort looked where Louis was pointing, as though the assassin might already be there, peering down his sights.

"Think about it," said Louis. "First of all, you are a witness to crime in high places in American government. And don't think that not knowing who hired you will protect you. It won't. Once they dispose of me, then you become a liability for them. Second, once your neighbors know that you are an agent for the Americans, they will despise you and want you dead. Both of these groups—my killers and your neighbors—are deadly players, and one or the other of them will get you. Why do you think they picked you to do the robbery? Do you think it was because of your great skill in these affairs?"

"You tell me," said Lefort, smiling uneasily. He shifted from one foot to the other.

"They picked you," said Louis, "because you were just skillful enough to do what they wanted, but you were also known to be lazy and uncurious. You aren't one to ask questions or to try to look behind the scenes, are you? They knew you'd take their money without being too interested in why you were being paid such a large sum. It was a lot of money, and that was all you really wanted to know.

"You are indifferent to the identity of your masters. They must have liked that about you too. And finally, and most importantly, you are dispensable. No one will care if you disappear, besides your mother and your son, of course.

"Frankly, I don't care either," Louis said. "My only interest is in how you might be helpful to me. You have knowledge that will help me fight back and perhaps even gain an advantage. I am at their mercy at the moment, but if I knew what you had done in my house, I could at least fight back.

"I don't expect you to help me out of any concern for me. You aren't a good or compassionate man. Am I wrong about that?" Louis paused. "I didn't think so. And I don't have any money to pay you with. But if I can disrupt their plans, then that might make it possible for you to save your life. Your son might not end up an orphan. Your mother might not have to grieve for her lost Pierre."

Lefort laughed. "Fight back? You are an old man. What do you think you can do against them?"

"I'll show you," said Louis. He turned and pointed to the rocks again. "If you go up there, you will see that we are being watched." Lefort did not move. "Go ahead," said Louis. "Overcome your laziness, for once. Then ask yourself: who would be watching me, and why?" Lefort stared into the rocks. "You spent several months in jail, Lefort. You were paid a lot of money for your time. So why are they watching you? Do you think it is out of concern for your well-being? Do they think I will harm you? Or maybe their reasons are less benevolent."

Lefort straightened up and dropped his arms to his side. "Go ahead," said Louis. He looked up the twisting road. There was nothing to be seen. "I did not see them on the way in. But I am sure they are there. And," Louis added, "don't let them catch sight of you."

Lefort disappeared into the rocks. In five minutes he was back. "So what?" he said. "Two men in a Ford. They could be anyone. Maybe they're scavengers. Scavengers come out here all the time. How do I know you didn't bring them?"

"You don't," said Louis. "Unless you bother to think about it."

Lefort thought for a moment, looking first at Louis's face

and then back to the rocks. Louis waited before speaking. "I am just guessing, Lefort. But I think *you* may appear on the surveillance tape that was made in my house. Doing . . . something. I don't know what.

"In fact," said Louis, "it doesn't much matter what it is. You know, if you're on the tape, then it might as well be your death warrant. Signed and sealed. Your being in my house links us together in the eyes of anyone watching the tape, doesn't it? When they see you there, that makes you my accomplice, deserving of the same fate as awaits me."

"Terrorists," said Lefort after a long silence. "We were supposed to be terrorists."

"We? There were others? Who were they?"

"I don't know. I didn't know them."

"How many were there?"

"There were three of them."

"Did you hire them?"

"No. They found me."

"How did you know what to do, what to say?"

"They had a sort of plan. Like a script. They told me what to say."

"Were they caught too? Were they paid?"

"The robbery came afterwards. I did the robbery, but they were gone by then. So, no, they weren't caught." Lefort's face changed suddenly, as though something had dawned on him.

"And," said Louis, "you can be sure they weren't paid. Do you know why?" Lefort was thinking and didn't seem to hear. "Well, do you?" said Louis.

"Because," said Lefort. He stopped and then started again. "Because they were already on the payroll."

"Exactly," said Louis, as though he were revealing to Lefort what had gone on and not the other way around.

"We were pretending to plan a terrorist attack," said Lefort. "At the tennis matches or something like that. But we talked as though the decision hadn't been made yet . . ."

Louis interrupted. "So that a strong preventative response would be required?"

"A preventative response?" said Lefort.

Samad had stood silently until now, but suddenly he threw his hands in the air in exasperation. "Don't you see?" he shouted at Lefort. "*Can't you see?* My God! Are you a complete idiot?! You have not only engineered Mr. Morgon's assassination. You have engineered your own as well. You are recorded on tape as a terrorist. Presumably, someone was acting the part of Mr. Morgon?"

"That is true," said Lefort.

"Well," said Samad, stepping up close to Lefort so that he was looking hard into his eyes, "did it ever occur to you exactly *who* you might be dealing with, who might *want* such a thing done?"

Samad continued before Lefort could speak. "Government spies do these deadly tricks. Now, Mr. Morgon is, as you know, an American. Or maybe you don't know. Maybe they didn't even tell you *that* much. And, as it turns out, to your great misfortune, he is an *important* American. Now, this is obviously a well-organized and highly planned operation. It comes from a high level. Even you can see that. Am I correct?"

Samad spoke as though he were leading a schoolboy through a not terribly difficult math problem. "Now, which American agency do you think might do such a thing? Which agency might want to eliminate one of its own troublesome operatives"—Samad gestured toward Louis—"and want to blame it on the FLN or al Qaeda or some other terrorist organization? Which one?"

Before Lefort could pronounce the dreaded initials, Samad placed his hand in front of Lefort's lips. "Do not even say it," said Samad. Lefort looked around nervously, as though someone might actually be listening.

"I did not know," said Lefort. "They did not tell me anything. How could I know?"

There was not much more to be said. Lefort was desolate, and neither Louis nor Samad said anything to offer him any comfort. He summoned his son, who drove the two men back to the gas station. Moamar was waiting for them there. The three men took the next bus back to Algiers. "He saw you in the rocks," said Samad to Moamar. "In the car with the guy that drove you there."

"That was a gamble," said Louis. "I'm glad you were there."

"He is convinced that you were spies from the CIA," said Samad.

"Your father convinced him," said Louis. "You were really quite expert, Samad."

Samad chuckled and folded his hands across his belly. "You are not the only one with secret talents," he said.

"Don't be so pleased with yourselves," said Moamar, scowling. "We may not have been CIA spies sitting there in that car, but the plot that you surmised appears to be true. You are marked as a terrorist, and an assassination target. And now it is likely that we are too."

IX

Hakim, the man in the Ford who had driven Moamar, was more than satisfied with the day's accomplishments. He rehearsed his report as he drove back to Algiers. He did not want to leave anything out. He had followed the three men from the hotel and had photographed them getting on the bus. He had followed the bus out to the Al Harib crossroads, where he had photographed the men getting off the bus, then waiting in the shade and drinking juice. He had noted down the make and license number of the van that had picked up the two older men. He had made himself available to the younger man when he wanted to hire a car and had sat with him while the two older men talked with Lefort.

Hakim telephoned his handler and told him everything he had seen, as well as a few things he had not. He said, for instance, that he had seen weapons in the van and more weapons at Lefort's house. He wanted to make sure that he would be handsomely paid for his information. Hakim's report quickly found its way up the line, and even before Louis was back in Saint Leon, the report, translated into English and typed, sat beneath a TOP SECRET cover sheet on Hugh Bowes's desk.

Hugh was certain there had not been any weapons in the van or in the house, but it did not matter. With or without weapons, there was, as he put it in his own assessment to the president, "strong and compelling evidence of imminent terroristic activity. Louis Morgon can have had only one reason for going to Algeria and meeting with one of his co-conspirators, and that is to plan terroristic acts. We must intensify our surveillance of him and his co-conspirators, and, when the moment is right, terminate their operation."

The following morning—it was still the middle of the night in Washington—a man and a woman arrived in Saint Leon sur Dême and took a pair of rooms at the Hôtel de France. The rooms looked out on the square, but the man and woman closed the shutters and drew the curtains. Later that morning two more men arrived and took a pair of rooms. And that evening two pairs of men arrived and took rooms on the floor above. They all parked their cars on the square in front of the hotel.

"See?" said Penont, the hotel clerk, pointing at the cars. Renard was standing at the hotel bar, having a cup of coffee. He turned and looked. "It is unbelievable," said Penont. "The hotel is full. We went from empty to full, just like that."

"Really?" said Renard. "Who are they? I wonder what brought them to Saint Leon."

"I have no idea," said Penont. "But they have lots of luggage. And whatever brought them, I hope it continues. When business is good, madame is happy."

Madame was Madame Chalfont, who had run the hotel

ever since her husband's death. At first, the place had languished under the burden of her loss, for it reminded her too much of her dead husband. After all, it had been their joint project for the last forty years. But then one day she decided she could get beyond her grief only by making the Hôtel de France a sort of monument to him. She hired a new chef and trained him to prepare the Chalfont recipes. She refurbished the lobby and redid the rooms. And she planted so many vines and flowers in the flower beds and window boxes that in spring the hotel all but disappeared in a cascade of blooms and greenery. When guests opened their windows, they were all but overwhelmed by the scent of the flowers and the sound of the bees. "The bees will not hurt you," Madame Chalfont assured them. "And the flowers . . . well, I simply cannot help myself. They remind me of him."

"It's summer," said Renard. "The Le Mans races start soon. It's a little early, but maybe the guests are here for the races." The hotel had long been a favorite stopping place for British drivers and their fans. The walls of the bar were covered with signed portraits of generations of drivers, looking handsome in their coveralls, with their helmets tucked under their arms. "Maybe they're drivers," said Renard, looking out at the cars in the square. Penont laughed.

On his way home from the airport Louis stopped to see Renard.

"What did you learn?" Renard wanted to know.

"That they—whoever they are—have made me out to be a terrorist," said Louis. "By playacting for the camera in my kitchen. They are laying some kind of groundwork."

"Playacting? Groundwork? For what?"

"That's not entirely clear," said Louis. "But I think it includes my assassination."

Renard stared at Louis. "I have decided," said Louis, before Renard could say anything, "to get rid of the camera and the microphone."

"Is that a good idea?" Renard asked. "I mean, as long as the camera and mike remain undisturbed, it allows them to think that you do not know. They can continue to pretend to be gathering evidence."

"They can no longer imagine that I don't know. Besides, if they want evidence," said Louis, "they'll find evidence, whether there is any or not. They'll manufacture it. What is evidence, anyway, but accrued superstition and rumor? If they want to do away with me," said Louis, "they'll do away with me. They have that kind of power."

"Then we have to take it away from them," said Renard angrily.

"That's *exactly* what we have to do," said Louis. "Which is why, when I get back to the house, I'm going to get rid of the camera. I've got to get them to reveal themselves. Whether they do anything about it or not could tell us something about what they're thinking."

Louis removed the microphone first, tearing it from the wall beside the stove. Then he stepped up on a chair and removed the camera. He smashed them both with a hammer. In what seemed like the next minute, he heard sirens.

My God, it's unbelievable. They were here all the time. Will they arrest me or just shoot me down? Hugh will want me shot down. I thought I had some time. A little time anyway. Louis decided he had the best chance to survive if he waited out in the open. He walked to the top of the driveway and stood there. He would raise his arms to surrender as soon as they appeared. What else could he do?

The sirens came closer. Then they stopped. Louis could see

the blue lights flashing down below. They were at Solesme's house. "Oh my God," he said, and ran down the hill. He ran so hard that he stumbled and nearly fell. He arrived in time to see Solesme on a stretcher being loaded into an ambulance. He ran to her side. She was barely conscious. Her eyes were glassy, and her mouth hung open. Her skin was chalk white except for bright red spots on each cheek. Her hair, wet from perspiration, was spread about her head. She had grown so thin lately that her body barely showed beneath the sheet.

"Monsieur, stop," said one of the attendants. He raised his hands and stepped in front of the stretcher. "Please, monsieur, she is very ill."

"I know," said Louis. "I am her . . . Please. I have been taking care of her. Let me go along."

Louis was allowed to ride in the back of the ambulance. They placed an oxygen mask over Solesme's face. A machine monitoring her vital signs whirred and beeped. Her faint heartbeat showed up as a jagged green line on a screen. Louis held her hand. "Forgive me, Solesme," he said. "Forgive me for going away, for being so absorbed in myself. Please, Solesme, don't leave. Stay with us. Stay with us. Stay with *me*." He spoke to her all the way to the hospital while the attendant watched the monitors and tried not to listen.

Solesme regained consciousness in the emergency room. She smiled at Louis, but soon lost consciousness again. Later, upstairs in a ward, she regained consciousness again and this time she remained awake. "Tell me about Algeria" were her first words. She smiled weakly.

"Algeria?" said Louis. He had almost forgotten that he had been there.

"Is it very beautiful?" she asked. "Tell me."

"It was once very beautiful," said Louis, forcing his mind

back there. "Algiers is an old French city. Like Nice or Marseille. But its grandeur is gone. It is run-down; it is dirty. Still . . ." Louis described the Hôtel de Boufa, the reunion with his friend Samad al Nhouri, the sardine dinner, the trip out to see Pierre Lefort. "You should see the color of the desert," he said, "against the color of the sky." He thought that if he could only talk forever, Solesme would have to stay alive.

"I would like to have gone with you," she said. "I should have gone with you." Then: "I am sorry I'm going to miss everything from now on. That is the worst part. The worst part is not knowing how it will all turn out."

Louis could only nod numbly and say, "Yes."

Later that evening, when the lights in the ward had been dimmed and the curtains had been drawn around the beds, Louis slipped off his shoes and climbed onto the bed beside Solesme. She lay on her back. Her mouth was open, and her breaths were shallow and far apart. Louis lay as close to her as he could manage without disturbing her. He placed one of his hands on her pillow and stroked her hair.

When he woke up a few hours later, his arm was asleep, and his back hurt from having lain so awkwardly. While he had slept, Solesme had laid her arm across his chest and her lips were pressed against his forehead. He knew right away that she was dead.

Solesme's brother, François, came from Lyon and led the funeral procession from the church to the cemetery. Louis walked in the middle of the large group of mourners. Afterwards, they all went to the town hall. Everyone greeted François and Louis and embraced them sympathetically. Tables of food had been laid out. People stood about in groups, eating from small plates and talking. After a while, Louis sat down on a folding chair beside François.

"She did not suffer, you know," said Louis. "I'm sure of that. She was serene to the very end." His hand went to his forehead involuntarily. He could still feel her lips there, as though they had left a mark.

"I'm glad she had you," said François. "So was she. Glad, I mean. Happy really. She told me so. More than once."

"Thank you, François. I know she was happy," said Louis. "And I was too. She made me happy. She knew me and knew how to make me happy. Oh . . ."

Once everyone had left, Louis walked home. He turned up the hill past Solesme's house. Her flowers were in bloom, and her rosebushes had been pruned and tied up to their trellises, as though she had just worked on them. How could she be dead and her garden still be so alive? Her life was still there, still going on, after she was gone. At any moment, he thought, she would open the window and invite him to stop for a cup of tea or a glass of raspberry juice. *How can I ever pass this way again?*

Louis went into the barn and leaned a large, blank canvas against the wall. He laid brushes on the table and filled several jars with clean water. On the paper palette, he mixed all the gorgeous colors he could come up with, one after the other. He mixed the colors he remembered from the Algerian desert. He squatted down and brushed paint onto the canvas. He painted as though his life depended on it. But as vibrant as the colors were, as heartfelt the brushstrokes, they did not add up to anything. When his brushes touched the canvas, the color seemed to go flat and turn to mud.

It was late afternoon when Louis finally gave up. He felt suddenly as though he could not stand up for another minute.

He slid the brushes in jars, climbed the stairs in the barn, and collapsed on one of the guest beds.

When he awoke the next morning, he imagined that he was back in Virginia and it was thirty years earlier. He waited to hear Sarah's voice telling him he would be late for work. He had to sit up and hear the birds singing before he realized where he was. Louis got a pen and paper, went to the small metal table on his terrace to write.

Dear Jennifer,

Solesme died Wednesday night. I was with her. As I wrote in my last letter, her cancer had gotten worse. She knew it would take her, and now it has. I am desolate, and yet I still do not comprehend her absence. I cannot even believe she is dead. I see her walking up the driveway, or I see her sitting across the table from me. It is stronger than imagination. It is like an afterimage, a hallucination, except it is real.

What is the difference between death and simply being apart? I don't know. There doesn't seem to be any difference other than my knowledge that our being apart is irrevocable and absolutely permanent.

Forgive me. I know these are not the kind of things you want to hear from your father. It must sound morbid to you, or embarrassing. Maybe you think I am really talking about my own death, but I promise you, I'm not.

As I write this, I realize that, even in this awful moment, my desolation has limits. It will end because it is surrounded by a large measure of good fortune. Not the least because of you. I am so proud of you, and so grateful. Among the long list of good things which are mine, but which I am not entitled to, is your generous treatment of me.

I hope you are well and happy and that the clinic is going well.

Love,
Dad

Louis wrote a similar letter to Michael. He walked to the post office, then to Renard's office. Renard rose from behind his desk and embraced Louis awkwardly. Then the two men sat in silence. Sunlight streamed through the front window, and Louis closed his eyes and waited while it warmed his back. But it did not seem to do so.

Finally Renard lit a cigarette and stepped to the window. "Come here and look at this," he said.

"What is it?" said Louis without moving.

"Come look," said Renard. Louis walked over and stood behind Renard.

"The cars," said Renard. "Do you see them?"

"The blue one?"

"And the sedan next to it. And there are two more in the parking lot behind the hotel."

"What about them?" said Louis.

"They all belong to hotel guests who all arrived on the same day."

"I am not following you."

"See the plate numbers?"

"Paris," said Louis. He turned away from the windows.

"They got here the day before . . . Tuesday was it? And they hardly ever leave."

"I'm sorry," said Louis. He passed his hand in front of his eyes. "I'm too tired for this. I'm still not following you."

"Well, it went by me too, at first," said Renard. "When Penont first told me. But then . . . well, you tell me. What kind of tourists come to Saint Leon with a lot of baggage and then hardly ever go anywhere?"

"Baggage?" said Louis.

"Oddly shaped suitcases," said Renard.

"Now who is being overly suspicious?" said Louis. "I'm sorry, Jean, I can't . . ."

"Not suspicious exactly," said Renard. "But curious. So I checked. The cars are all four rentals. All four from Paris."

"What else does Penont say?" said Louis, looking out the window once more.

"They don't make any calls on the hotel phones. They act as though they don't know one another, but they keep similar hours and take their meals at the same time. It's as though they are waiting for instructions."

"So you think they are watching me," Louis asked.

"They hardly go out, but who knows?"

"Maybe they are," said Louis. He thought for a moment. "But three or four people are enough to watch someone around the clock. This is . . . how many?"

"*Eight*. Eight people. And they mostly stay in the hotel. With a lot of luggage."

"So, what are you thinking?" said Louis.

"You *know* what I'm thinking," said Renard. "They're waiting for orders—or they have orders and are waiting for the right moment—to assault your house. Perhaps they'll arrest you, or maybe they'll kill you. Eight people and a lot of odd-looking luggage . . . containing assault weapons, if I had to guess."

Maybe, Louis thought, he was all wrong. Maybe *nothing* was going on and he had just enlisted poor Renard in his ridiculous fantasy. Or maybe they *were* assassins and he should just allow them to play out their absurd drama, kill him, and then it would be done. But then he remembered Solesme's words. "The worst part is not knowing how it will turn out." *I owe her a good ending,* he thought.

"Look," said Renard. He stepped back from the window and nodded toward the square. A man had walked out of the hotel. He wore khaki slacks, a T-shirt with a picture of a racing car on it, and sunglasses. He unlocked one of the cars and sat down inside. He seemed to be studying something, a map maybe. He spoke on a portable telephone. When he looked in their direction, Renard dodged backward.

"What if they *are* planning an assault on your house?" said Renard. "They have proof that you're a terrorist, and they're waiting for a moment that will somehow conform to their evidence. They have invented a story that proves your guilt, so sooner or later they can launch their assault and confirm their story."

"Then," said Louis, after a moment's hesitation, "we have to begin *our* assault first."

"Our *assault*?!" said Renard.

"Well," said Louis with a faint smile, "perhaps assault is too grand a word for it." He thought for a moment. "We have to force them to do something to reveal themselves before they want to. I tried ripping out the bugs . . ."

"Maybe that is what they are waiting for," said Renard, "for you to do something . . . incriminating."

"Maybe. But if they'd show their cards, we'd have a better idea of what they're up to. Maybe they really are just odd tourists . . . But I think I know how we can find out."

A short time later, Louis was sitting under an umbrella on the terrace in front of the Hôtel de France. Penont had just brought him a cup of coffee. Madame Chalfont arrived at the table and offered Louis her condolences, and he invited her to sit down. "Ah, monsieur, it is all so sad." She recalled how he and Solesme Lefourier had met on that very spot over thirty years earlier.

"There were lights everywhere," said Louis. "The town never looked more beautiful."

"Remember the gypsy violinist?" said Madame Chalfont.

"I do," said Louis. "Henry Kadusco."

"And you and I danced," she said. "Do you remember?" Her eyes shone. "I remember it as though it were yesterday."

Louis smiled at the recollection. "It was your hospitality, madame, that changed my life. Yours and Monsieur Chalfont's."

She smiled and took Louis's hand in hers and squeezed it. At that moment Renard stepped through the door of the police station and marched across the square with such a grim expression on his face that Madame Chalfont let Louis's hand drop. She rose from her seat and took a small step backward. "*Mon dieu!*" she said.

Renard pulled up in front of their table and stood at attention. "Monsieur Louis Morgon," he said in a loud voice and the most official tone he could manage, "I am placing you under arrest. Will you come with me please?"

'What is the charge, Renard?" said Louis.

"I am arresting you for the murder of Solesme Lefourier."

Madame Chalfont let out a cry and sank back onto the chair.

Louis stood up. "It is a mistake, madame," he said, as though he had ordered tea and Penont had brought him coffee. "A mistake. I assure you, it will be sorted out in no time. If you will excuse me."

"As though he had ordered tea," said Madame Chalfont, "and Penont had brought him coffee." People had gathered in front of the hotel almost immediately. The whole of Saint Leon was talking about the arrest of Louis Morgon for the murder of Solesme Lefourier.

"Of course it is a misunderstanding," said Penont. "Why would anyone kill someone who was already dying?"

"To help them die, of course," said Lansade, the *boulanger*. "To spare them the agony and pain. That is the only logical explanation. That must be what happened."

"Aha," said Penont. "Well, that is a humane thing to do if they are in pain."

"Humane perhaps," someone else said, "but still against the law."

A debate erupted on the merits of helping someone die, whether pain was sufficient justification, whether that person, while perhaps not legally culpable, was culpable in the eyes of God. "He is an American," someone said. "Monsieur Morgon is American. They think differently about such things."

"Oh, but he has been here a long time."

"That he has been here a long time does not change the fact that he is still an American." The arguments came fast and furious. They washed over one another and masked the sadness and confusion that everyone felt.

"We shall have to wait and see," said Madame Chalfont. "Life certainly has a way of taking a strange turn."

Louis was taken to a cell in Tours. "May I stop at home and get a book?" he asked Renard.

"I will get it for you. What do you want?"

"It's on the kitchen table," said Louis. "Dostoevsky, *Crime and Punishment*."

Renard sighed and rolled his eyes. "Of course. Why am I

not surprised?" Now he sat in his office and waited. He tried to do paperwork, but he could not concentrate. The telephone rang. "Finally," said Renard, but he hesitated a moment before he lifted the receiver.

"Renard," he said.

"*Inspecteur* Renard, this is Captain Montfort." It was his superior in St. Calais. "I will get straight to the point, *Inspecteur*. Regarding the arrest you just made: you are to secure Mr. Louis Morgon's release immediately," he said.

"But, Captain, he has—" Renard was not permitted to finish the sentence.

"All charges are to be dropped. Immediately. Is that clear? Louis Morgon is to be released. I am faxing you the paperwork," said the captain. Renard's fax machine began humming before he had hung up the telephone.

"So, it is as bad as I feared," said Louis when Renard came to the prison to see to his release. "They don't want me in the custody of the police. They prefer to have me out and about, where they can do whatever they want, whenever they want."

"That is one possibility," said Renard, but he could not think of any other. For once he could not disagree with Louis's grim assessment. "What do we do now?" he asked.

"You go home to Isabelle," said Louis.

"And what about you?"

Louis looked at the prison guards standing by the door. "I think it is best that I disappear," he said softly. "I'll be in touch with you." Louis looked into the policeman's eyes.

"Shouldn't you . . . ?" Renard began. But he did not have any suggestions, so he looked away.

The two men walked slowly through the front door. Louis's shoulders were slumped. He even took Renard's arm for support as they descended the stairs. They crossed the gravel courtyard and reached Renard's car. *Is he up to this?* Renard wondered. But a moment later when he turned to look, Louis was gone.

"How can he bear it?" Isabelle wondered that evening at dinner. "Solesme's death, this terrible vendetta. And then arresting him for . . ."

Renard raised his hands in self-defense. "That was his idea. I was against it. In fact, I couldn't believe it when he proposed it. As for how he can stand it, that's beyond me too. I just don't know."

"But why the murder of *Solesme*?" Isabelle wondered. "If you had to accuse him of a crime, why that in particular? It seems so cruel."

"Because," Renard said, "it is plausible. In the first place, she just died. And, in the second, because he had apparently thought of helping her die. They had talked about it. She thought that she might want him to do that someday. To help her die. Of course, he couldn't bear the thought of it. And she didn't want it, at least not yet. 'As long as *I* can stand the pain,' she said, 'then so must *you*.' "

Isabelle still found the whole idea shocking and terrible. "What if Solesme knew you were doing this?" she said.

"Louis thinks she would be pleased," Renard said. He thought about it for a moment. "And you know what? He might actually be right. You know Solesme. She would be thrilled to have a part in this whole business. She never wanted to miss out on anything."

The day after Louis was released from jail and disappeared, the strange tourists checked out of the Hôtel de France and disappeared themselves. "They all left at the same time," said Penont. He paused in his sweeping and leaned on the broom. "It was like a small convoy. They just got in their cars and sped away. Madame is desolate. They were the perfect guests. Clean. Quiet." He began to sweep the bar floor, then paused again. "And they paid in advance. In fact, they paid through the end of October. Full daily seasonal rate. Imagine that. It is a large sum."

"Through the end of October?" said Renard.

"Of course madame will return their money."

"Let me know if she is successful," said Renard.

"If she is successful?" Penont did not understand.

"If she is able to find them, to return their money," said Renard, taking a sip from his coffee.

"You think they were up to some mischief?" Penont wondered.

"I have never known innocent people to pay in advance," said Renard.

X

Pierre Lefort was lazy, just as Louis had said, but he was not stupid. On the morning after Louis's visit, before the sun had even risen, Pierre packed the white van with some clothes, bottles of water, and cans of food. Then he took a flashlight and went out to the small shed behind the house. He pushed aside some garden tools, hose, and bits of plastic; moved some empty cartons and an old wheelbarrow; and pulled a small white plastic tub out of the corner. Pierre set the light on the wheelbarrow so that it was pointed at the tub. He pried up the lid, peeled it back, and withdrew a thick bundle of dollars and euros from the bucket. Then he returned to the house and woke his son.

"Get dressed, Zaharia," he said.

"Why?" said the boy, trying to rub the sleep out of his eyes.

"We have to leave," said Pierre. "Hurry up. Get dressed."

"Why?" said the boy again. But Pierre did not answer, and

Zaharia did as he was told. A short while later, still drowsy and confused, the boy climbed into the van. They drove away from the house, leaving everything as it was. Pierre could not bear to look back. He knew he would never see this place again.

The headlights of the van swept across the stony landscape as they jolted and lurched up the road. The shadows shifted as they passed, and the familiar cliffs and boulders took on strange and menacing shapes.

"Papa," said the boy, "I'm scared."

Pierre did not respond at first. But then he reached over with his right hand, stroked the boy's head, finally pulling him to him. "I know," he said.

Pierre did not call his mother to tell her of his decision to disappear. He did not dare tell anyone where he was going, and he knew his mother would beg him to tell. Nor did he tell the boy's mother that they were leaving. When she learned finally that Zaharia and his father had vanished without a trace, she was beside herself. But whom could she turn to for help in finding them? There was no one.

The eastern sky began to turn pink as Pierre pulled onto the main road and headed south. Apart from a few trucks, there was very little traffic. He and the boy ate some apricots and figs. They drank juice from paper cartons. The sun rose high into the sky and hung motionless above them as they drove into the mountains. Late in the afternoon, they turned onto a smaller road and, after half an hour, onto a narrow stone track. After lurching along the track for about an hour, they arrived in the village of Al Ghargourat.

Al Ghargourat, which is not even on most maps, consists of a few round stone huts huddled under a cliff and surrounded by miles of undulating stone and sand. The people of Al Ghargourat have a few small olive groves and keep some chickens and a skinny goat or two. Summers are scorching and winters, bitter cold. Pierre had not been there for more than twenty years, but he especially remembered the summers, when everything shimmered in the heat.

When Amir opened the door and recognized his boyhood friend Pierre standing there, he smiled broadly, spread his arms wide, and enfolded Pierre in a warm embrace. "Welcome in Allah's name," said Amir, and kissed Pierre on both cheeks.

"My son, Zaharia," said Pierre, motioning toward the van. The boy climbed down and came forward.

"You have a son?" said Amir in astonishment. "Has it been that long?"

"Can we stay with you?" Pierre asked. "Just until I figure out my next move. I think," he said as though it had just occurred to him, "we are going to France."

The boy's eyes widened, but he did not speak.

"France?" said Amir.

"I lived there for a while," said Pierre. "I will tell you all about it." Later, when they had eaten and the boy was asleep, Pierre and Amir sat outside and smoked. Pierre told Amir about his time in France and about how well his life had been going, until now. But now they had to leave.

"Maybe I can help you," said Amir. He explained how he drove oil tankers all over North Africa and the Middle East, and he offered to take Pierre and Zaharia along on his next trip. No one would know or care. "I go to all the ports and I know people at all of them," Amir explained. "Getting on a ship to France should be easy. The only thing is, it will cost you." He named a large sum.

"All right," said Pierre. "Thanks, Amir. I knew I could count on you."

"Here is how it works," said Amir. "I get a call. A couple

of times a month I get the call. There's going to be a shipment from, say, Algiers to Tripoli, or from Benghazi to Port Said. I've been all those places," he said proudly. "And then some."

Amir would be told when and where to show up, and he would be given the name of a contact. When he got there, the tanker truck would be waiting. "Good new trucks, too. The best. There's a lot of money involved. There are hundreds of these trucks going back and forth." He would be provided with shipping manifests and customs documents.

The tanker he was to drive was filled with off-the-books oil that had been skimmed from the production of a Saudi company. The Saudi princes, who were also the oil company executives, and their cousins, who were oil ministry officials, were thus able to exceed export quotas and avoid the price controls that had been agreed upon by OPEC. They also avoided taxes and other duties, and enriched themselves in the process.

The oil was bound for the United States and Europe, where it eventually ended up being sold and distributed on the black market. "Oil prices are political dynamite over there," Amir explained. "They'll do almost anything to keep the costs down. So this way the Europeans and Americans can keep the lid on prices, the Saudis keep the oil flowing and the pipelines open, I make some money, and everybody is happy."

When Amir delivered a tanker to his assigned destination he was handed an envelope filled with money. "*Good* money," he said. "*Very* good money." He then found his way back to Al Ghargourat and waited for the next call.

A few days after Pierre and Zaharia arrived, the call came. Amir, Pierre, and Zaharia got into Amir's Toyota truck and drove north and then east. "You didn't tell me why you're going, what you're running from," said Amir. They had stopped for gas. He and Pierre stood behind the pickup.

Pierre looked to see that the boy was out of earshot. "I'm in trouble," he whispered.

"I know that," said Amir.

"That's all I should say about it," said Pierre.

"You should have told me," said Amir. "What kind of trouble?"

"I can't say. It's big. Believe me, it's best for you if you don't know."

Amir gave him a long look. "Still, you should have told me," he said. "I'm risking my neck, you know."

The shore west of Tripoli was lined with rows and rows of gigantic steel storage tanks connected to one another by an impenetrable tangle of valves and pipes. Pipes of every size climbed over one another like steel vines, twisting and turning corners and going up and down and in every direction. Here and there steam escaped from valves, making a hissing noise and shooting up jets of vapor. A tall, narrow stack at the water's edge spouted blue flames high into the air. Beyond the tanks and pipelines enormous tanker ships sat at anchor, riding low in the water.

Amir pulled into a vast, unpaved lot between two sets of storage tanks. He stopped next to a line of tanker trucks parked side by side. Amir punched some numbers into his satellite telephone and waited while it rang. He listened and then hung up without speaking.

After a short while, a Land Rover appeared on the road. It turned into the lot and came toward them, leaving great clouds of yellow dust in its wake. "Wait here," said Amir. He got out of the Toyota, and two men got out of the Land Rover. They looked in Pierre's direction and gestured with their heads as they spoke with Amir. Pierre looked straight ahead and tried not to watch. After a while, the men handed Amir a packet of papers. They got back in the Land Rover and drove back the way they had come.

Amir helped Pierre and the boy load their things behind the seat of a tanker truck. He drove the Toyota under a shed, and Amir, Pierre, and Zaharia climbed into the cab of the tanker truck. Amir turned the ignition, and the engine roared to life. He put the truck in gear and drove out onto the highway.

"Why France?" said Amir.

"I told you," said Pierre. "I lived there."

"You did time there," said Amir.

"Please, Amir, don't . . ."

"I just want you to be straight with me," said Amir. "I'm taking a big chance for you."

"Please, Amir," said Pierre. "My son. Not in front of the boy."

"Suit yourself," said Amir with a shrug, and gave himself over to driving. They rode in silence.

The engine hummed. It was warm in the cab. They rocked forward and back as though they were in a cradle. Pierre woke up as they came to a shuddering halt. He had been dreaming of France, and for a moment he did not know where he was. He looked over at Zaharia. The boy was asleep. He murmured and turned his head back and forth restlessly.

It was the middle of the night, but it was as bright as day. They were surrounded by brilliant orange lights mounted on top of tall masts, and Pierre could hear the loud electric hum of the lights. He could smell salt in the air, and he could hear the sea slapping in the darkness somewhere below them.

They had stopped at the head of a long concrete pier. A great tanker ship loomed above them, groaning and creaking where it rubbed against its moorings. Fat hoses and thick ropes hung down her side and snaked, in random patterns, back and forth across the pier. The words *Miss Chastain* and *Libya* were painted in white on her black hull.

When Amir climbed down from the cab, he was met by two men who appeared from behind the truck. One was in shirt-sleeves, while the other wore a uniform and a pistol on his hip. The two men went over the papers Amir handed them. The men spoke for a while, then gestured toward Pierre and the boy. Amir returned to the truck. "Give me the money."

Pierre reached inside his shirt and took out an envelope. Amir opened it. He counted the bills quickly, as though he was used to handling large sums of money. He climbed down and handed the envelope to the man in uniform, who put it in his pocket without looking inside.

"This ship is bound for Marseille," said Amir, handing Pierre a fat envelope. "Inside you have crew papers that should get you ashore. Once you're in Marseille, though, you're on your own. But France is easy. By then you should be home free."

"Thank you, Amir. I owe you a lot."

"Go with Allah," said Amir. He embraced Pierre and patted his shoulder. He did not look at the boy but turned and walked away.

The journey to Marseille took five days. The seas were calm. The nights were clear and still, and the days were sunny. During the day, Pierre and Zaharia sat on deck in the shade of a lifeboat and stared across the flat, green water. Gulls followed the ship the entire way, swooping and diving whenever the garbage was thrown overboard. Zaharia stood at the back of the ship and watched the gulls glide above his head. He held out his hand as though he had something to give them, but they knew better.

"What is France like?" Zaharia wanted to know.

"You will see," said Pierre. Then: "It is hard."

"Why is it hard?"

"The French make it hard. They hate us. The French hate North Africans."

"Why?"

"They think we are all criminals," said Pierre.

"Is everyone in France rich?"

"No. But a lot of people are."

"Amir said you were in jail."

"That is true. I was in jail. Stop asking so many questions."

The crew consisted entirely of Pakistanis, thin, hard men who kept to themselves. They did not seem surprised or even curious about the father and son who had joined them. They did not ask questions because they did not want anyone asking questions of them.

Among the crew, there was a boy who looked to be not much older than Zaharia. He was even smaller than Zaharia and had large, dark eyes. His dark hair lay in a great tangle on top of his head, and he had the wispy beginnings of a mustache. He wore the same filthy clothes day after day and shoes that were much too large for his feet.

Most meals aboard ship consisted of curried stew, which simmered in a great pot and to which the cook added potatoes and carrots and other vegetables throughout the voyage. Pierre and Zaharia ate with the crew, seated around a long table covered with a tattered sheet of oilcloth. The Pakistani boy leaned over his plate and ate ravenously, as though he had not eaten for days. Even while he ate, he could not take his eyes off Zaharia. He seemed astonished to see another boy aboard ship, and a privileged child at that. Zaharia did not even have to work.

Pierre and Zaharia slept on thin, soiled mattresses on metal bunks in the ship's small dormitory. Like everyone else, they slept in their clothes. The room was steamy and smelled of sweat. Men snored and sighed and groaned in their sleep.

The night before they reached Marseille, Pierre took Zaharia up on deck. He looked around to make certain they were alone. "Here are some people you can contact in France," he said, and pressed a paper into his son's pocket. "In case you have to. And here is some money. Put it away where it will always be safe."

"Why?" said Zaharia.

"Just in case," said his father. "Do as I say." His face was serious and stern, and he watched as Zaharia stuffed the money deep into his pants pocket.

Zaharia lay awake late into the night, trying to imagine what France might be like. He pictured it as a sort of paradise, with big shiny cars everywhere and plentiful food and palatial homes. Pale, handsome people smiled at him and said, "Welcome, Zaharia."

It was already late in the morning when Zaharia woke up. He was alone in the dormitory. Sunlight found its way through the hatch and onto the dormitory floor in bright, thin strips. He heard the hollow sound of the ship grinding against the dock. He heard the muffled noises of the harbor and ran up on deck to find his father. Father and son gathered their belongings together and lined up with the crew. After showing their papers to the immigration officials who came on board, they were allowed ashore.

One of the Pakistanis had written the name of a cheap hotel on a piece of paper. "It's a good place, and cheap," he said. Pierre and the boy walked through the streets of Marseille following the Pakistani's directions. This did not seem like France to Zaharia. It seemed more like North Africa. He heard Arabic everywhere, and the streets were filled with people who looked North African. It looked just like in Algiers. There was lots of noise and dirt. It did not seem like paradise.

There were open-fronted shops, food stalls, and restaurants everywhere, and the smell of cooking filled the air. Pierre bought two meat pies, and they sat in a small park eating them. Beggars sitting under trees nearby eyed them as they ate. "Let's go," said Pierre, throwing the rest of his pie in a trash can. A man in rags dug it out and began eating it as they walked away.

Pierre saw the fear and consternation in his son's eyes, but he could think of nothing he could do or say to comfort him. *If only they do not find me,* he thought. He did not know whom he should fear more: the Americans or the Arabs. He wondered whether he should have trusted the Pakistani crewmen as he had, or Amir, for that matter. He only knew that he had left a broad trail behind him, which anyone wishing to do him harm would have little trouble following.

In fact, they did find Pierre, and they did so with relative ease. And even in his last seconds alive, as he saw their knives slashing down upon him, he still did not know who they were.

The Hôtel St. Denis, which the Pakistani had named, was in a narrow building on the rue St. Denis, in a residential quarter inhabited mainly by poor Arabs. The hotel was the only commercial establishment on the block, which otherwise consisted of shabby apartment blocks and an abandoned factory that had once made umbrellas. The tiny hotel lobby, a step up from the sidewalk, contained a small, chipped Bakelite table and two overstuffed chairs covered in green leatherette that was splitting at the arms. The proprietor was sitting in one of the chairs reading *Le Monde* when they arrived. In the other chair sat a huge Persian cat with green eyes and matted white hair.

The only decoration in the place was a framed reproduction

of da Vinci's *Last Supper,* hanging above the front door. It had evidently hung there for years, for the color had faded almost entirely, and everything was one shade of brown or another. The picture had apparently once been part of an advertising poster, for the words *QUI SAIT?* (who knows?) were still visible in large type across its center. The proprietor rose slowly from his chair as Pierre and Zaharia entered. The cat raised its head and looked at them. Pierre asked for a room and paid cash for four nights. The proprietor counted the money twice.

Their room was small and clean and sparsely furnished. There was a sagging iron bed, covered with a chenille bedspread, positioned against the wall to the left as you entered. A dresser with a mirror attached was against the opposite wall, and a wooden straight-back chair and a sink stood like sentries on either side of the door. The wooden floor had been scrubbed and polished over the years until there was no finish left on it, except around the edges of the room.

The high ceiling was painted white, and a plaster medallion in the center suggested that the building had seen better times. A small glass lamp hung from the medallion and, along with the pale yellow wallpaper with its pattern of little pink roses, somehow gave the room a cheerful aspect for which Pierre was grateful.

There was one small window, which did not close properly, opposite the door. It looked out onto an adjoining roof and, beyond that, to a tall building across an alley. That building's windows were all sealed from inside with what appeared to be blue plastic. Ropes hung from the roof and ended halfway down the building. The plastic rattled and the ropes swung slightly when the wind blew. Pierre pulled down the window shade. There was a toilet just at the head of the stairs.

Early on their third morning in the St. Denis, just as the sun was coming up, Zaharia awoke to the sound of a commotion in the hall. His father was not in bed. Zaharia was about to open the door to see what was going on, but decided instead that he had better look through the keyhole first. He saw two men in policemen's uniforms and two other men. Their faces were contorted and their brows were furrowed in concentration as they held his father down against the floor. Pierre was struggling mightily, arching his back and then collapsing, then arching again. He tried to kick out but they held his legs.

Pierre's body arched one last time, and he seemed to remain in that position for a long time before his body sagged and he was finally still. Zaharia did not know what to do. He did not know whether the men would come for him, so he turned the key in the lock as silently as he could and got back into bed. He pulled the covers up and pretended to sleep.

Before long he heard sirens and the sound of men running up the stairs. Zaharia understood some French, but everyone was speaking at the same time and too quickly for him to make out what they were saying. Then there was a knock at the door.

Zaharia turned the key in the lock and opened the door. A tall policeman stood in front of him. The hallway was filled with police. Beyond them the toilet door was open. Blood had dripped down the sides of the toilet bowl and was splashed about on the door. At that moment a stretcher was being lifted by two attendants in yellow coats. Pierre lay on the stretcher, his head turned sideways, facing the boy. His skin was gray, and his open mouth had been stuffed with a huge wad of blue plastic. His wide eyes looked straight at his son, but they saw nothing. Zaharia knew his father was dead. Pierre's head bobbed as he was carried down the stairs.

The tall policeman went down on one knee. His face was

right in front of Zaharia. It looked like a kindly face, but it belonged to one of the men who had killed his father. "What's your name, son?"

"Zaharia," said the boy.

"Do you know what happened?"

"No."

"Did you see or hear anything?"

"I was asleep."

The policemen thought for a moment. "Your door was locked?"

"Yes," said Zaharia.

"Do you have anyone you want us to call? Do you know anyone in Marseille?" said the policeman.

"No," said the boy.

"Well, we're going to finish up out here, son, and then we'll come take you someplace where you'll be safe. In the meantime, go back in your room and get your things together. I'll be right back."

Zaharia rolled his things into a bundle. He did the same with Pierre's things. He sat on the bed and waited. He opened the shade and looked out the window at the building with the ropes hanging down. After a while, he heard a sound at the door. He looked through the keyhole but didn't see anyone.

He opened the door, and the large white cat walked into the room. Zaharia watched the cat cross the room and jump onto the unmade bed. He walked over and sat down next to the cat. The cat looked up at Zaharia, and the boy thought of his father's terrified eyes. He could not stop seeing them. He could feel the blue plastic as though it were in his own mouth, and he began to cry. Tears rushed down his cheeks and splashed on his shoulder blades. He wept bitterly, and yet he did not make a sound. He stroked the cat while he wept.

When Zaharia went downstairs, the cat followed. In front of the hotel, policemen were interviewing the proprietor and writing down his answers. Others were talking to neighbors, asking them what they might have seen or heard. The policeman with the kindly face was still there, so Zaharia went back upstairs. He picked up his small bundle of things, opened the window, and stepped through onto the roof of the adjoining building. He crossed the roof and found an unlocked door that led into a stairwell and down two flights to another door that opened onto the alley.

An hour later, Zaharia had found his way to the train station, where he sat on a bench, eating a *pain au chocolat* and wondering what he should do. There were crowds of people coming and going. He took the list of names his father had given him "just in case" from his pocket and studied them one by one. There were six names on the list, but they were all unknown to him, except for one: *Louis Morgon,* followed by the words *Saint Leon sur Dême.*

XI

The village of Pen'noch sits alone, out of the way and almost forgotten, among the stony cliffs at the southern end of the Bay of Audierne in the Finistère. The villages to its north and south are not only more attractive and more accessible, but they are also served by small, efficient hotels and several restaurants. And these towns have beaches that attract a regular stream of visitors. Pen'noch has none of these things.

You can get to Pen'noch by any one of three small roads, all three of which come from small villages inland, and all of which wind and twist their way along ancient rights-of-way through fields and marshes and woods. When the ocean is finally within sight and you imagine you have reached your destination, the three roads converge, and it is only at this point of convergence that a small sign announces the village of Pen'noch. You must still pass over the cliffs and descend toward the harbor, and only then does the village finally reveal itself. This particular configuration of roads suited Louis's purposes well. There was only one way into Pen'noch, but there were three ways out, not counting the path along the coast heading north and south.

Of course, Louis knew that his arrival in Pen'noch would not go unnoticed. Like the inhabitants of small villages everywhere, and particularly those off the beaten track, the citizens of Pen'noch made it their business to scrutinize every stranger. If he did not stay, they watched him leave. If he *did* stay, they made it their business to know what had brought him. And they were unabashedly straightforward in this pursuit. They asked direct questions, they stared, and they exchanged information. They seemed to consider it their obligation and moral duty to know who was in their town and why. Though it might seem otherwise, this also recommended Pen'noch to Louis as a suitable hiding place. He knew that once he had told them his story, he could depend on the citizens of Pen'noch to establish his false identity for him.

Louis stepped from the cab in the Pen'noch square just above the harbor, and a group of three women and a man broke off what had, until that moment, been an animated conversation. They watched Louis pay the fare—they noticed that the taxi was from Quimper—and gather his things from the trunk. They watched as he crossed to the *mairie*—the town hall. He carried a knapsack on his back, a small suitcase, a plastic bag of groceries, and what appeared to be a large wooden briefcase.

When Louis left the *mairie* a short time later, they stared at him again. He nodded in their direction, but they did not smile or otherwise acknowledge his greeting. Nor did they avert their eyes until he was out of sight.

In the ten minutes it took Louis to walk along the path

above the sea to a gray stone cottage with blue shutters and to turn the key in the lock, they had learned from Natalie Lechamp, the secretary on duty in the *mairie,* that he was Louis Bertrand, an Irish painter, and he had rented the small cottage owned by the mayor. The odd wooden box he carried held his paints and brushes. It had legs that unfolded so that it also served as an easel. Monsieur Bertrand spoke excellent French, but with a slight accent. He appeared to be an amiable man. He had not said how long he intended to stay, but he had rented the cottage for two months with the provision that he could extend the lease.

That evening Louis stood in line at the bakery behind the same three women. He greeted them as though he knew them. "*Mesdames,*" he said, and tipped his hat. This time they nodded in return. Within not too many days, almost everyone in Pen'noch had laid eyes on Louis and thought they knew his business.

Another thing about village life in France, and perhaps everywhere else in the world as well, is that a stranger, no matter how long he stays, remains a stranger. Even if he is accepted and becomes part of village life, it is as the village stranger, which is not unlike the village pharmacist or the village doctor or the village teacher or, in some cases, the village idiot.

If the stranger is accepted over time, the people of the village become his mentors and protectors. They take great satisfaction in teaching him their ways. They correct the errors and missteps that he commits with astonishing regularity, and they praise his astuteness when he does or knows something a stranger might not be expected to do or know.

One sunny day shortly after his arrival, Louis carried his paint kit to the dock. He extended the legs under the portable easel, placed a canvas on the tray, and began to paint. He had not painted the ocean before, and he found the constantly changing light frustrating and difficult. After a time, Louis turned to see a man standing behind him, studying the canvas he was working on. "You've gotten the prow wrong," said the man. "The arc of her. You've got her like this, but she's more like this." The man moved one hand and then the other to show Louis what he meant.

"Ah," said Louis. He studied the boat and then the painting. "You're right."

"Of course," said the man. "And the mast is a bit too far forward." The man paused. "You see, I built her," he added finally, half by way of explanation, and half as apology.

"You built her?" said Louis. He lowered his brush and turned to face the man again. "You have built a beautiful thing, monsieur. I take my hat off to you." And Louis actually lifted his hat.

The man smiled in return. "Forgive me for speaking up. I could not help myself, monsieur. I apologize. I am not a critic. I can see you are an excellent painter. But"—the man shrugged—"I built her."

"Have you built many boats, monsieur?" asked Louis.

"I have," said the man. "Thirty-six, to be precise. I am Jean Pierre Lamarche, monsieur. I live just over there."

"I am Louis Bertrand," said Louis. The men shook hands. "May I invite you, monsieur?" said Louis, motioning with his head to the small bar that faced the *mairie*.

The men sat at one of the tables on the square. Jean Pierre drank a glass of beer and Louis drank cold cider from a small ceramic cup. The sharp, sweet taste bit into Louis's tongue. He closed his eyes and felt the sun on his arms.

It turned out that Jean Pierre Lamarche was also a stranger. He was originally from Paris, where he had been a professor of literature at the Sorbonne. He had left Paris in 1978 and come to live in Pen'noch full-time, more or less. "My grandparents were from the Finistère, near Douarnenez. My fondest memories are of summers spent at their house. My grandfather built boats, and when I was a teenager, he began teaching me. I helped him in his workshop and learned from the ground up. I suppose it was all but inevitable that I would build boats, once I came to live in the Finistère, that is."

Over the last twenty-five years, Jean Pierre had acquired a reputation in this corner of Brittany as a builder of fine small sloops. He built them using only hand tools and traditional methods, and he had orders for as many boats as he wanted to build.

Jean Pierre's wife had died a year earlier. And so, while the two men took an immediate liking to one another, it was sadness that cemented their friendship. "Marianne and I were married forty years. We spent great blocks of time apart. She adored Paris and I did not. She did not like the sea. She was cold most of the time she spent out here. She couldn't wait to get back to Paris.

"She stayed in Paris most of the time, and I stayed here in Pen'noch. But only now that she is dead do I notice and comprehend her absence. Her absence is complete and total. It cannot be undone. I cannot go to Paris and find her there. A day apart from someone who has died is far worse than a day, or a month, for that matter, apart from someone who is alive. When someone is alive, there is always the possibility that the absence will end."

Louis spoke only reluctantly about Solesme. Her death was more recent, and he feared the power it held over him. The thought of her touch, the feel of her warm skin beneath his fingers, rendered him almost incapable of speech. But he found, at the same time, that speaking of her with Jean Pierre, who was gentle and understanding, revived for him somehow the happiness he and Solesme had shared. He was grateful to be able to speak of her and to recollect their shared life.

One day Jean Pierre invited Louis to visit his workshop. It was in a large, tin-roofed shed behind his house on the southern edge of the village. The two men stopped and admired the view of the sea from the doorway. Inside the shed a small sloop was in the early stages of construction. The stays and beams of the vessel were in place, resting on wooden supports and held together by shims and pegs, looking like the skeleton of a large sea creature. The dirt floor underneath was littered with wood shavings and sawdust, and lights with broad metal shades hung from the ridge of the roof. Drawknives, wood planes, mallets, spoke shaves, and adzes of various sizes and configurations were suspended from pegs on the wall over the long workbench. The place smelled of shellac and wood. Jean Pierre explained the double rigging of a sloop, the special shape of the hull, and how it all came about. He described the purpose of the various tools he used.

"Would it disturb you, Jean Pierre, if I were to paint your workshop while you worked?"

"It would not disturb me in the least," said Jean Pierre. "On the contrary. It would allow me to make certain that you got it right."

Louis invited Jean Pierre for supper. He built a fire in the small iron grill on the terrace in front of the cottage and grilled mussels until the shells popped open. Then he drizzled wine and butter over them and served them with roasted potatoes. Jean Pierre savored the wine Louis served. "To be honest," he said, "I have never liked cider that much."

The two men sat on the terrace gazing over the low stone

wall at the sea. The evening air was chilly, and there was fog over the water. The sound of a foghorn drifted in, and another, more distant horn answered. "The second one comes from the light," said Jean Pierre, "The Pointe du Raz."

"That far?" said Louis.

"When the wind is right, and when there is a cold fog, the fog carries the sound great distances."

"Have you ever painted?" Louis asked Jean Pierre one day. He had set up his easel in a corner of Jean Pierre's workshop and was sketching a row of tools onto a fresh canvas. He was using a thin wash of blue paint, and streaks of blue ran down the canvas as Louis's brush moved quickly across the canvas. "Those drips will disappear into the painting," said Louis.

"I have never painted," said Jean Pierre, watching Louis. "I am not much of a sailor either. I am a dilettante. In the best sense of the word, I hope. And you? Have you always been a painter?"

"No," said Louis. "I traveled for a living. I only discovered painting after I retired and started coming to France. I am like you with your boats. I love the act of making the painting. I love using the tools and materials, and I love pursuing a sense of competence. Now that I am retired, I do what I love."

"And how did you find Pen'noch?"

"I hiked through here some time ago. I started at the Pointe du Raz. It took me three days to get this far. I was charmed by the place. The view from the cliffs to the north is enchanting. I could only see the church and a few of the houses situated on the highest ground. And then the lower town and the harbor came into view as I got nearer. I remember thinking, at the time, that the harbor and the town were timeless. But not picturesque, if you know what I mean. That suited me."

Louis thought of Samad. *I am lying again to someone I*

like. How can I do it so easily? How easily he became someone else and abandoned who he had been, like he was changing clothes. He was hiding, but it required little effort. Hiding took no time, it required nothing of him except lying. And forgetting.

Louis tried not to think of his house in Saint Leon or of his garden going to waste, day by day, certainly by now overgrown with weeds. Soon it would disappear altogether. He tried not to think of Renard, of Isabelle, of the Hôtel de France. He did not want to forget them, but when he remembered them, his mind filled with anguish and longing.

Louis was shocked one day to realize that he could not quite picture Saint Leon, which had been his home for the last thirty years. Even after being gone such a short time, he could not remember it exactly. He still knew the layout of the place, of course, but some details eluded him when he tried to fix them in his mind. He could not quite see Renard, who was his best friend, or even Solesme, whom he had loved. Her face swam uncertainly in his memory. He did not know for sure the color of her eyes. He closed his eyes and reached out with his fingers as though he might still be able to touch her. But, as Jean Pierre Lamarche had said, her absence was complete.

Walking home from buying groceries one day, he saw a young woman coming toward him with a red and white spaniel on a lead. The woman had short, dark hair and large eyes. She was slender and had a halting gait that caused her body to turn in a strange, but all too familiar, way. Louis stopped in his tracks. The young woman stopped too, since Louis was staring at her.

"What is it, monsieur?" she said sternly.

"Excuse me, madame. I am sorry for staring, but you remind me very much of someone very dear to me." The young woman's eyes flashed and she did not smile.

"In fact, the more I see you, madame, the more you remind me of her. I apologize. Please forgive me."

"I accept your apology, monsieur. But it is alarming nonetheless to be stared at in that way." The woman walked on and Louis watched until she disappeared over the next rise.

Once the strange tourists had left the Hôtel de France, Renard let some time pass before he paid a visit to Louis's house. He was busy with other police work, and he did not think the matter was urgent. But when he got there, he found that the lock had been forced and the front door was broken in. He pushed against the door and it swung open to reveal the devastation inside. Shelves and bookcases had been emptied onto the floor. Drawers had been dumped out, and mattresses had been pulled from the beds and slit open. Pictures had been torn from the walls, and their glass and frames had been crushed on the floor. This was not just a search; this was intimidation. Renard took photographs of the destruction and filed the appropriate reports.

His reports elicited a telephone call and then a visit from Paris. The visitor presented himself one rainy morning at Renard's home. He wore a dark suit, a white shirt, and a dark necktie. "I am from the *Sécurité nationale*," he said, although in truth he looked more like a funeral director. He showed Renard his badge and waited to be invited inside. Instead, Renard stepped out into the rain and pulled the door closed behind him. The two men stood in Renard's garden. The visitor did not seem particularly put off by Renard's unfriendliness. He squinted up into the drizzle and smiled an indifferent smile.

The man recounted for Renard some vague details of Louis's

infamy—his consorting with known terrorists, his being armed, his being a danger to the community—while Renard listened in silence. Finally Renard said, "I cannot believe it. We have been friends for a long time."

"We know that," said the visitor. "That is why I am telling you these things. You must be alert and vigilant. With your help we can bring him in—without harming him, of course, and without endangering the community. He must be brought to justice and made to answer for his crimes."

The man paused for a moment. "I wonder," he said. "Have you heard from him?"

"No, I have not heard from him," said Renard.

"Well, keep an eye out and let us know if you do hear from him." The man handed Renard his card.

"I haven't heard from him," said Renard again. He looked at the card.

The man studied Renard. "Do you expect to hear from him?" he asked.

"I don't know. I do not know what to think."

Renard said the same thing to Isabelle that evening "I don't know what to think." She did not respond at first. They had finished eating but remained at the table. Renard had told her about the visitor from Paris. He regarded her now with an expression of faint astonishment, as if to say, *I no longer understand the world. The simplest things, which I once thought comprehensible, have become mysterious and impenetrable to me.* "I do not know what to think," Renard said again, in order to force a response.

"About Louis?" said Isabelle finally.

"Not about any of what the guy from Paris says," said Renard. "No. That is all nonsense. But, yes, about Louis. Where is he? *How* is he? What is he doing? *How* is he doing? It is the not knowing that I find difficult. Does he need me to do something? And what? *What!?*"

"I will tell you," said Isabelle, and Renard looked at her as though she might actually know the answer to his questions. "No, no," she said with a laugh. "But I know and *you* know that he is doing all right. Otherwise we would have heard something. He would have been in touch somehow. If he needs you to do something, he will tell you what it is. I would guess that, for now, he simply needs you to wait."

Renard did not find her assurances comforting. "He can't call here," he said. "They would know if he did. He can't write; they would know that too. As long as he is out of touch, they can't reach him. If he tries to contact me, though, he risks letting them know where he is. I am not good at waiting."

Renard looked at Louis's mail on the side table. The stack of envelopes and circulars he had been picking up at the post office had grown quite large. He removed the rubber bands holding it all together and leafed through everything yet again. Suddenly he paused, leafed backward through the stack and then forward again. "Look at this," he said. "I missed something." He held up a letter. Then another. Then yet another.

"Here are *three* letters from Jennifer, his daughter."

"So?"

"Three letters from your child, all within a matter of two weeks?"

"Maybe it is good news," said Isabelle.

Renard held up the first letter and studied the envelope. He hesitated a moment before slitting it open with a dinner knife. "Louis will not mind," he said, and began reading. "She is happy," he announced after a few sentences." Then: "She has met someone."

"There, you see?" said Isabelle. "Just as I said." She watched his eyes scan across the page. His mouth moved silently. Finally he said, "He is young and handsome and intelligent. His name is also Louis. Lou, that is. Lou Coburn." Renard looked at Isabelle and shrugged. The name Louis Coburn meant nothing to him.

"Louis is a common name," said Isabelle. "Now that you have started, you have to open the next one."

Renard read the next letter. "This young Lou Coburn works for some government agency. His work is very important." Renard smiled. He felt relieved. "Young women *always* think their young man's work is important."

"I never did," said Isabelle, smiling at him. "Go on. Open the next one."

Renard read the third letter. His mouth stopped moving. He reread what he had already read. He hesitated once more before he began reading aloud. He pronounced the English words slowly and with difficulty. "Dear Dad. You won't believe what has happened. What a small world it is!! Lou invited me to a big engagement party for one of his coworkers. It was at Cincolini in Georgetown in a private room. Cincolini is just about the fanciest place in town at the moment. It's in an old town house. The dining room has lots of brocade and gold and heavy draperies and lots of candles everywhere. It was packed with people. There were, maybe, a hundred people there. And right there, at somebody else's party, Lou asked me to marry him. Things are moving way too fast for me, and I told him so. But it was a wonderful moment, and I told him that too. He was very sweet and promised to wait until I was ready.

"Then this man walked up who looked very familiar and, guess what? It was Hugh Bowes, the former secretary of state!!! I couldn't believe it. But he was so sweet. He put his arm around

Lou and congratulated me on finding such a fine young man. But here was the real surprise: he remembered working with *you*!! He told me how the two of you had been close associates!!! I didn't know any of that!! You worked with the secretary of state??! My gosh! Why didn't you tell me? He made me promise that I would say hello. 'Give my very best regards to your father,' he said."

XII

After putting away leftovers and cleaning up the dishes, Isabelle lingered in the kitchen. She was expecting Renard to call, and she wanted to be near the phone. When the phone rang, she picked up immediately. There was silence at the other end, and then she heard her name. "Isabelle." A pause. "How are you?"

"Louis! My goodness!" she said. She immediately regretted saying his name; she did not know who might be listening. "How is your mother?" she said, saying the first thing that came into her mind, trying to sound casual. "Has she . . . recovered?"

"My mother? Not entirely," said Louis. Isabelle thought she heard him smiling at her effort. "But she is much better, thank you. And you? How are you?"

"Fine," she said. "It must be difficult for you . . . and for your daughter."

Louis was silent.

"Are you well?" Isabelle asked. She did not know what to say.

"Yes," said Louis. And after another long pause: "Is Jean there?"

"He is not."

"Will he be back tonight?"

"He won't. He has been away for several days. First Paris, then your old hometown."

"My old . . . ?"

Isabelle did not know how these things were done. She wanted to make herself clear to Louis, without making herself clear to his enemies. Would Louis sort out her meaning? Renard himself had made no great secret of going to the United States. He had ordered his tickets and made hotel reservations by telephone. And yet Isabelle felt compelled to conceal everything she could conceal, as though even repeating mundane facts could place Renard's life in danger. The world had become such a strange and treacherous place, and she needed to learn how to find her way in it.

"Isabelle," said Louis. "Listen: I sent Jean a postcard. I didn't have your address, so I sent it to his office. Did he see it?"

"No," said Isabelle. "I don't think so. He would have said so. And Jean is gone."

"Yes," said Louis. "I see. Well, I sent the card to his office."

As soon as they had hung up, Isabelle drove to Renard's office. The night was warm, and the windows in the hotel dining room were wide open. You could hear the clatter of china as the tables were being cleared, and there was laughter coming from the bar.

Isabelle turned the large iron key in the old lock, and the door to Renard's office swung open. Even before she switched on the light, she saw the stack of mail Marie Picard had left on the corner of the desk. Isabelle leafed through the mail, but there was no postcard.

Isabelle took the mail home and sat at the dining table, turning it over, piece by piece, spreading it across the table as though she were playing solitaire. But the mail seemed like nothing more than the guileless accumulation of a village policeman's daily business. There were official documents and circulars that were undoubtedly meant to be posted on the bulletin board. Most of these, she was certain, Renard would throw away. There were commercial circulars advertising mattresses and potted plants. There were court notices and schedules of hearings.

She turned over a small brown envelope that Renard appeared to have mailed without sufficient postage. It had been returned, stamped, front and back, POSTAGE DUE. The ten-centime stamp was obviously insufficient. What had Renard been thinking? In fact, was that even his handwriting? After a moment's hesitation, Isabelle tore open the envelope and found a picture postcard of the French Alps. Written in block letters on the back of the card was a telephone number and 13:15. There was no other message and no signature.

The next afternoon Isabelle drove to Tours. At exactly one fifteen, she placed a call from one of the public booths outside the main post office to the telephone number written on the postcard. Louis answered immediately. Before she could say anything, he asked where she was calling from. Next he wanted to know what on earth Renard was doing in Washington. "And when did he go?"

"He went," she said, "by way of New York actually. He went two days ago, because . . ." She hesitated briefly. "Because he knows you will go. He wants to be there when you arrive."

"When I arrive?" said Louis. "Why does he think that I will go? Why would I go?"

"Because . . ." Isabelle took Jennifer's three letters from her pocket. She took a deep breath. "You received three letters from your daughter, Jennifer," she said. She read the letters to Louis. She paused once or twice in her reading, but when she did, she heard only silence from the other end of the line. When she had finished reading, she waited. She thought she heard Louis breathing, but he did not speak. Finally she heard him say in a faint and strangled voice, "I cannot talk right now. I am sorry, Isabelle." He hung up the phone.

As Renard entered the customs hall at John F. Kennedy International Airport along with crowds of other arriving passengers, a large woman in uniform instructed everyone to sort themselves into two lines—one for citizens and one for noncitizens. The lines were long and snaked back and forth past rope barriers before arriving at a yellow stripe painted on the floor two meters in front of a row of glass booths.

When Renard finally arrived at the front of the line, a customs agent, a burly man in a tight white uniform shirt, signaled him to step forward. The man held out his hand and Renard handed him his passport. The agent leafed through the pages of the passport, then looked at Renard, comparing his face with his photo in the passport. The agent slid the passport through an electronic scanner. Renard had hoped to escape discovery by passing through customs in New York instead of in Washington, but he realized now how naïve he had been. It was a futile gesture. Undoubtedly his information was already finding its way into computers in Washington. After studying the screen of his computer for a few seconds, the agent handed the passport back to Renard. "Enjoy your stay," he said, looking past Renard to the next person in line. "Next?"

After collecting his small suitcase and passing through another checkpoint, Renard found the line where people were waiting for taxis. When his turn came he stepped into the assigned cab, pulling his suitcase in with him, and said, "Take me to the Hotel Cliffton," enunciating each word as carefully as he could. Despite his best effort it still sounded like *tek mee to zee ot-el-cleef-TONE.* The driver wore a turban. His eyes appeared in the rearview mirror. Renard said, "It is at East Eighty-seven Street by Lexington Avenue." The taxi roared off, finding its way somehow into an apparently endless stream of traffic.

They bounced and rattled along one great boulevard after another at what Renard considered to be excessive speed. There were traffic cones everywhere, and temporary concrete barriers, and arrows and flashing lights. The roadbed dipped and buckled like a living thing. Everything seemed under construction. It had just rained, and the rough, uneven streets were slick and shiny. The cab was swept along in an endless river of cars and trucks and buses, honking and growling and roaring, crowding in on one another, weaving in and out with what seemed like the greatest urgency and impatience.

The sky was gray and heavy. Suddenly the city appeared through the mist before them, spread across the entire horizon, tall and jagged and immense. Renard leaned forward and peered hard through the Plexiglas barrier and the windshield as the buildings rose up larger and larger. Renard had feared going to this huge city, but now, instead of dread, he felt excitement rise in him. "It is beautiful, the city," he said, smiling. The driver's dark eyes glanced back at him, but the man did not speak.

The Cliffton Hotel was all but hidden under ugly scaffolding that rose along the front of the building, casting the entry in darkness and concealing entirely from view whatever charms the narrow town house might have to offer. In an incongruous gesture the management had strewn rose petals on the front stairs, making it seem to Renard as though he had arrived in a fairy tale and were walking into an enchanted cave.

The lobby was small but attractive, with bright spotlights in the ceiling and shiny black lacquer everywhere. Vases of flowers on the front desk and on a side table were reflected again and again in the square mirrors mounted on opposite walls.

"Welcome to the Cliffton," said the desk man in a strong East Indian accent. Renard filled out a form, and the man gave him a card that he said would open the door to his room. The room on the third floor was small but comfortable. Its window was covered with a gauze curtain. When Renard pulled the curtain aside, he found himself looking out at a brick wall.

After walking around the neighborhood, Renard found a small fish restaurant on Third Avenue. He sat at a tiny round table by the bar and ate a meal of mussels and French fries. He had a half bottle of Muscadet, which he was amazed to find on the wine list at a decent price. "In fact," he told Isabelle on the telephone the next morning (it was already afternoon in Saint Leon), "everything was reasonably priced, and the food was excellent."

"I am not at all surprised," she said.

"You should see New York," he said. "It is like an entire country of its own. It is unimaginable."

"It sounds as though you are right next door," she said. But of course he was not. "What are you going to do next?" she asked.

"I will go to Washington," said Renard. "But beyond that I

don't know what I will do. I will just have to see what I can find out."

Renard checked out of the hotel and took a taxi to Pennsylvania Station, where he caught the next train for Washington. He watched the passing landscape in wonderment. They emerged from the tunnel and sped across marshlands, past factories and refineries whose smoke turned the sky yellow, past truck depots and shipping docks with endless stacks of rust-colored containers. He wanted to remember it all so he could tell Isabelle everything. He kept a map unfolded on his lap and followed the route with his finger.

Newark came and went, then smaller cities whose odd names he had never heard before, then Trenton, which was marked on his map with a star. He saw the dome of the state capitol flicker in and out of view between office buildings. The train slowed as they approached Philadelphia. The boarded-up buildings and junk-strewn lots of North Philadelphia seemed endless.

In Wilmington, an enormous mural of a sounding whale covered the entire side of a building. Renard could not begin to imagine what it meant. They crossed the Susquehanna River, which was very large, and which he had never even heard of. They rode for nearly four hours and covered only one small corner of this enormous country. Renard measured the distance on the map with his thumb and index finger. "This much only," he said to himself. The man across the aisle raised his head from his book and turned to look at him, but Renard did not notice.

Renard took a taxi from Washington's Union Station to Jennifer's address—5440 Powhatan Street, Arlington, Virginia—which he read to the driver from a slip of paper.

"POWhatan," said the driver. "It's pronounced POWhatan. You French?" he asked, turning around and looking at Renard.

"Yes," said Renard. "I am French."

"I thought so," said the driver. He paused. "The French was right, you know. I said so from the start. You don't just go into that part of world over there . . ." That was all Renard was able to understand, even though the driver spoke continuously for the rest of the trip.

The cab stopped in front of a small apartment building near the Ballston Metro station. "Here we are," said the driver. "Fifty-four forty Powhatan." He remained seated while Renard lifted his suitcase from the trunk. The Prescott, as the low brick building was called, had been built fifty years earlier, when this had still been the outer edge of the city's suburbs. It had been an early harbinger of the city's expansion, but now it sat in perpetual shadow, surrounded by tall apartment towers.

Renard found a hotel a few blocks from the Prescott. It was an ugly, peculiarly American place of the sort he had seen often in American movies, with a brick façade dressed up with cheap colonial trim and false shutters. "All our rooms are non-smoking," said the clerk, a short-haired young man wearing a bow tie and a name tag that said ROBERT.

Renard's room was outfitted with blocky, anonymous furniture designed mainly to withstand the assault of endless numbers of hotel guests. A television, bolted high up on the wall, was on when Renard entered the room. The remote control was cabled to the nightstand, which was bolted to the floor. Renard turned off the television. He turned off the air conditioner, which was on high. The room smelled like disinfectant, but the windows would not open, so Renard lit a cigarette.

After unpacking, Renard bought a newspaper at the front desk and walked to a coffee shop across the street from Jennifer's apartment. He sat in a booth watching through the window while he sorted out what he should do. He was a stranger here, and everything felt unfamiliar and slightly dangerous. He ordered a sandwich and a soft drink. The sandwich was tasty, and Renard felt better.

After a while, he dialed Jennifer's number from the public phone by the restrooms. He got an answering machine. "I'm not here right now. Please leave a message." Renard and Jennifer had met years before, so he thought he recognized her voice, but he did not leave a message. He ordered a cup of coffee and sat with the cup between his hands. He hoped he would recognize Jennifer if he saw her, but he did not know what he would do if he recognized her. Should he warn her about Bowes? And what about Lou Coburn? She would think he was insane.

"Heat up your coffee, hon?" said the waitress.

Renard gave her a baffled stare.

"More coffee?"

"Yes, please," he said. Although he had drunk only a few sips from the first cup, she poured new hot coffee into the old. This was just one of countless American habits Renard found astonishing. Heating up coffee.

At three thirty in the afternoon, after Renard had been in the coffee shop for nearly two hours, he paid his check and left. He dialed Jennifer's number from a different telephone and again got her answering machine. Again he left no message. He waited for a while on a bench at a bus stop. He watched as buses came and went and passengers got on and off. He tried her number again at five thirty. She did not answer.

Renard was walking back toward his hotel when he saw her coming up the escalator out of the Metro station. She had a bag of groceries in one arm, and her other arm was linked through the arm of a tall young man also carrying groceries. They leaned toward one another, talking and laughing at the same time. Anyone could see they were in love.

Renard waited nearby while they went into the Prescott before he dialed Jennifer's number once more from the phone beside the bus stop. "Hello?" she said. She sounded out of breath.

"Yes," said Renard. "I would like to speak to Lou."

"Who's calling?" said Jennifer.

"I would like to speak to Lou."

"Just a minute," said Jennifer, and Renard hung up the phone. He walked a short distance down the street and waited. After a few minutes the young man came through the door of Jennifer's building and looked up and down the block. He crossed the street to the telephone by the bus stop and studied the street again. Then he returned to the Prescott and went inside.

Renard smiled and spoke to himself in English. "Finally," he said. "I have learned something."

Renard resumed his watch early the next morning. The young man left the Prescott shortly after eight, and Renard followed him onto the Metro and from there to an office building on K Street. After the young man got on an elevator, Renard entered the lobby and studied the directory. "Can I help you?" said the guard at the desk. Renard pretended as though he had not heard. "Sir! Can I help you?" said the guard, speaking more forcefully this time.

"I am sorry," said Renard. "I am looking for . . . a man. He works here. In this building. He is Lou Coburn."

"It doesn't ring a bell, buddy."

"I'm sorry?" said Renard.

"I don't know everybody that works in this building. What company is he with?"

"Oh, I see. I am very sorry," said Renard, and left the building.

Renard went back to Jennifer's building. He approached

the entry just as a young woman was leaving. "Please," he said, and quickened his step. She smiled and held the door for him. "Thank you," he said, and stepped inside. He went to Jennifer's apartment and studied the door. There were two locks showing. He went to the floor above and the floor below, which were identical to Jennifer's floor. He went to the basement and to the roof terrace. Over the next two days Renard did as thorough a reconnaissance of Jennifer's life as he could without having any contact with her or alerting her to his presence. He went to the clinic where she worked and watched from outside the building. He saw where she shopped. He sat a few tables away from Jennifer and Lou Coburn on the terrace of the Starlight Restaurant, where they ate supper. They held hands and spoke in whispers. They touched wineglasses and laughed.

Two days later, and just five days after Renard's arrival in New York, Air India flight 1618 from Paris arrived in Toronto. A short time later, Louis came through the doors into the terminal's waiting area. Though Renard was standing behind a barrier along with the friends and families of other passengers, he did not have to wave. Louis found him in the crowd.

THE CURRENT ALERT STATUS IS ORANGE.
PLEASE REPORT ANY UNUSUAL OR SUSPICIOUS ACTIVITY TO
LAW ENFORCEMENT OR SECURITY OFFICIALS.
The Department of Homeland Security

The enormous sign hung where it was easily visible to all traffic waiting to enter the United States. After a perfunctory look, Canadian border agents waved everyone forward. But now all traffic stopped and waited to be scrutinized by the Americans. There were six lanes of cars, trucks, and buses, and because of the additional precautions brought about by the recently declared orange alert, traffic was backing up.

Sergeant William Terrell, of the United States Border Patrol, leaned forward and peered into the next car in his lane. The man in the front passenger seat—a slightly addled-looking older man with unruly white hair—leaned forward, looked into the agent's eyes, and smiled. "Hello," said the man. Sergeant Terrell did not smile back. Instead, he turned his attention to the driver. "Your papers, sir," he said, and held out his hand.

Renard handed Sergeant Terrell his passport along with the car rental agreement. Sergeant Terrell examined the rental papers and handed them back. He studied the passport, turning the pages until he found the American visa. He studied it for a moment. He compared Renard's face with his picture, then handed the passport back. "Your papers, sir," he said, turning his attention to Louis, who was still smiling at him. "Hello," he said again.

"He has no papers," said Renard. "He is my cousin." He pronounced it *coo-zang*. "I visit him in New York. He is in home . . ."

"In *a* home," said Louis, grinning even more broadly at the customs agent. "Sunset Years Retirement and Care," he said. "Armonk, New York."

"He is in *a* home in New York," said Renard. "I am visiting him. He run away. To Toronto. I don't know how he get Toronto. I go . . ."

"Sunset Years Retirement and Care," said Louis. "Armonk, New York." He brushed his hands through his hair so that it stood up even wilder.

"Sir," said Sergeant Terrell to Renard, "would you step out of the car, please, and open the trunk?"

"I'm sorry?" said Renard.

"Armonk, New York. Armonk, New York," said Louis in a singsong voice.

"The trunk, sir. Please, step out of the car and open the trunk." The border agent pointed to the rear of the car. The Frenchman got out of the car. He fumbled with the key and finally managed to unlock the trunk lid. "It is rental car," he explained. "I am sorry." The customs agent opened the two suitcases in the trunk and found that they contained men's clothing and toilet articles. He pulled them aside and lifted the floor of the trunk and looked at the spare tire compartment.

Sergeant Terrell looked up in time to see Louis walking, faster than anyone might have guessed he was able, *back* toward Canada, past the long lines of vehicles waiting their turn to cross into the United States. "Sir!" said Sergeant Terrell. "Sir, you'll have to come back." Louis walked even faster.

"Mon dieu!" said Renard, and he and Sergeant Terrell took off after the old man, who was now nearly running. Louis zigzagged in and out between waiting cars and did not allow himself to be caught easily. When they finally got him, with the help of Canadian agents, Sergeant Terrell and Renard took Louis by both arms and walked him back to the car. "Armonk, New York. Armonk, New York," he said. With Sergeant Terrell's help, Renard finally managed to get Louis buckled into the passenger seat. Once the sergeant was sure that both doors were securely closed, he slammed the trunk and, without another word, waved Renard ahead while he turned his attention to the next car in line.

"You didn't have to run quite so fast, did you?" said Renard. He was still out of breath.

"We'll turn in the car in Armonk," said Louis, "and rent a different one. Just to be safe."

As they drove, Renard told Louis what he had learned from watching Jennifer and Lou Coburn. "Her phone is tapped. When I rang them from a phone booth, Coburn came out and checked the booth. He learned very quickly which phone I had called from. I doubt that Jennifer knows her phone is tapped.

"He works at 116 K Street, on either the eighth or tenth floor. I watched the elevator numbers light up. The eighth floor is a law firm called . . ." Renard steered with one hand and pulled a slip of paper from his pocket. "Addison, Goldstein. The tenth floor is . . . Tetra Trading."

"That will probably be it," said Louis. "Tetra Trading. They always choose names like that. It's supposed to sound anonymous and vague. And they like top floors. Besides, law firms are too public. Anyone can walk in."

"Coburn lives at—"

"His name is not Coburn," said Louis. "Louis Coburn . . . that was *my* name when I was undercover with the Agency—the CIA—many years ago. This is Hugh Bowes's way of taunting me. And threatening me. He is saying that *this* Coburn is *his* man. He enticed Jennifer to send me his veiled threat in order to draw me into the open, to get me to come here. Which he has succeeded in doing. By now he will be reasonably certain that I am in the United States."

"If I had known, I could have . . ."

"You couldn't have done anything other than what you have done," said Louis. "I have no doubt that they will harm her if they think it will serve their purposes," Louis said. He paused only briefly to collect himself. "They want to make me desperate. And they know harming her or threatening to harm her will . . . have the desired effect." They drove on in silence.

The following afternoon, when Renard and Louis arrived in Washington, they drove straight to Jennifer's clinic despite the risk in doing so. Jennifer was not there. In fact, they were told, she had not appeared at an important appointment that morning. "She was supposed to meet some people from Arlington Hospital about funding. It's just not like her not to show up," said her assistant. "And usually when she's not coming in, she calls. I'm worried. It's just not like Jennifer. I called her apartment. Do you think she's all right?"

"I don't know," said Louis. He turned away and stood looking out through the storefront of the clinic. He saw the backward words *Arlington Nursing Clinic* on the plate glass in front of him, and he saw them again reflected on the shiny side of a bus rolling past just at that moment. It seemed as though he were in a hall of mirrors, and if he walked outside and turned around, the words would *still* be backward, as though everything he saw was a distortion or a reflection of something else.

"I blame myself," said Renard. "I gave myself away. The telephone call to Jennifer's phone. The cameras at Tetra maybe. I don't know. I'm sorry. Forgive me."

Louis called Sarah to warn her. After hearing that Jennifer had not showed up for work and might be in danger, Sarah began shouting at Louis. He had brought this all down on their heads by leading a life of duplicity and intrigue. He had placed the lives of his own children in jeopardy. What kind of insane person was he? What kind of insane people had he been involved with? How could anyone do such a thing? Finally she just wept.

Louis could think of nothing to say that might console her. "Please, Sarah," he said finally. "I am doing what I can to find her. The best thing you can do for her is to protect yourself. Please. Leave town. For yourself and for the children. Go somewhere where you don't know anyone or have any connections. Do it as quickly as you can manage. Just for now. Will you do that? Sarah? Please."

She had stopped sobbing. "Yes," she said. "I will do that."

Louis called Michael, who listened to his admonitions and

to his apologies in silence. When Louis had finished, Michael said, "Well, what are you going to do?"

"Me? I'm going to try to find Jennifer," said Louis.

"How? Do you even know where to look?"

"No, not exactly," said Louis. "But I have some leads."

"Leads?" said Michael.

"Ideas," said Louis.

"In other words, you don't have anything," said Michael.

Louis was silent.

"Meet me," said Michael.

"What?"

"Meet me. Meet me. Right now."

"Michael, I can't . . . They're probably listening to us right now. You should stay out of it. You and Rosita should leave town if you can. You shouldn't . . . *Wherever* we chose to meet, they would be there before we were."

"Come on, Dad, you're a stranger here. You think you know your way around, but you don't. Listen, I *know* the city, and I can help you. Don't be so . . . stubborn. Meet me. Rosita is away," he added. "She's safe. I'll tell her to stay put."

"You'll be followed."

"*Right* now, Dad. The rope swing where we used to swing."

"Michael, do you have a passport?"

Michael was silent for a moment. Then he said, "I'll bring it." Before Louis could object, Michael hung up the phone.

It had begun to rain by the time Louis and Renard pulled up at Potomac Heights Park. "Wait here," said Louis. "I'll be right back." Louis turned up the collar of his jacket and hurried across the playground and playing fields. No one was there. From behind the picnic shelter, trails led off in different directions, and, after a moment's hesitation, Louis followed one into a grove of sycamores. The rain rattled on the thin canopy above his head, and a few sycamore leaves drifted to the ground.

After a short distance the ground began to fall away more steeply, and the river came into view below the trees. Beyond the river he could see Georgetown. Louis stopped. Though it had been thirty-five years, he suddenly saw himself pushing Michael on a rope swing until the little boy seemed to fly out over the river: a few running steps and then the big pushing motion. "Higher," Michael would cry out in his high, sweet voice. "Come on, Dad! *Higher!*"

An airplane passed low overhead on its way to Reagan National. "Dad," said a man's voice from behind him. Louis turned and embraced his son.

"Michael, you don't have to . . ." Louis tried to object one last time, but Michael would not let him.

"Come on. Stop it. Let's go." The two hurried back to the car.

"Michael," said Louis when they arrived, "this is my friend, Renard."

"The French cop?" said Michael.

"The French cop," said Renard with a laugh. He liked the sound of it.

Michael suggested they go to a small Lebanese restaurant in Arlington where they could eat something and make plans. "You better tell me what's going on, Dad." Louis hesitated once again. He wondered whether there was any way he could avoid endangering his son. But it was a foolish thought; it was too late for that. As they drove, Louis told Michael about the burglary, about Hugh Bowes and Pierre Lefort, and about having been Louis Coburn many years ago.

They found the restaurant and took a corner booth. They ordered quickly and then sat gazing through the window. It was dark outside, and the rain was coming in torrents. Michael studied his father's face, then he looked at Renard. But Renard just looked back at him, his eyebrows raised in a sort of shrug, as if to say, "Don't ask me. I don't understand it any better than you do."

"I never met this Coburn," said Michael. "Never even saw him. Jenny said he was very shy. I couldn't figure it out. Now I know why. She said he was good-looking too. Clean-cut, athletic. A good tennis player. Looks really young."

"That's right," said Renard. "I saw him. He is tall and handsome. I saw them together."

"The son of a bitch," said Michael. "Who do you think he is? What do you think he's up to? Do you know what's going on?"

Louis put his fork on his plate and looked at his hands. "He might be an earlier me," he said, drawing small circles on the damp tabletop with one finger. "Maybe he is the wages of my sins, the payback for my earlier life," he said. "Divine retribution, or something like that. Other than that, I don't know who he is. Whether he's a freelancing renegade or simply a straight-up agent who has been persuaded that I am a dangerous terrorist . . . an abduction like Jenny's doesn't imply one explanation or the other . . . I just don't know who he is. The thing is, you *never* know who *anyone* is in that world, so it doesn't really matter.

"What we have to do is find Jenny before they even know we're getting close. They know we're here, and they know we're looking. But if they even *think* we're close, they'll . . . I don't think they have . . . done anything to her yet. I believe she is more useful to them alive . . ." How could a father even think this way about his own daughter? Tears welled in Louis's eyes. He continued looking at the two men across the table, though their faces swam in front of him. He pressed ahead. "They are using her to draw me further into the open. I have . . . I *may* have a plan. Or at least it *seems* like a plan. Or maybe it is just my own desperate madness."

The man known as Lou Coburn sat in a wingback chair in Hugh Bowes's Watergate apartment. He sipped from a glass of ice water while Hugh Bowes sat at his dining table and ate his dinner. Coburn uncrossed his legs and smoothed the crease on his khaki slacks. "Morgon's ex-wife has left town," he said, "although we can find her if we have to. It means Morgon warned her, which is good. He's afraid. That's what you hoped would happen, isn't it?" Coburn shifted slightly in his chair, so he would not have to watch Hugh Bowes eat. Outside, the rain was flying past the window in sheets and washing across the balcony.

"We know Morgon's here," Coburn continued. "He's in Washington. And the French cop is here too. He—the cop—showed up at our Tetra office. We've got him on videotape. A few nights after he showed up, the alarm at Tetra went off. I don't know whether that was Morgon's doing or not. There's nothing on tape. If they did it, I don't know how they did it, but it accomplished nothing. Also, a window was broken at Jennifer's, the daughter's, apartment. The father got in. He left fingerprints everywhere, like he didn't even care."

Hugh took one more bite, chewed a few times, swallowed, and looked up. He put his fork down and took a sip of water. "If he left fingerprints," said Hugh, "I promise you it was not because he didn't care. It was because he meant to."

"He also took the telephone," said Coburn.

"The telephone? For the caller ID?" said Hugh.

"Maybe," said Coburn.

"And last-call redial. And the programmed numbers. And the wiretap," Hugh said.

"The phone was clean," said Coburn. "I cleaned it."

"What does he know about you?"

"Nothing," said Coburn, smiling.

Hugh gave Coburn a long look. He took the heavy white napkin from his lap and wiped it across his mouth in two deliberate motions, from right to left, then from left to right. He placed it back on his lap and smoothed it with both hands. He studied Coburn's face.

"Coburn," he said finally, "he knows where your office is. I'm guessing he knows where you live. He may even have been inside your place by now."

Coburn sat up straight in his chair. "I'd know if he had," he said.

"Would you," said Hugh. It was not a question. "You know, Coburn"—Hugh did not want to know the man's real name—"you worry me. I'm quite certain you are good at what you do. You came to me highly recommended and with an excellent record. But Louis Morgon is a serious adversary, and you had better take him seriously. He did what you do long before you ever did, and he was very good at it. He knows all the tricks, and then some.

"He may still be here, or he may not. At any moment he may be where you think he is, doing what you think he is doing. But chances are, he will be doing what you *don't* think he is doing, somewhere where you *don't* expect him to be. Killing his daughter will rattle him, but it won't stop him. It won't put him off course. Be very careful. And do not be smug."

"No sir," said Coburn.

At that very moment Louis was inside Coburn's Dupont

Circle apartment. He had simply rung the bell, and when nobody answered, had let himself in. Coburn lived alone and kept a clean and orderly place, but it was also a completely anonymous place, a home without an occupant. There were no pictures of family or loved ones, no notes by the telephone, no files or folders, in fact, very few papers of any kind. Michael checked the computer as best he could and found nothing there. "Sorry, Dad," he said. "I don't know how to hack computers. And his e-mail is secure."

In the top dresser drawer Louis found half a dozen cell phones. *What is it,* Louis wondered, *that makes dresser drawers so appealing as hiding places?* He took the cell phones, turned them on, and spread them out on the dining table in case any of them rang.

The telephone answering machine was clean, and there were no numbers on the telephone speed dial. The caller identification did not show any calls from Jennifer's number or from the clinic. "He probably uses a cell phone for the stuff that would give him away," said Michael.

"Let's try these numbers anyway," said Louis. First he pressed redial, to dial the last number Coburn had dialed, then, one by one, he dialed the numbers on the caller ID.

Some of the numbers had answering machines. When a person answered, Louis listened in silence for a long moment. "Hello? . . . Hello?" the other person said and then hung up. Louis went through all twenty-five listed numbers.

"Shouldn't we go, Dad?" said Michael, sounding nervous. "We've been in here a long time."

"We're fine," said Louis. "Renard will let us know if anyone shows up. Let's just wait a minute and see if anyone calls back." And a moment later, the telephone rang. Louis picked up the receiver. "Yeah," he said softly. There was silence at the other end of the line and then that person hung up. The caller ID revealed the number and its address: Perryville, Virginia.

Louis gathered up the cell phones and put them in his pockets. He unplugged the telephone from the wall and tucked it under his arm. "I can't believe we're doing this, Dad," said Michael, his voice a mixture of astonishment and excitement. "I can't believe that you did this for a living . . ."

"Don't be charmed by it, Michael. It's a reprehensible business. I am ashamed that I ever did it and that I have to do it now. I am ashamed that I ever thought it was a good or useful thing to do. They call it intelligence, but it seems just the opposite to me now. To my way of thinking, it is stupidity. It is nothing but lies stacked upon lies. We're finished here. Let's go."

Once they were in the car, Louis turned back to Michael. "If we were gathering intelligence, then that would make us smarter, wouldn't it? We should know more now than we did when we started. But look at us. If anything, we know less. And it's always that way. We think we know more, but we know less."

"And what do we do now with our tiny knowledge?" said Renard.

Louis gave him a look. "I can tell you what *might* have happened, what I *hope* has happened, but it would just be a guess. I hope that the person who called back called because he was surprised or alarmed to receive a call from Coburn. Then that person called back and realized it wasn't Coburn, and realized he had given something away by calling back. Then, with any luck, whoever it was called Coburn on his cell phone to tell him what had happened and that someone was in his apartment using his phone. Now, whoever it was gave away three things. He gave away his phone number, which is of little use to us. He gave away his address, which he must believe to be of some use. And he gave away the fact that he believed this connection to Coburn was secure. Otherwise, he would have suppressed his number and location.

"The only reason the number or location could be of any use would be that something secret or important is going on there. Although it might have something to do with us, chances are it doesn't. Still, I suggest we go to Perryville."

"Perryville? That's a long way off. And how do we even know where to look once we're there?" said Michael.

"And we have no reason to think that Jennifer is there," said Renard.

"That's all true. It's a wild-goose chase," said Louis. "I know that. But it's all we've got. Wild-goose chases are for when you only have guesses and no facts. My recollection is that Perryville is a small town on a through highway. If we get there quickly and wait on the north end of town, and if Coburn, once warned, rushes down there from here, then we have a chance of picking him up as he goes by." Louis paused. "I know it's not much," he said again.

"It is nothing," said Renard.

"It's a lot of ifs. But what else have we got?"

"And I am getting a tour of America," said Renard as he started the car.

Louis would have been surprised to learn that luck had fallen his way, although it had happened differently than he imagined, and nothing would have come of it if Lou Coburn had not made two mistakes. Coburn had been walking through the basement garage of the Watergate apartments on his way to his car when his cell phone rang. He was alarmed to see his home telephone number flashing on the blue screen.

He thought of Hugh Bowes's admonition that Louis might

have already been in his house. He did not answer. Instead, he clapped the cell phone shut. "Son of a bitch!" he said. Then he made his first mistake. If Louis already had this number, he thought, then he gave nothing away by calling his house. He heard a soft voice say "Yeah," and realized too late that Louis would see Perryville on the screen, which was where this phone was registered. He hung up.

"Son of a bitch!" said Coburn again, slamming his hand against the steering wheel. The parking garage gate went up. Coburn pulled out into traffic, turned right, accelerated past the Kennedy Center, and sped across the Roosevelt Bridge. In another minute he was on Interstate 66 going west. Going to Perryville was his second mistake.

Louis, Renard, and Michael were crossing the Roosevelt Bridge barely five hundred yards ahead of the man who called himself Lou Coburn. "Slow down," said Louis. "The last thing we need is to get arrested." Renard slowed down. But then he sped up again.

"Slow down," said Louis again.

"Do you want to get to . . . ?"

"Perryville," said Louis.

"Do you want to get to Perryville before this Coburn does?" said Renard.

At that moment a large, white SUV sped past them on the right and maneuvered into the left lane in front of them.

"Look how fast *he* is going," said Renard.

Louis leaned forward. A small sticker on the right of the SUV's rear bumper had caught his eye. It had no identifying logo or words, only a number. Louis recognized it as being like the sticker he had had on his car when he had been at the CIA. He was about to urge Renard to catch up so that he could get a look inside when a police car passed them, switched on its flashing lights, and directed the white SUV to the shoulder. Louis tried to see the driver's face as they passed, but the windows were dark, and he could not even tell whether it was a man or a woman.

XIV

By the time Louis, Renard, and Michael drove into Perryville, Lou Coburn had already sped through the village despite having been stopped by the state police. After going a few miles on State Road 17, he turned onto an unmarked gravel road, which he followed steeply up the side of the mountain. He stopped at a green metal gate, got out, and swung the gate open. He drove through and got out again to close the gate behind himself. He continued up a narrow dirt drive, and a log cabin came into view in a small clearing in the pine trees.

Good. No one was there. He had been unnecessarily alarmed. Everything looked all right. Jennifer would be asleep inside, happy in the belief that she was on her honeymoon. Coburn congratulated himself on his successful ruse. He parked the car, climbed the stairs to the porch, and let himself into the house. He latched the door and went to the bedroom at the back of the house. Without turning on the light, he leaned over the bed and kissed Jennifer's cheek. She stirred briefly. "Hi, honey," he whispered. "I'm back."

She moaned happily and smiled in the dark. "Oh, good. Did everything go all right?"

"Perfectly," he said.

"The clinic?" she said.

"I told you already. They were fine with everything. I promise. They got Sally to fill in. They just want us to have a wonderful time, that's all. They were delighted. They're a bunch of romantics. Just like you."

"Are you sure, Lou? Shouldn't I call?"

"Don't be silly, honey. It's all squared away. Anyway, who are you going to call in the middle of the night?"

"You're so sweet, Lou. Come to bed."

"In a little bit, honey."

Jennifer propped herself up on her elbows. "It's our honeymoon, Lou. C'mon. If I can skip out of work, so can you."

Coburn laughed and gently pushed her back onto the pillow. "In a little bit."

Louis, Renard, and Michael sat in their car in front of a darkened service station at the northern edge of Perryville. After thirty minutes, Louis knew they were waiting in vain. If Coburn had even come, he could have taken any one of a number of routes. Louis's speculations had been off; his guesses had been all wrong. His shoulders sagged and his head slumped forward. He pressed his fists to his eyes until he saw colors. He had tried everything he could think of to find Jennifer.

"Wait a minute, Dad," said Michael. "The cell phones. Why does this guy have so many different phones?"

"They're probably off-the-book phones—stolen or confiscated," Louis said. "Coburn is careless. He should have thrown them away."

"I mean, there are how many different phones here? Cell phones automatically keep logs of all calls made on that phone—calls dialed, calls received, calls missed—all of them. There could be lots of phone numbers listed in the logs. Did you check those?"

"No," said Louis, sitting up. "I didn't know about those. I don't use a cell phone. Show me." He handed the phones to Michael.

Michael turned on the phones, and the three men sat in the dark, their faces lit by the soft glow of cellular screens while Michael pushed buttons. Different telephone numbers kept coming up on the screens. "What if we just call all the numbers we find and see what happens?" said Michael.

"That is risky," said Louis. "We need to find someone who can get us to Coburn without letting him know we're here."

"*If* he's here," said Renard.

"Wherever he is," said Louis. "We need to find him to find Jennifer." They divided the phones among them. "Look for phone numbers here in Perryville—703 area code, 855 exchange. If he's got a place here, those could be handymen or plumbers or property managers, that sort of thing. That's who we need."

"Here's a number," said Michael. "It was called several times in the last few weeks, and it's a Perryville number. There's no indication who it is. And look: the same number is listed in the logs for received and missed calls."

Renard spoke up. "Here's a Perryville number. Coburn called this number three times. It's on two other phones too. Here it is in the main directory too, under Riley. No missed or received calls for that number, though. He calls them, but they don't call him." In all they found eight local numbers, four identified by name.

"The ones with the names listed are most likely civilians. Let's try those first," said Louis. "Drive to the center of town."

Renard drove a few blocks and parked in front of the church. You could see both ends of town from where they stopped as well as the post office and the police station across the street. Except for streetlights along the main street and a red bulb above the police station door, the town was dark. "Renard and I will get out and watch for lights being switched on and listen for phones ringing while you make the call, Michael."

Renard looked skeptical. "It's all we have," said Louis yet again. "Okay, Michael, call the first number. If someone answers, don't say anything, wait five seconds, then hang up."

Michael punched in the number. "There's no answer," said Michael. They heard no phones ringing. No lights came on. "Hang up, Michael. And wait. Let's see if anyone calls back." No one called back. Michael tried the same number again after a few minutes. No one answered or called back.

"Try the next number," said Louis. Michael poked away at the keypad while Louis and Renard peered up and down the street. This time he got an answering machine. Michael hung up. "Try the next number," said Louis. When Michael called the fourth number on the list, a light came on in the small woods behind the post office. "Hello?" said a woman's voice. "Hello? Is anybody there?" Michael waited five seconds and hung up. "It was a woman," he said. "She sounded old."

Louis stepped across the street and peered in the direction of the light. It came from a trailer no more than two hundred meters from where he stood. You could just make out a flower garden in front of the trailer. There was a white birdbath. "Wait here," said Louis. He could see as he approached the trailer that there was a name beside the door. He crept closer until he could read the name, then he returned to the car. The name matched the one in the directory. "Give me the phone, Michael." Louis dialed the number again. "Hello?" said the woman.

"Hello," said Louis. "Mrs. Price? This is Louis Coburn. I'm terribly sorry to bother you at this late hour, but we have had a family emergency, and I was hoping you could help me."

"An emergency?"

"Yes, ma'am. My son Lou is in Perryville and—"

"Who is this?" A man's voice came on the line.

"I'm sorry to bother you, Mr. Price, but my name is Louis Coburn and—"

The man interrupted. "You ain't Lou Coburn. I know Lou Coburn . . ."

"Yes, I know you know him, Mr. Price. He's my son. I'm Louis, his father. That's how I got your number. I think you and I may even have met once before when I was down here for a visit."

"We did?" said the man. "I can't say as I remember that."

"Yes, sir. I think so. Anyway, I'm very sorry to bother you so late. As I told your wife, there's been a family emergency, and I need to get in touch with my son immediately. He's supposed to be at his place. I've been there a couple of times in the past, and I thought I could find it this time. But now I'm here, and, I confess, I'm a little lost and just can't seem to find my way there . . ."

"An emergency? Well, where you at? He's up there all right. He called a little bit ago from the road. I can run you up there easy enough. I hope it ain't nothin' too serious."

"There's no need for you to come out, sir. Really. It isn't that complicated as I recall . . ."

"Well, it ain't complicated at all. South on State Road 17, about four miles once you leave town, then left on Mountain Road—there ain't no sign, but it's the only road on the left for a good ways. There's a boulder marks the corner. Go all the way up Mountain Road to the green iron gate on your left, and there you are. You'll recognize it, I'm sure."

"You're right. I will recognize it. In fact, I remember the way now that you describe it. I'm very grateful to you, Mr. Price. And once again, my sincerest apologies to you, sir, and to your wife, for calling so late."

"Oh, that's all right. I guess we'll survive. I hope everything turns out all right."

"Thank you again, sir. And good night."

Louis hung up the phone. The three men sat in the car and waited. After a short time the light in the trailer went out. No one came out.

"What unbelievable luck," said Renard.

Louis could not disagree.

Louis, Michael, and Renard drove to the foot of Mountain Road. Louis peered up the steep road into the darkness. "We should wait for daylight," he said.

"But if we wait, we're giving him more time, and Jennifer . . . ," said Renard.

"I think we should go up now," said Michael.

"Daylight changes everything," said Louis. He did not elaborate.

Renard pushed the driver's seat as far back as it would go and drew his jacket more tightly around himself. Louis sat upright with his hands folded on his lap. Renard listened to Michael's slow, deep breathing coming from the backseat.

Outside there were night sounds: the flutter of invisible wings, crickets chirping rhythmically, breaking off, then starting up again, an occasional wavering cry from an owl.

Renard was determined to keep watch. But the next thing he knew, he was waking up from a deep sleep, and the first morning light was seeping into the sky. His neck and back were stiff from having sat so awkwardly. He pushed himself upright in the seat. The seat beside him was empty. Renard swept his hand back and forth across the steamy windshield and peered out into the twilight. Louis stood next to the boulder and faced into the woods, his back to the rising light. Renard opened the door and stepped out into the cool, damp air. He took a deep breath and stretched his arms above his head. "Did you sleep?" he asked.

"No," said Louis without looking in Renard's direction. "It's almost morning," he said. "In a little while I'll go up the mountain. You and Michael stay here and wait for my signal."

"Your signal?" said Renard. "Alone? Do you want—"

Louis did not allow him to continue. "I have programmed the telephones. I think I've done it correctly. Before I go, we'll check with Michael to make sure they do what we want them to do. If he's there, maybe we can use his phones against him."

"Why go alone?" said Renard. "You know he will be armed, and—"

"He may not even be there. If he's not there, then we can search the place together. But if he is there, I think I have a better chance of succeeding if I have you both in reserve. He knows I'm not alone, and if you aren't with me, then he has you to worry about."

"*Succeeding?*" said Renard. "At what?"

"That depends on what I find," said Louis.

Michael woke up, and the three men went over Louis's plan.

The sky lightened some, but it remained steely gray, and a few drops of rain began to fall. It was seven thirty. "Early, but not too early," said Louis, and he set off. Michael and Renard watched him go until he disappeared into the woods. Then all they could do was wait.

Louis walked up the gravel road, his hands jammed into his jacket pockets, peering into the woods ahead of him. The road was rutted and stony, and he walked slowly. The only sounds were the rain hitting the leaves and the crunch of his footsteps. When he reached the green gate, he lifted the metal latch, stepped through the gate, and latched it again. It made a small click as the latch engaged.

There was the white SUV with the small decal on the bumper. Coburn was here. Which could mean Jenny was too. *We should have stopped when the police pulled him over. But what were the odds?* Louis thought. *But then, what were the odds of finding him at all? And yet here we are.* It only remained to be seen whether finding Coburn would be good luck or bad. Louis crossed the clearing to the front of the cabin. The windows were dark. There were no sounds, no signs of life coming from inside.

Louis climbed the stairs onto the porch and knocked firmly on the door. He heard some movement inside, and a short time later Jennifer opened the door. She was wearing a T-shirt and sweatpants. Her hair was tousled. She was rubbing one eye with her fist, as though she had just gotten up. Coburn immediately came up from behind and stood beside her. He was tall and muscular and had a boyish face. He had a coffee mug in his hand. Jennifer and Coburn stared at Louis.

"Daddy!" said Jennifer finally. Then again. "My God. *Daddy!* What on earth . . . ?!" She turned to Coburn and grinned. "Lou, did you . . . Is this your doing? Oh, Lou!"

"Hello, Jennifer," said Louis. "I'm glad to see you. I'm *so* glad to see you."

"And I'm glad to see you, Daddy." She hugged Louis happily. She looked at Lou, but he was not smiling. Neither was Louis. "Is everything all right?" she asked.

"And you must be Lou," said Louis, and held out his hand.

Coburn hesitated and then took Louis's hand. He did not say anything. He set down his coffee mug on the table behind him.

"Come in, Daddy," said Jennifer. "I can't believe it. You didn't even say you were coming . . . Lou, I can't believe it. Did you arrange all this? You're so sweet!"

"Lou didn't tell you?" said Louis. He turned toward Coburn. "You didn't tell her I was coming?"

Coburn looked from Louis to Jennifer and back again.

Louis spun around suddenly and opened the door. "Come outside, Jennifer. I need to talk to you," he said.

"Stay here," said Coburn, his voice sounding sharper than he meant it to. "Jennifer, don't go outside. *I'll* go outside with him. *You* stay here."

"Why shouldn't she come outside for a minute, Lou?" said Louis. "I just want to talk to my daughter . . ."

"Stay here, Jenny," said Coburn. His voice had an urgency that caused Jennifer to turn and look up into his face. "Stay here," he repeated, taking her by the arm now and trying to lead her away from the door.

"Why?" said Jennifer. "*What are you doing?* Stop pushing me, Lou. What . . . ?"

"Stay here," said Coburn. He was commanding her now, and he did not loosen his grip. "I said, stay here." He took her by both arms and turned her to face him. "Listen, Jennifer, I'm sorry you have to hear it like this. I hoped . . . I didn't want you to find out. But listen: your father is a . . . a wanted man, a *dangerous* man . . ."

"A . . . a wanted? *What?!* Stop it. Are you kidding? Why are you saying that? What are you talking about?"

"Come outside with me, Jennifer. Please. I . . ."

"He's a terrorist. He's dangerous. Don't go," said Coburn, making one last effort at persuasion. He tried to sound reasonable and undramatic. The honeymoon had been the perfect ruse to get her here without a struggle, and, until now, it had worked. But Jennifer was becoming agitated, and he realized that, if he were to alarm her, things could go wrong in a hurry.

Coburn had been prepared for every eventuality except for Louis walking right up to the door and into the cabin in broad daylight. *God damn it! Bowes was right.* "He's a wanted terrorist," Coburn said again. "Listen to me, Jennifer, he's wanted for terroristic activities against the United States. *He's al Qaeda.* He's in charge of an important cell of terrorists in France. They're planning a big action. I couldn't tell you, Jennifer. *Of course,* I couldn't tell you. You can see that. I wanted to, but I couldn't. But he's wanted by us and by the French. He's a fugitive."

"And you," said Louis, "have been on my trail. Is that it, Coburn? Well, then, here," he said, taking a cell phone from his pocket and pushing the call button. The automatic dialer started beeping. Coburn stared at the phone. "Here," said Louis again, thrusting the phone toward him. "It's dialing the police. Tell them you've caught a terrorist." They heard the phone ring and then a man's voice. It was tinny enough so that Michael's voice was unrecognizable, but loud enough so that Coburn and Jennifer could hear. "Virginia State Police," it said. "May I help you?" Louis held the phone out. "Take it," he said. Coburn just stared at it. The voice spoke again: "You have reached the Virginia State Police. May I help you?"

"Go on," said Louis. "Tell them."

Coburn snatched the phone out of Louis's hand. He fumbled to turn it off.

"You know, Coburn, cell phones all have GPS now," said Louis. "It stands for Global Positioning System. I'm told the police can pinpoint exactly where a call comes from the instant it enters their switchboard. Did you know that?"

"You smart son of a bitch," snarled Coburn, and swung a huge fist at Louis, catching him on the temple. Louis staggered. The pain of the blow made his ears ring. As he was going down, his head hit the thick leg of the kitchen table, and he lay on the floor, stunned. When he looked up, he could only see out of one eye.

Coburn had one arm clamped tightly around Jennifer's neck and held a large black pistol against her head. "Is this what you wanted?!" said Coburn. "To bring harm to your daughter? Are you happy now, you smart son of a bitch?"

"Let her go," said Louis. He raised his hands. "Please. Take me. You've got me. That's what you wanted, isn't it? She's no use to you now that you've got me. Isn't that what you wanted all along? *Take me."*

"Get up!" said Coburn. "Get up, you son of a bitch. Get on your fucking feet, or I will kill you *and* her. GET UP! I said."

Jennifer had begun crying. "Oh, Lou," she said. "Lou, stop. Please, stop, Lou, please. What are you doing? No. You're hurting me. No. Oh, Lou, stop . . . please, you're hurting me . . ."

Louis struggled to get to his feet. He could feel blood trickling down his cheek from somewhere above his eye. He could taste blood where his lip was split. His head was buzzing, and the room seemed to be turning around him. He tried to see

Jennifer's anguished face, but it drifted in and out of focus. He tried to pull himself upright by holding the edge of the table, but his legs kept collapsing under him.

"GET UP!" screamed Coburn. "GET UP."

"*Please,* Lou," said Jennifer. "Oh, Lou, *please. Please.*"

At that moment, Renard came through the front door. He pulled up short. "Finally," said Coburn, "the gang's all here. All right, *now* we go outside. Outside. Let's go." No one moved. "OUTSIDE!" shouted Coburn. He waved toward the front door with the pistol. Renard stepped forward to help Louis. "Leave him alone," said Coburn. "You better worry about your own ass. Outside! Now!"

"I warn you," said Renard without moving. "I am a policeman."

Coburn stared at him in disbelief. "Just move," he said finally.

Renard went through the door first and down the porch steps. Louis followed as best he could, taking one step at a time and pausing at the bottom to get his balance. Coburn pushed Jennifer ahead of himself. He kept his arm around her neck and the gun against her head. Renard started walking toward the gate.

"Not that way," said Coburn. He motioned with his head toward the side of the cabin. "Back there," he said. Renard led the way around the corner and then, following Coburn's gestures and nods, into the woods. There was no path and the hill was steep. The four struggled under low-hanging pine boughs, through briars, and across tangled undergrowth that tore at their clothes. The ground was uneven and muddy, with sticks and stones hidden in the leaves. The going was slow. Louis stumbled more than once, and each time he fell Coburn screamed for him to get up.

It was raining steadily now, and the rain cooled Louis's head and washed the blood from his face. His right eye was swollen shut, and he tried to follow in Renard's steps.

Renard could not tell how far they had climbed, but it seemed like a long way. He hoped they might go on forever. If they did not stop, then nothing bad would happen. But Coburn finally said, "All right. That's far enough." There was a deep hole in front of where they stopped. A large grave had been dug in the earth. It was meant for one, but it would do for three.

Louis turned slowly to face Coburn. "Coburn," he said, "do you know how telephone messaging works?" His split and swollen lip got in the way of his words.

"*What?!*" said Coburn, not quite believing what he was hearing.

Louis reached into his pocket and pulled out another cell phone. He held it toward Coburn. "Telephone messaging." He pronounced the words as clearly as he could manage. "When it is on, the phone records everything you say. Long or short. And the message is always there in someone's mailbox. It can be retrieved at any time. And it's accessible to anyone with the access code. It is amazing, isn't it? This phone has been recording a message since I walked into your cabin. Everything that we say is being recorded," said Louis, and held the phone directly in front of Coburn's face.

This time Coburn hit Louis with the pistol. Louis's head whipped to the side, his legs buckled, and he collapsed and rolled into the muddy grave. Jennifer began moaning. It was a low, piercing, animal sound, a sustained note of agony, and it went on and on. Coburn grabbed her tighter, but she did not stop.

"Kneel down," Coburn said to Renard.

Renard looked puzzled. *"Nil?"* he said. He did not understand.

"Down!" said Coburn, pointing toward the grave with the pistol. Renard understood this time. He got on his knees at the edge of the grave. He closed his eyes and prepared, as best he could, to be shot. He tried to picture Isabelle and everything he loved, but all he could see was the grave in front of him with Louis lying on the muddy bottom, his body twisted crazily and blood seeping from the gash in his head.

When the shot came, it rang like a great brass gong beside Renard's ear. It echoed in his head and through the woods, and died out slowly. Renard knew he had not been hit. And in front of him he saw Louis struggling to climb out of the grave, so he had not been hit either. He was clawing at the dirt, a look of wild determination and horror on his face. Jennifer had stopped shrieking.

Renard was afraid to turn around and see what he knew he would see. But when he turned, Jennifer was still standing, her head buried in her hands, and it was Coburn who was lying on the ground. His face was white, his eyes had rolled back in his head, and his mouth opened and closed soundlessly like the mouth of a fish. His hands clutched at his middle, opening and closing and opening again, grasping at air, not knowing what to do, as though they had forgotten how to be hands. He rocked back and forth on the ground. He might have been rocking himself to sleep, except that his back was arched grotesquely.

Michael stood over Coburn, holding the iron shovel above his head, ready to hit Coburn again and break the rest of his ribs if he even threatened to get up. But Coburn just moaned. His breath came in short, jagged gasps. Then he fainted. A small trickle of blood seeped from his nose and from one corner of his mouth. His hands dropped to his sides and turned skyward like two dead birds. His gun lay in the leaves beside him, still smoking. It had fired into the trees when the shovel had slammed into his ribs.

Renard climbed down into the hole and lifted Louis out. Louis knelt on all fours for a while with his head hanging down before rising unsteadily to his feet. He picked up Coburn's pistol and, without a word, handed it to Michael. Michael looked at his father in horror.

"No, no," said Louis. "Don't shoot him. Just keep the gun."

With Renard and Michael supporting Louis and Jennifer, the four made their way slowly down the hill. When they reached the cabin, they stopped long enough for Michael to tear out the telephone connections and to take the two cell phones he found. He let the air out of the SUV's tires and ripped out some wires under the hood. Halfway down the mountain, he hurled Coburn's car keys into the woods. Finally, they reached their car.

Michael sat in the backseat and held Jennifer in his arms while she sobbed. "It's okay, Jenny," he said over and over. "It's okay."

Renard drove and Louis sat beside him, gazing straight ahead. He held a towel against the side of his head. Every part of him hurt. He leaned back against the headrest with a groan.

"Should we find a doctor," asked Renard.

"No," said Louis.

They drove back through Perryville. People stood about chatting in front of the church. A man wearing a baseball cap and a puffy red vest crossed in front of them, his hands stuck into his vest pockets. Renard wondered whether that might be Mr. Price.

They drove back to Washington in silence, each lost in his

own thoughts. When they were on the Beltway on their way to Baltimore, Louis fished Coburn's two phones from his pocket and examined them. Each had quite a few local Washington numbers stored in its directory. Many were identified with names, and one was listed as HB. Louis selected that number and pressed the call button. After a few rings, Hugh Bowes answered.

Louis was silent.

"Coburn? Is that you?" said Hugh. "Hello? . . . Coburn?"

Louis hung up the phone.

XV

For hours Coburn lay on his back in the mud beside the empty grave. It was raining steadily. His clothes were soaked through, and after a while he began to shiver, occasionally at first, but then continually. This slight, involuntary motion caused his broken ribs to saw back and forth inside his body, stabbing at his lungs and other organs, and sending him into paroxysms of agony. He cried and moaned without knowing he was doing so.

As night began to fall Coburn groped about gingerly until his hand found the shovel. He pulled it to him and, using it as a prop, managed, with great effort, to pull himself to his knees and then, after a while, to his feet. He stood there for a long time, swaying back and forth. Then, using the shovel as a kind of crutch, he began staggering down the hill. It was growing dark, and the ground was treacherous. Coburn slipped and slid in the mud until his feet went out from under him. He collapsed with a cry onto a clump of brush.

He lay there without moving, his moans being the only indication that he was still alive. Finally he got on his knees and back on his feet. He took a few unsteady steps and fell again. Each time he fell, he remained where he fell for a long time, thinking he would die there. But each time, he managed to pull himself upright and make it a bit further, only to fall again. After two hours of this terrible journey, Coburn crawled up the front stairs of the cabin and collapsed on a bench on the porch.

The next morning Ed Price, who worked at the cabin as a handyman and caretaker, and who had given Louis directions up the mountain the night before, tried to call Coburn on his cell phone. There was no answer. Ed and his wife, Merleen, who did occasional housekeeping at the cabin, had received strict instructions not to call or go up to the cabin when Coburn was in town. But now, after some discussion, they agreed that, in light of the fact that Lou's father had said there was a family emergency, it might be a good idea if Ed were to drive up and make sure everything was all right.

Ed Price found the man he knew as Lou Coburn lying on the porch floor beside the bench. His face was pale and swollen, his lips were peeled back from his teeth, his eyes were rolled back in his head. His body was grotesquely twisted, and his hands were knit into tight fists. At first Ed thought he was dead. Coburn was, as Ed later told Merleen, "a right pitiful sight."

He tried to help Coburn into his truck to drive him to the hospital, but even just touching Coburn's arm caused him to scream out in agony. Ed didn't have a cell phone, so he drove back down the mountain to town and called 911. Then he drove back up to sit with Coburn until the ambulance came. It seemed to take forever, but finally he could hear the siren down below. Mountain Road was a muddy mess from all the rain, and it took the ambulance a good ten minutes to work its way up to where they were.

Two emergency medical technicians covered Coburn with thermal blankets and gave him injections to ease the pain. They put an oxygen mask over his face and carefully slid him onto a stretcher, which they then loaded into the ambulance. One of the men described his condition over the radio as the other drove back down the mountain. They took Coburn to the hospital in nearby Warrenton. But by the time Ed and Merleen Price tried to visit him there, Coburn had already been airlifted to Washington. Nobody could tell them which hospital.

Ed and Merleen Price learned later that Coburn did not die, although he had been suffering from severe hypothermia and his injuries were grievous. One day a man in a dark suit appeared at their door. Ed and Merleen were thanked for their work and told, regretfully, that their services would no longer be needed. The man gave them both generous severance bonuses in cash. The Prices never saw or heard from Lou Coburn again.

When Ed went back up Mountain Road to collect some tools he had left there, the cabin had been cleaned out, including his tools. Not a stick of furniture was left, and the electricity was off. Even the curtains and curtain rods had been removed. The cabin, which it turned out had been owned by a corporation in Maryland, was eventually sold.

Coburn stayed in Walter Reed Hospital in Bethesda, Maryland, for three weeks. Early in his convalescence he was visited by two Agency officials, who inquired after his injuries but did not ask about the events that had brought them about. The next day the phone by his bedside rang. He struggled to lift the receiver. "Yes," he said, his voice a raspy whisper. When he recognized Hugh Bowes on the other end of the line, he hoisted himself up into a half-sitting position, even though it hurt him to do so. "Yes sir," said Coburn.

"How are you doing, Coburn? How are you recovering from your injuries?"

"I'm getting better, sir," said Coburn. "The doctors say it could take months to recover completely." Then he gave Hugh an honest and unsparing description of events as he remembered them. He could not remember what had happened at the end, how he had been knocked down, or by whom, although he assumed he had been struck with the shovel and that it was the son, Michael, who had hit him. "Jennifer is still alive," he said. "They all are."

"The main thing is that you are still alive," said Hugh. "These are very dangerous people, Coburn. We have issued a countrywide alert. All airport and railroad personnel have been notified, and police and border crossing agents have been alerted. They will undoubtedly try to leave the country, but an all-points bulletin has been issued. Morgon and the others have been described in detail, and photos have been supplied. They have been described as armed and dangerous, and their capture and arrest has been given the absolute highest priority. We will get them. They will find it absolutely impossible to escape. The war on terror has been brought home to American soil. These terrorists will be apprehended.

"I am grateful for your work and sacrifice, Coburn." Hugh continued. "The president has asked that I express the country's gratitude on his behalf. I have recommended that you be given the distinguished service medal and a promotion. The United States of America cannot thank you enough. The war against terror is long and difficult and will exact many sacrifices."

Coburn listened to this peculiar speech in puzzled silence. It was not until Hugh Bowes mentioned the war on terror's many sacrifices that Coburn realized Hugh was speaking for someone else's benefit, someone who was there with him, and that he, Coburn, was being hung out to dry.

After they left Washington, Louis, Jennifer, Michael, and Renard proceeded past Philadelphia and New York, and headed north on the New York State Thruway. They stopped at a shopping mall near Albany, where Jennifer and Michael bought clothes, toiletries, and suitcases.

Louis got out of the car in Plattsburgh, just below Montreal, and Renard, Jennifer, and Michael continued across the border into Canada. The all-points bulletin had, of course, not been issued. They showed their passports—Louis had gotten Jennifer's from her apartment—and were waved through by the Americans and by the Canadians. They abandoned their rental car in a fast-food parking lot on the outskirts of Montreal and continued by taxi to the Hotel Terminus, a small establishment adjacent to the train station.

The three were having dinner in the hotel restaurant when Louis came through the door. He had a plastic bandage on his forehead, and his lip and right eye were still bruised and swollen. It hurt to do so, but he smiled broadly when he saw them.

Later, in his room, Louis described for them how he had crossed the border on a bus filled with elderly Americans on their way to Canada to buy prescription drugs. He had signed up for their excursion in Plattsburgh. At the border, American and Canadian border guards entered the bus, looked at all the gray heads, and got off.

Louis opened his knapsack and took out Coburn's pistol.

He gave it to Renard who, as a policeman, was permitted to carry a pistol in his checked baggage. "But why?" Renard wondered.

"Coburn's prints will be all over it," Louis said. "It is one more piece of evidence." The next day they purchased separate tickets on separate flights, Renard filled out the appropriate papers to transport a firearm, and by the end of the following afternoon they had all four cleared customs at Charles de Gaulle Airport. They caught a train for Quimper. Renard left them in Le Mans. "*A bientôt,*" he said, and then added in English, "I will see you soon."

When Louis and his children arrived by taxi in Pen'noch, people in the square, including the women he had seen on the day of his first arrival, greeted him by name. "*Bonjour, Monsieur Bertrand.*"

Louis introduced Michael and Jennifer to his neighbors. "They have come to stay with me for a while," he said. The fact that he had children, there in the flesh, had the effect of erasing any remaining doubts the people of Pen'noch may have harbored about Louis Bertrand, the Irish painter. A few congenitally suspicious souls struggled to keep their suspicions alive, but to little avail.

Monsieur Bertrand's daughter seemed very sad. She had obviously suffered some terrible loss, which disposed people kindly toward her. Despite their natural curiosity, the villagers were discreet and protective toward Louis and his family and did not inquire too closely about whatever tragedy might have befallen Jennifer. After all, tragedy and unhappiness were not strangers in the Finistère.

"If there is something we can do . . . ," they offered, but Louis graciously declined their help, as everyone knew he would. Of course people speculated among themselves. Perhaps her husband had been killed. Perhaps she had lost a child. But each speculation only increased their sympathy for her.

Louis invited Jean Pierre Lamarche for dinner. Louis steamed a large pot of mussels in white wine and roasted Brussels sprouts and tossed them in vinaigrette. Jean Pierre arrived with a bottle of Chinon and a bouquet of violets, but Michael and Jennifer stayed away.

"I apologize for Michael and Jennifer," said Louis. "The cottage is small for three people, and they feel they need time to themselves."

Jean Pierre shrugged. "These are for you then," he said with a smile, handing the violets to Louis. "There is no need to apologize."

Jennifer left the cottage each morning and took long, solitary walks along the cliffs and the beach while Michael disappeared with his drawing kit. The days grew shorter and the fog drifted ashore earlier in the day.

Louis went to Quimper each week to pick up the mail, and Jennifer and Michael went along just to get away. In Quimper they went their separate ways, walking through the city, or visiting a museum, or shopping, or just sitting in a café and watching people leading their ordinary lives. What could possibly be more wonderful than leading an ordinary life?

"I can't stay here," said Jennifer one afternoon. They had just returned to Pen'noch, and she took off her jacket and shook the rain from it. Louis put the mail on the table. "I just can't live like this," said Jennifer.

"Like what?" said Louis.

"Like *this,*" said Michael. "Jenny's right. We're stuck here. I can't stand it either."

"We have no choice," said Louis. "It won't go on . . ."

"Yes, we do," said Michael. "We have a choice. And yes, it

will go on. What's going to change? Nothing. *Nothing* will change. It could go on forever."

"Is it really that hard on you?" Louis wondered. "It has only been—"

"What?! You're kidding, aren't you? Or you have no idea," said Jennifer. "No idea at all." She stepped toward him and made him look at her. "Spies, assassination, murder, that's what *you* know. That's *your* life. But it's not mine. I never wanted it to be mine."

"That's not fair . . . ," Louis began.

"What the hell does fair have to do with it?!" Michael was suddenly on his feet and shouting. "We're hiding out in this godforsaken corner of the world because of the life YOU chose to live. YOU put us in danger. We were safe when you were gone from our lives."

"You know what, Dad?" said Jennifer. "Your whole life is about deceit and betrayal. You betrayed Mom. You betrayed us when we were little. Maybe that's why I fell in love with . . . Jesus, I don't even know what to call him. Who is he? I don't even know. Maybe I fell in love with him because he was treacherous like you. Who are you? I don't even know that either. Are you Louis Bertrand? Is Louis Morgon even your real name? Who are you? You are the master of betrayal. That's who.

"I've lost my clinic. It was my life, and now it's gone. And Michael has a wife he can only talk to by telephone and write letters to through a mail drop. She doesn't even know *where he is*. And why is that?"

"I can't argue with you," said Louis raising his hands. "I wish I could . . ."

"You can't," said Michael.

"I can't," said Louis. "Listen: I wish I could free you from this predicament. But I can't. I might be able to soon. But right now I can't. I'm trapped in hiding, and because I'm trapped, so are you."

"It isn't fair," said Jennifer.

"It isn't fair," said Louis. "That's true. Where would you go?"

"What?" said Jennifer.

"Where? Where will you go? I think you're safest here, but I can't force you to stay. I'll help you as best I can."

"Quimper," said Jennifer. "Maybe I'll go to Quimper." Her voice had softened and tears welled up in her eyes. She stepped to the table where Louis sat. He hoped she would reach out for his hand, but she didn't. She jammed her hands in her pockets and stopped crying. "Quimper. Okay?"

"I can help you find a place." said Louis. "It would be—"

"No," said Jennifer. "I'll find my own place."

Jennifer went back to Quimper the following morning. She searched the ads in the paper and found a small apartment in the center of town. It was available immediately, so she returned to Pen'noch for her clothes and left again at the end of the day. Encouraged by Jennifer's success, Michael followed her a few days later and found his own place. "Call when you're in Quimper," he said as he was leaving, and gave Louis his number.

Louis went to Quimper more frequently than he had before, and he and Michael met for lunch. Jennifer joined them occasionally, but not often. She did not want Louis to have her phone number. "If only I could betray you, I mean *really* betray you . . . I wish I could," she said. "So you would know how it feels."

I know how it feels, thought Louis. *I know betrayal from every angle.* The next time Jennifer accused him, Louis said, "Can we talk about it?"

Jennifer looked suspicious.

"I don't want to argue with you," said Louis. "I just want to talk."

"I'm listening," she said.

"Okay. So. You said, I made betrayal my occupation, and that's true. When I started, though, it was patriotism that drove me. Then it was ambition. Only later, when I thought about it, could I see the betrayal in it. But even then I saw it as something else, as a distortion of love maybe, as the shadow of love, its dark side, its mirror image. I thought, where there's love, there's always betrayal. They sweep back and forth like the tide. Betrayal always follows love.

"A husband betrays a wife, or a wife betrays a husband out of love for someone else. A double agent betrays his country because he loves a woman or money or even, in some rare cases, another country. Love is part of us all; it is who we all are. But so is betrayal. I mean, don't we all betray everything and everyone we love somehow, at some time or another?"

Jennifer leaned forward toward her father. Michael slid back in his chair, waiting for the explosion. They were having lunch in a small tearoom whose walls were decorated, floor to ceiling, with Quimper pottery, and Michael could imagine Jennifer standing up and, with a huge, sweeping gesture, sending the entire collection shattering to the floor.

Instead, Jennifer said, "Will he find us here?"

"Who?" said Louis, taken unawares.

"Will . . . Lou Coburn find us here?"

"I don't know. It depends on whether he comes looking."

"But *if* he comes looking." Jennifer was insistent. "Will he find us, *if* he comes looking?"

"If he comes looking," said Louis, "then eventually he will find us. But I am hoping—"

"Why didn't you kill him?" Jennifer's eyes were hard.

"Maybe we *should* have," said Michael, recalling his earlier horror at the thought.

"Not you, Michael. Why didn't *you* kill him?" said Jennifer, looking at Louis. "You, my father. Why didn't *you* in particular kill him? He hurt me terribly and he almost killed me. Was it because you thought of his betrayal as love, as 'the mirror image' of love, as growing out of his love for me? Was *that* what you were thinking?"

"Of course not. You know it isn't—"

"*I know* it isn't," she said. "But I want *you* to say it. I want to hear you dispute your own sophistry."

Louis looked sharply at Jennifer. He knew she was right immediately. Sophistry. How did she see that? And how did she have the courage to call it by name? He should have felt ashamed, but instead he felt proud of his daughter.

"You are right," he said. "And I am wrong. Love is complicated, and betrayal . . ." But he decided to forego the rest of his analysis. Instead, he reached across the table and took her hand in his.

Jennifer did not withdraw her hand, but neither was she going to be distracted by Louis's affection. "And what about Bowes?" she said. "Will Bowes find us?"

"He will," said Louis. "Sooner or later he will." He thought about it for a moment, wondering how much he should say about what he had in mind.

"Say everything that you are thinking," said Jennifer, as though she could read his hesitation.

"All right," said Louis after a moment. "I owe you both that. Here is what I am thinking. The trick is to make certain that Bowes finds us when *we* want him to find us and not before."

"*Do* we want him to find us?" Michael said.

"Of course we don't," said Louis. "But the fact remains that he *can* find us eventually. You can find almost anybody eventually. And Bowes has tremendous resources. But I'm thinking if we can arrange things so that he finds us . . . *me*, that is, when we have the initiative and he is off balance, then we will gain, if not an advantage, at least a fighting chance."

"A fighting chance?" said Michael.

"A fighting chance to return to life as it should be," said Louis. "To have our lives back. Yours, Michael; yours, Jenny; and mine. I had a life too."

Everyone else had left the tearoom and they were alone. Even so, Louis leaned forward and, speaking in a low voice, told Michael and Jennifer everything he had not told them before. He told them about the earlier murders, about his career with the State Department and the CIA, about being Louis Coburn, about Algeria and Samad al Nhouri and Pierre Lefort, and about Hugh Bowes's apparently boundless enmity.

They listened with astonishment while he spoke, not interrupting, hardly daring to breathe, almost as though they were children again, and he was their father telling them tales from *A Thousand and One Arabian Nights*.

XVI

The vacation season had been over for weeks. The seaside hotels at La Baule were nearly empty, and some had already closed for the winter. The broad beach was not quite deserted, but those few souls strolling there wore jackets and hats. A lone horse and rider galloped along at the edge of the surf, sending great showers of spray into the air. Louis and Renard sat inside a restaurant, la Maison des Huîtres, regarding the blustery scene. It was a little risky to have a regular meeting place, but La Baule was located more or less halfway between Pen'noch and Saint Leon. It was an added benefit that the mussels at la Maison des Huîtres were fat and tender, the *pommes frites* crisp and hot, and you could order an excellent Muscadet by the pitcher. A great mound of mussel shells lay in a large bowl between the two men. They were sipping the last broth with silver soup spoons.

"Maybe," said Louis, "this is the moment."

"The moment," said Renard, looking bored. He lit a cigarette and blew smoke into the air. He was tired of Louis's guessing games, and he refused to play.

"The moment to let Hugh Bowes find me." Louis waited, but Renard did not respond. "My children are out of harm's way but not permanently. There is an American election coming."

"I read the newspapers," said Renard.

"Bowes might see the election as offering him some cover for a nice anti-terrorism move. To finish the game."

"The game?" said Renard. "The *game*?"

"I think it *is* a game for him," said Louis.

"Just tell me," said Renard, still sounding annoyed, "what you have in mind."

"I have in mind turning myself in," said Louis.

Renard just looked at Louis and waited.

"Surrendering," said Louis. "But not just to anyone. I will only surrender to Hugh Bowes."

Back in his office in Saint Leon, Renard searched through his top desk drawer. It was where he kept everything he did not know where to file. He finally found the card that had been left weeks earlier by the visitor in the dark suit. "Pénichon," he muttered as he punched numbers into the telephone. "Lieutenant Pénichon, please," he said.

"Monsieur Pénichon," said Renard when the lieutenant answered, "this is *Inspecteur* Jean Renard, gendarme at Saint Leon sur Dême."

Pénichon needed reminding. "You were here some weeks back," said Renard. "On the Louis Morgon case."

"Ah, yes," said Pénichon, "the American terrorist."

"Yes," said Renard. "The American terrorist. Lieutenant Pénichon, I promised I would call if I was contacted by Louis Morgon. I have been contacted, and I think you should come down here immediately—or I can come up there if you wish—in order to discuss the matter. I believe it is an important development."

A few hours later Renard watched from his office window as Pénichon eased his official black sedan into a parking space in front of the Hôtel de France. Pénichon stepped from the car and used the car window as a mirror to straighten his tie and smooth his lapels. He walked across the street and through Renard's office door. He wore the same dark suit and the same bored expression as he had on his previous visit.

Renard rose from his chair. The two men shook hands. Renard thought it wise to be more hospitable than he had been on the occasion of the lieutenant's previous visit, so he suggested they go for coffee. The two men walked across the square to the Hôtel de France and took a table in the front corner of the bar.

"Tell me everything," said Pénichon. He emptied three envelopes of sugar into his coffee. "This made me hopeful," said Renard later when he spoke to Louis by telephone. "Michel makes the best coffee in France. What kind of idiot puts three sugars in Michel's coffee?"

Renard explained to Pénichon that the telephone in his office had rung the previous afternoon at exactly four fifteen. He had picked up and had immediately recognized Louis Morgon's voice. In his opinion, Morgon had sounded distraught.

"Really?" said Pénichon. "Distraught?" He opened a small notebook and wrote the word on the first page. "This gave me further hope," Renard said to Louis, "and it enlivened my imagination. I told Pénichon how, at one point in our conversation, you began crying. I told him you were not only distraught, but that you might be desperate. I have to confess I was disappointed that Pénichon did not write the word *desperate* in his notebook."

Pénichon stirred his coffee. "He cried?" he said. "Well, he has a great deal he might cry about."

Renard went on to explain to Pénichon that, while Louis thought he would be able to hide indefinitely, he found such a life all but unbearable. He was separated from his home, from his friends, from everything and everyone he loved. "He might be willing to surrender under certain circumstances."

"Under certain circumstances? He should not be trying to negotiate," said Pénichon. He had been raising his coffee cup to his lips, but he set it back on its saucer. "He has little on his side to negotiate with."

"I agree with you entirely," said Renard. "I told him so. I said that I thought the best thing for him would be to simply surrender. But he seems to believe otherwise."

"And so?" said Pénichon. He was growing impatient. He had just driven all the way from Paris, and, thanks to traffic, a trip that should have taken two hours had taken three.

Renard reached inside his jacket pocket and withdrew an envelope, which he laid on the table between them.

"What is this?" Pénichon said, regarding the envelope suspiciously.

"This morning when I arrived at my office, I found it on the floor. It had apparently been slid under the door during the night."

"Then," said Pénichon, "he cannot be far away." The lieutenant glanced out the window, as though he might actually expect to see Louis scurrying away.

"He was here last night," said Renard. "Or perhaps he had

someone deliver the letter. In either case, he could be halfway around the world by now. After all, in three hours you came all the way from Paris."

"Yes, you are right, of course," said Pénichon. He looked at the envelope in the middle of the table.

Renard continued. "Wherever he is, this letter was delivered to me, and I was instructed to deliver it, or rather to arrange to have it delivered, to . . ." Renard pushed the letter toward Pénichon.

Pénichon bent forward to look at the envelope. In blue fountain pen ink in a neat hand it had been addressed to *The President of the United States of America*. Pénichon sat bolt upright, almost knocking over his coffee cup. "He's insane," he snorted.

"Undoubtedly," said Renard. "Still, you probably know from your investigations that Morgon was in government service in the United States. That was many years ago, of course, before he came to France."

"I do not know much about that," said Pénichon, as though such facts were above and beyond the scope of his investigation.

"Well, it is true," said Renard. "For a time he worked as a presidential adviser. I believe he was quite high up in the administration. It was an earlier administration, of course. And Morgon could be exaggerating about all this. But I have seen some indication that it is true: certificates, letters of gratitude, photos, and the like. I'm sure you can easily check for yourself. He has many former acquaintances and friends still in high government service. Hugh Bowes, the former secretary of state? . . ."

Pénichon gave no indication that the name meant anything to him.

"Hugh Bowes was once the American secretary of state—which is like our foreign minister—and was a close friend of

Louis Morgon's. Anyway, Morgon has valuable information about terrorist activities, and he believes that the president of the United States will find his . . . offer an interesting one. He asked me to deliver the letter to someone who could deliver it to the president."

"But I am a police lieutenant," said Pénichon. "A small fry. I cannot deliver this letter to anyone who will be able to deliver it . . . into the proper hands." Pénichon suddenly found himself in deep water, and the chill he felt rising from the depths frightened him.

"You only have to read the letter to see that it will quickly find its way to the American president once you present it to your superior. Go ahead. Read it. It is not sealed."

Pénichon reached for the letter. He pulled it toward himself with one finger. He opened the envelope and withdrew the letter as though it were a precious and fragile manuscript. "It is in English," he said.

"Do you read English?" asked Renard.

"Yes," said Pénichon, and it sounded to Renard as though he wished he didn't. Pénichon read the letter very slowly. When he had finished, he folded it and reinserted it carefully into its envelope. He let the envelope sit faceup on the table for a while. He studied the writing on the front, and then, finally, picked up the envelope and slid it into his inside jacket pocket.

The two men finished their coffee while Pénichon continued to contemplate what he had just read. They were walking back to Renard's office when Pénichon broke his silence. "By the way," he said in an almost lighthearted tone, "what were you doing in Canada recently? Were you on vacation?"

"Of course not," said Renard, looking at the lieutenant sideways. "I was doing my own investigating into this case. I was not only in Canada. I was also in the United States—in New York and Washington, D.C."

"Were you, really?" said Pénichon. He sounded pleased with himself at having forced Renard to admit to these facts. "And what were you doing in those places?"

"I was trying to discover Louis Morgon's whereabouts. I had met his daughter and his son before. I hoped they would know where their father was."

"And were they helpful?" Pénichon wondered.

"They weren't," said Renard. "Michael and his father have been estranged, and Jennifer was missing."

"Missing?" said Pénichon. He smiled. "Perhaps she has just run off with a lover."

"Perhaps," said Renard. He could not tell whether Pénichon was joking or whether he actually knew something about what had happened. With his next question, however, Pénichon put Renard's mind at ease. He withdrew the notebook from his jacket pocket, opened it, and asked, "What is the daughter's name?" He also wanted to know the names of the hotels where Renard had stayed.

"Are you interrogating me?" Renard said.

Pénichon's friendly smile disappeared. He closed the notebook and put it away. It was time for him to reassert his authority. "Monsieur Renard," he said. He took a step closer to Renard. "*Inspecteur* Renard, you have exceeded your authority in so many ways, I don't even know where to begin. Louis Morgon may have been a friend of yours, but if that is so, then my best advice to you would be to choose your friends more wisely. But regardless of your friendship, his criminal activity has not occurred within your area of responsibility."

"Saint Leon is where the crimes were committed," Renard protested.

"But these are not crimes which come under your purview," Pénichon continued. He was gaining momentum. "Nowhere near it, in fact. Do you still not realize that this is a matter of international concern and import? This is a case *crucial* to the war against terrorism. It involves murder and espionage and numerous acts of terrorism. It most certainly does *not* involve village policing and amateur sleuthing. We are not talking about missing cows or stolen chickens. You must cease all your efforts immediately if you do not wish to find yourself up to your neck in trouble. Is that completely understood?"

Pénichon continued before Renard could respond. "You have behaved properly in passing information along about your contact with Morgon, and you will continue to notify us of any further contacts. You are right that the letter"—here Pénichon patted his jacket—"is of great importance. We will see to it that it finds its way swiftly and safely into the appropriate hands. But, as for the rest of it, these are matters you must leave to the experts, those of us who have trained and prepared for such occasions. I hope that is well understood, *inspecteur*." Renard had no other choice. He saluted Lieutenant Pénichon, who responded with a crisp salute of his own.

XVII

Every morning at seven thirty a member of the president's national security staff entered the Oval Office to deliver the daily security briefing. This was usually the president's first appointment of the day, and they were usually alone together. On this particular Monday morning, however, the security adviser was surprised to find the Oval Office buzzing with activity. The president was at his desk looking through a stack of papers while his chief political adviser murmured fervently in his ear. Other political advisers and strategists hovered nearby, talking on the telephone or huddled in groups of two or three.

Over the weekend the president's reelection, which, until now, had seemed a foregone conclusion, had suddenly been cast in doubt. Several leading newspapers, including some friendly to the president, had published reports that important intelligence used to justify a particular military action had either come from an unreliable agent or been an outright falsification.

Despite the best efforts of spokesmen from the Department of State and the White House, a political firestorm was brewing around these revelations.

The president's opponent, whose campaign efforts up to now had been mostly futile, had seized the opportunity and charged that the president's policies had not only been ineffectual in the battle against terrorism, but had actually made the country more vulnerable to a terroristic attack and less safe. "I believe that this president has put politics before national security," he said, "and, in doing so, has placed the country at risk."

Moreover, the latest polls showed that, for the first time, the challenger's charges were sticking. In just a few short days the race had tightened up to such an extent that the outcome now appeared to be within the margin of error; that is, the race was too close to call.

For that reason Carl, the political adviser, and his staff were preparing the president for a whirlwind campaign foray. A helicopter waited on the South Lawn to take the president to his plane for a tour of three of the so-called battleground states, where polls showed the election to be a dead heat.

"I know, *I know*. God damn it, Carl, I know," said the president.

"I know you know, Mr. President," said the political adviser. "That's why I'm reminding you." The adviser's phone chirped, and he turned away. "Talk to me," he said, stepping into the small alcove that had become his temporary operations center.

"Phil!" said the president, looking expectantly at the security adviser. "How are you? What's up? What have you got for me?" The security adviser passed the briefing folder across the desk to the president.

"It's pretty much what we've been seeing for a while, Mr.

President," said Phil. "The hot spots are North Korea and Iran with their nuclear aspirations. The North Korean program has stopped moving for the moment, contrary to what they're saying. We believe that what we're hearing from them is mainly for Asian consumption. The Iranians, on the other hand, have continued assembling nuclear materiel. The Russians have been worrisome in that regard. We've followed several shipments of nuclear materiel—"

"And the war on terror?" The president leafed back and forth through the briefing book. "What about the war on terror? I don't see anything here on the war on terror." The president slapped the briefing papers with the back of his hand and looked up.

"No sir, Mr. President." Phil removed his glasses and put them in his pocket. "Al Qaeda has not been heard from for a while. Suicide bombings in Iraq and Israel both are down. It's been quiet on that front lately, I'm happy to say."

"Well, I'm happy about that too, Phil. I believe we've got them on the run. But . . . listen, Phil: fighting terrorism, that's supposed to be our strong suit, damn it. I realize everyone is putting in long hours, Phil. Believe me, I know that, and I appreciate it. You don't know how much I appreciate it. I mean, all I want is an all-out effort to win this war on terror, to finally smack these bastards into oblivion.

"We've got al Qaeda on the run, but things are kind of stalled right now, aren't they? We've got to keep the heat on them so they don't have time to regroup. What the hell ever happened with that thing Hugh Bowes was working on, in . . . ?"

"In France?" said Phil.

"France. Right," said the president. "If we could destroy a cell right under Chirac's nose . . ."

"Yes sir, Mr. President. The investigation is still very much alive, very much in play. But nothing is happening there at the moment. That cell dispersed suddenly, and pretty much vanished from sight for the moment."

"Vanished?" said the president. "How the heck could *that* happen? I know, Carl, I'm coming." The political adviser had just whispered urgently in his ear. You could hear the *thwak-thwak* of the helicopter.

"Louis Morgon, the ringleader—" Phil began.

The president was on his feet, slipping his arms into the jacket that an aide was holding. "I don't care about that. I just want some results. Jesus, that guy's *still* on the loose?"

"Central Intelligence, the FBI, everyone is all over it, sir. It's only a matter of time until we smoke him out."

"Smoke him out? Hell, I thought we *had* him. The Agency? Well, forgive my scepticism, Phil, but I don't want to leave *anything* up to those guys. And damn it, Phil, we don't have a hell of a lot of time. I want you and your people all over this thing. And I've already told the secretary of state and everybody else the same damn thing."

"Yes sir," said Phil.

That evening when the president arrived back at the White House, Phil was waiting. He asked to see the president urgently and was summoned to the residential quarters. The president was in shirtsleeves when Phil was escorted into his office.

"Mr. President, good evening." Phil passed an acetate folder across the desk.

"I'm worn out, Phil," said the president.

"Yes sir, I know," said Phil. "And I'm sorry to interrupt your evening, but—"

"What's this?"

"This couldn't wait, sir. It's a letter, sir, that came in just this afternoon. It's a stroke of luck, really. It was forwarded to us through the French *sécurité*. It's from Morgon."

"Who?"

"The terrorist, sir. Secretary Bowes's terrorist. Louis Morgon. We were speaking about him this morning."

"A letter?"

"Yes, sir."

"To whom?"

"To you, sir."

"To *me*? The son of a bitch sent me a letter?"

"Yes, sir. If I may, sir, I believe this may be just what you've been looking for, Mr. President."

The president read the letter. Then he read it again. He looked up at Phil. "God damn! Jesus H Christ! Is this for real?"

"It checks out, sir. All the *bona fides* are there."

The president turned to his aide. "Get Carl in here. Does the secretary of state know about this? Get him in here too, the CIA chief . . ." He named other senior officials. "And Hugh Bowes. Find out where Hugh Bowes is, and get hold of him as soon as you can."

The political adviser's limousine was halfway to his house in McLean when the phone in the armrest rang. "What is it?" he said. "Yes. I'll be right there." He hung up the phone. "We're going back," he said to the driver. The secretary of state and the other senior officials had been sent transcripts of the letter, so as soon as word came that the president had returned, they hurried to the White House.

Hugh Bowes was in Mexico City, where he was negotiating a large and complicated deal between AmericaBank and some large Latin American financial institutions. Hugh's assistant entered the conference room and whispered in his ear. "Right now?" said Hugh.

"Yes, sir," said the assistant. "He said it was urgent."

Hugh excused himself from the table. "Gentlemen, if you will excuse me. I have to take an urgent call from the president."

"It has to do with your Louis Morgon," said the president, once he had Hugh on the line.

"Louis Morgon?" said Hugh.

"We found him," said the president.

"You *found* him? Did you? That *is* good news, Mr. President."

"I need you back here, Hugh. ASAP."

"I am at your service, Mr. President. I'll be there as quickly as I can."

"Time is of the essence, Hugh."

Hugh's clients did not mind his sudden departure. In fact, it pleased them, despite the inconvenience to their enterprise. After all, they had engaged his services mainly because he was at home in the halls of power in Washington and had access to the highest decision makers. What better demonstration could there be of his value to them than a summons from the president of the United States?

A police escort and limousine met Hugh's Gulfstream on the secure apron at Reagan National Airport. They raced to the White House with sirens wailing. The president rose to greet Hugh as he was wheeled into the Oval Office. "Great work, Hugh," he said, walking forward and clasping Hugh's hand in both of his. "Thanks to you, we've reeled this son of bitch in, this Morgon character. You spotted him, and now we've got him."

"Have you been able to interrogate him? Or is he dead?" Hugh raised his eyebrows slightly, as though the matter were only of passing interest to him.

"Dead? No, he isn't dead. It's a whole lot better than that. He's alive and ready to talk."

"To *talk*?" said Hugh. "That *is* a surprising development."

"He wants to give up his al Qaeda comrades. I don't know how much he knows, but somebody *that* high up in al Qaeda has got to know *something*. Right? He should know who's where. Hell, maybe we can finally get that son of a bitch, bin Laden. This is a huge break. Of course, Hugh, it still all depends on you."

"I fail to understand, Mr. President, just how it depends on me."

"Show him the letter, Phil."

Phil stepped across the room and handed Hugh the acetate folder.

The letter had been written on three pages of white paper with a blue fountain pen in a careful hand. It's author, Louis Morgon, described how he had discovered that his house was under surveillance and how he had fled shortly thereafter in order to avoid being assassinated. He confessed that, at the moment of his flight, he had been serving as the chief of a terrorist cell that was in the course of planning various catastrophic events. He declined to be specific about these events.

He realized, he wrote, that once his identity had been revealed to the Americans, his value to al Qaeda was seriously, if not fatally, compromised. In that moment, he went from being an important asset to being a liability. His life was in danger, as much from al Qaeda as from the Americans. Maybe more so, since al Qaeda had, so far, been better than the Americans at searching out their enemies and destroying them.

Louis Morgon wrote that he was willing to reveal what he knew about the operations of al Qaeda, which, he promised, would be sufficient to cause large-scale disruption in that organization. He declined to go into further detail. Suffice it to say, he had information he knew would please the president and his administration and would offer them significant strategic advantages in the so-called war on terror.

He offered this information in exchange for safe passage into the United States witness protection program, although not in the United States. And there was one other condition. He would only give his information in person to former secretary of state Hugh Bowes. The reason for this, he explained, was that he knew Secretary Bowes from his earlier career in the State Department. He believed that Hugh Bowes had been the only official who had treated him fairly during and after his dismissal from government service. Secretary Bowes was the only American official he would trust.

The president should let Louis know his decision by publishing a small advertisement in the employment wanted section of *The International Herald Tribune*. Louis would then send instructions about how, where, and when he and Hugh were to meet.

Hugh continued to look at the letter long after he had finished reading it. Everyone in the room was silent. He looked up finally and smiled slightly. "Well?" said the president. "What do you think? This is what we've been waiting for, Hugh, and we owe it all to you. You discovered this guy, and you delivered him. I can't thank you enough." The men and women standing around the president nodded in agreement.

"Of course, Hugh, whether you meet him or not is entirely up to you. It is a mission not without risk. I would understand completely if you were to decide it's too dangerous to you personally. But if you agree to go, I promise you will be completely protected."

"I'm sure, Mr. President—"

"No, I mean it, Hugh. We won't let you go in by yourself. My thinking is, his days are over and he knows it. He'll have to make some concessions on where and how you meet. You'll have bodyguards with you. There will be sharpshooters standing by. We'll make certain the area is clear of any of his cohorts. I guarantee you, by the time we get it all set up, it will be the safest place on the planet . . ." The officials around the president's desk nodded again in agreement.

"I'm sure that's true, Mr. President; I have no hesitation on my own account. I only wonder whether he has the information he claims to have."

"That's a big if, Hugh. Frankly, I'd guess he probably doesn't. But he's still a big fish, and he'll know something. And info or no info, we'll have *him*."

"He's expecting safe passage, Mr. President . . ."

Phil jumped in. "Then he's a fool, sir."

"Phil's right," said the president. "He's not Osama or Al-Zarqawi, but he's a big enough trophy to mount above the fireplace."

"He's going to pick a meeting place where he knows there's a way out for him. He's a smart and clever man," said Hugh.

"Not as smart as you, Hugh. Hell, *you're* the one that caught *him,* Hugh. Not the other way around."

XVIII

The boy, Zaharia Lefort, was lost. He knew, of course, that he was in the main hall of the Gare St. Charles, the Marseille railroad station, and he knew Marseille was in France. The station, with its noise, its bustling crowds, its announcements, its rows of tracks and trains gave him some comfort. It seemed like you could go anywhere from there. But where should he go? Marseille and France were mere words to him, without any context. He did not know the names of other places in France, besides Marseille and Paris. He did not even know where the sea was; was it to the north or south? He was a world away from Al Harib and Algiers and everything else he knew.

To complicate things further, Zaharia did not have French identity papers, or Algerian ones, for that matter. He did not have a plan or a thought, even, beyond getting away from the police and whoever else had killed his father, and who were now undoubtedly looking for him.

Zaharia chose a ticket window with a sympathetic-looking woman behind it and got in line. When his turn came, he spoke to her in Arabic. "I want to buy a ticket to here," he said. He held his father's list of names against the glass and pointed to the words *Saint Leon sur Dême.*

The woman at the window leaned forward, squinted over her glasses at the words, and typed them into her computer. She waited for a moment and then typed something else. After studying the screen, she wrote something on a piece of paper and slid the paper through the slot to Zaharia. She said, in French, that he would first have to travel to Lyon, where he would have to change trains for Orleans. In Orleans he would have to change for Tours, and then from Tours he would have to take a bus or a taxi to Saint Leon sur Dême. The departure and arrival times were on the paper she had handed him. The ticket to Tours would cost 109 euros. She did not know how much the bus or taxi would cost.

She spoke slowly and, by studying the paper as she spoke, Zaharia was able to understand what she said. He looked at the sum she had written and considered the money in his pocket. He had enough to pay for the ticket, but some of the money his father had given him would then be gone, and he might need it later.

"No thank you," said Zaharia.

The woman asked him something he did not understand. She sounded concerned.

"No," said Zaharia quickly. "My parents are over there." He pointed toward a crowd of people and walked away from the window before she could ask any more questions.

Zaharia studied the sign with the departing trains. A destination city and a track number scrolled off the top of the sign as each train departed the station. The information on the remaining trains then scrolled up one slot. There was a train for Lyon halfway down the sign and another still further down.

Zaharia could see trains waiting like great, sleek beasts. Puffs of steam came from beneath them, and they made loud hissing sounds. Zaharia found the next train to Lyon on track eight, just as the sign had indicated. It was not scheduled to leave for another twenty-five minutes, but people were already getting aboard. Zaharia could see them through the windows, lifting their bags onto the overhead racks and settling down for the journey, eating sandwiches or unfolding their newspapers. He looked up and down the platform but did not see anyone in uniform.

Zaharia climbed onto the train and walked through the cars. At the end of each car there were luggage racks, and some people with especially large suitcases had lifted their bags onto these racks before finding their seats. Zaharia waited until no one was watching and climbed onto a luggage rack. He squeezed behind the suitcases, lay down with his head on his small bundle of clothes, and waited. Before long he felt the train begin to move. He remained hidden until they reached Lyon. Then he pushed the suitcases aside and got off the train.

Zaharia did not have any difficulty finding the train for Orleans. He got on that train and again climbed onto a luggage rack. Again he pulled the suitcases together to conceal himself, but a few moments later a policeman pulled them aside and ordered him down from the rack. The policeman asked Zaharia for his ticket, but Zaharia did not have one. The policeman asked the boy where he was going and why he did not have a ticket. "You cannot travel without a ticket," he said.

"I am going to see . . . my uncle," said the boy.

"Your uncle?" said the policeman. "Really. Well, I think you had better come with me."

The policeman and Zaharia stepped down from the train. The policeman kept his arm across Zaharia's shoulder and walked him out of the station.

"Please," Zaharia said, "my uncle will be waiting for me in Tours at the station."

The policeman did not speak. Instead, he steered Zaharia to a blue police car. He opened the door and waited while the boy got inside. "Have you ever been in a police car?" asked the policeman, and smiled at the boy in what was meant to be a friendly manner.

"No," said Zaharia. They drove a short distance to the precinct station. "Please," said Zaharia again, "my uncle is waiting for me. He will be worried if I don't arrive."

"So," said the policeman, "what's your name?"

"Zaharia Lefort," said Zaharia.

"And where do you live, Zaharia? Where are your parents?"

"I'm going to live with my uncle," said the boy. "My parents are . . . at home?"

"Your uncle? And where does your uncle live?"

"In Tours," said the boy. "I already told you."

"And who is your uncle? What's his name?"

Zaharia thought for a while but did not answer.

"If you tell me his name, Zaharia, then we can take you back to the train, and you can go see him."

"Louis Morgon," said Zaharia. "His name is Louis Morgon."

"And do you have a telephone number or an address for him?"

"He is waiting for me in Tours. At the station. He has a big car and a big house. With servants."

The policeman opened the door of the police car and got out. He stood there leaning on the open door while he kept one hand on the steering wheel and one foot in the car.

"Jean!" he called to a colleague who was having a smoke on the front steps of the precinct station. "Jean! I've got a runaway. Would you watch him while I go in and check out his story?" Jean, the man on the steps, dropped his cigarette and ground it out with his shoe. He took a step in their direction. The first policeman released the steering wheel, stepped around the door, and started walking toward the station house. As soon as he did, Zaharia slid across the seat, put the car in gear, and spun the car away from the curb and out into traffic, the open front door still flapping. The shouts of the two policemen running after him were lost in the sound of squealing tires.

Zaharia wove his way through traffic and circled back to the train station the way they had come. He left the car in an alley behind the station and ran inside. The train for Orleans had already left, and the next one was not leaving for another fifteen minutes. But the fast train for Paris was just about to leave, so Paris would have to do.

The police soon found the police car parked neatly against the curb, the keys still in the ignition. Four policemen ran into the train station. Two stood by the tracks watching the crowds pass, while the other two got on the next train for Orleans. They walked through all the cars and checked all the baggage racks, but they did not find the boy, so they got off. The four continued searching the station for some time. They walked up and down the aisles of those trains scheduled for imminent departure, scanning the crowds, watching people come and go, before they finally gave up.

Back at the precinct, the policeman named Jean and the one who had first arrested Zaharia did a computer search on the name Louis Morgon. Jean, the officer at the computer, let out a low whistle. "What is it?" said the other policeman, and leaned toward the screen.

"This kid's uncle? Take a look."

Now the other policemen let out a whistle.

"Do you think that's where this kid is really heading?"

"I think it probably is. I scared him. I think he was telling the truth. Not the whole truth, but some of the truth. Call headquarters. If they can find this kid, they might just be able to follow him right to his 'uncle's' doorstep."

"Do you think Morgon is really his uncle?"

"Who knows? I doubt it. The kid's North African; Morgon's American, it says here."

"Maybe the kid's a courier or a messenger or something."

"No. If that were the case, he wouldn't have given up Morgon; he'd have known to lie. Besides, he's too young. What do you think, twelve maybe? I could tell he was just plain scared. And especially of the police."

"Maybe so. But I'll tell you this: that little bugger sure can drive."

The first policeman did not find this amusing. "Call Paris," he said.

Louis went to the café by the Pen'noch harbor every morning. And every morning he bought *The International Herald Tribune* at the bar, whose proprietor now greeted him as though he had lived there his entire life.

"Et un café, Monsieur Bertand?"

"Oui, Pascal, un café noir," said Louis. He sat at a table by the window and looked out on the boats dipping and bobbing in the harbor while he sipped his coffee. He opened the newspaper to the employment wanted advertisements. When he did not find what he was looking for, he read the rest of the paper. He read with particular interest about the American presidential

campaign, about the back-and-forth accusations, the outrageous charges and countercharges, the appeals to patriotism and religious righteousness. "To think that I once thought I understood all this," he said to himself. Pascal was already accustomed to Monsieur Bertrand's occasional muttering and no longer looked up.

One morning—it was cloudy and cool, and the ocean had all but disappeared behind a bank of fog—Louis turned the pages of the newspaper and found the advertisement he had been waiting for: *Well-qualified international traveler in search of executive banking position. Specialty: import, export, tax law. Contact IHT Box KH4472.*

In Saint Leon, Renard saw the advertisement too. He folded the paper, took a last swallow of coffee, and stood up. He left the Hôtel de France and walked to his car. Three hours later, when he arrived in Quimper, Louis was waiting for him in the small park near the train station, just across from the Café Brezh. The two men shook hands and took a small table at the back of the café.

"I am sure," said Louis, "a lot of people are watching this particular advertisement. It is being scrutinized by those to whom it was not addressed as though it were a sacred text. The French *Sûreté* will certainly respond to the ad, trying somehow to entice the Americans to let them in on the game. I am not sure, but the Algerians may well know what is going on as well. And who knows how much al Qaeda knows. Or cares.

"It would be amusing," said Louis after a thoughtful pause, "to be able to see it all from above. It is like a game of Chinese checkers."

"I still don't know how you are able to do that," Renard said. "How do you stay so *detached* from such a deadly business? You're still a mystery to me, after all this time."

"I know, Jean. You don't like my calling it a game," said Louis. "You want me to take it more seriously. But you understand—don't you?—if I did, I would be overwhelmed by it. The only hope I have of solving things to my satisfaction is to remain fascinated.

"Of course, that is the great seductive fallacy, isn't it? The truth is, it can't be solved; there's nothing to be solved. Every mystery, even the most obvious, is too complicated and too simple to ever have a solution. An outcome, maybe. But an outcome is never a solution. It's just an outcome."

Renard reached for a cigarette.

Louis smiled at his friend before he continued. "Be that as it may," he said, "the Americans will almost certainly try to do things entirely on their own, without notifying the French, without notifying anyone else. I am certain Hugh Bowes does not want French special forces interfering with his assassins. The French, in turn, will not be keen on seeing me, or any other 'terrorist,' for that matter, gunned down on a beautiful French beach while they stand idly by. That is certainly in my favor."

"If that is in your favor," said Renard, "then that is all."

Louis smiled again in Renard's direction. "I think we can improve the odds," he said. "For instance, I'm depending on you to see that Pénichon is informed somehow, and that he figures out where and when this will all occur. The trick will be to make certain that he notifies his superiors, and that they organize a French presence."

"On the beach?"

"I've told you too much too soon," said Louis.

"Well, you have said it, and you can't take it back now," said Renard. He understood why Louis did not want to say very much, but he did not like it.

The two men stared across the table at one another. Finally Louis spoke again. "The great beach just north of Pen'noch. The one with the German bunkers. That's where I'll meet them."

"And why the beach?"

"Because it's wide open, so they can see that I'm alone. And because they'll have a clear shot. They'll love that about the choice. I want them to be happy."

Renard looked at his friend to be certain he was serious. "If you promise to explain yourself to me," Renard said, "I will figure out how to notify Pénichon."

"When it begins to unfold," said Louis, "if things go as I hope, the reasons for my choice of the beach will become obvious. If I am unlucky, well, . . . it won't matter."

Renard did not like the direction the conversation was taking, so he changed it. "If you could give me a letter or something for Pénichon, that would help."

"I had the same thought," said Louis. He reached inside his pocket and withdrew an envelope, which he handed to Renard. "Say that you persuaded me to send you a copy of my response to the advert. Mention my despondency again as a reason, if you like." Louis smiled thinly and added, "It would not be entirely untrue."

The two men ate the rest of their meal in silence.

XIX

It was barely five o'clock when Renard arrived back in Saint Leon, but it was already nearly dark. The time had changed from daylight savings time the week before. "Winter is coming," said Renard as he drove down the last hill. "The night season." The village was shrouded in dusk. Curtains had been pulled and shutters had been closed. The only light to be seen came in thin shards poking their way out into the evening from around the edges of shutters.

As he was passing on the road below Louis's house, Renard thought he saw a light showing through one of Louis's windows. But that was impossible. Still, he stopped, backed up, and looked again. He had not been mistaken. Someone had been inside and had left a light on. Or they were inside now.

Renard stopped in front of the house that had been Solesme's. It was shuttered and dark. The property had been sold, but the new owners had not taken possession yet. Renard left his car there and walked back up the hill to Louis's driveway. He could not see the house from the bottom of the drive. He stood for a while and listened, but he did not hear anything.

Slowly he climbed the hill, walking on the grass beside the drive to avoid making any noise. Where the drive crested the hill, Renard finally got a good view of the house. There was no car in the drive, so he stopped and listened again. Then he moved closer. The light he had seen was coming from a half-open shutter on the kitchen window. He had just about convinced himself that no one was there and was reaching into his pocket for the key when a shadow flickered across the window.

Renard stood against the wall and tried to look inside. But he could see only a narrow section of the kitchen. Then he heard the sound of water running; he moved sideways and the edge of the kitchen sink came into view. He saw an arm. The arm moved, and whoever it was turned toward the window. Renard ducked back out of sight.

After waiting a moment, Renard stepped to the door. Slowly he tested the handle. The latch was still broken and the door was open. He took a deep breath, held it, threw open the door, and lunged inside. A figure dove past him and was almost out the door, but Renard reached out and grabbed at its arm. He missed the arm, but his hand struck the person's shoulder squarely and knocked him onto the floor. Before he could scramble to his feet, Renard had a small, ragged boy firmly in his grip.

The boy kicked and struggled mightily. "Let me go! Let me go!" he shouted, lashing out in every direction. Renard wrapped his arms around the boy, pinning his arms to his sides. He lifted him completely off the floor and staggered backward into the living room, where he managed to get one leg around the boy's flailing legs. With that, the two of them collapsed onto the couch. The boy continued to struggle, but Renard held him tightly. The water was still running in the kitchen sink.

"Let me go," said the boy. "Please let me go. Don't hurt me." He had a strong North African accent. "I wasn't hurting anything," he said. "Let me go."

"Who are you?" said Renard.

"Let me go," said the boy.

"What are you doing here?" Renard demanded.

"Let me go."

"Don't you know this house belongs to someone? It is private property. You are trespassing on private property. Do you know what that means?"

"Yes, I know," said the boy. "Of course I know. It belongs to Monsieur Louis Morgon, doesn't it? I know him. I am waiting for him. For Monsieur Morgon."

"You are *waiting* for him? You *know* him?"

"Yes, I am waiting for him. I must see him."

"How long have you been waiting?"

"Since yesterday. I have been waiting since yesterday. Are you the police?"

"How do you know Monsieur Morgon?"

"I knew him back home. He is my father's friend. My father said, if I need help, I should find him. Where can I find him? Please tell me." The boy had stopped fighting. Renard loosened his grip. The boy hesitated, then gestured toward the sink. "The water," he said, and backed toward the sink to turn off the water—looking at Renard as he went. It looked as though he might bolt again, so Renard rose and stationed himself by the door. The boy was defiant. "Don't worry," he said. "I'm not going anywhere. I'm waiting for Monsieur Morgon. When will he be back?"

"Sit down over here," said Renard. In their struggle, Renard and the boy had knocked over a chair. Renard set it upright, and only then did he notice that the house was no longer in its ransacked state. The furniture had been set upright and straightened. Drawers had been replaced in the buffet, books had been stacked on the bookshelves.

"Did you clean all this up?" asked Renard.

"Are you the police?" asked the boy again.

"Yes, I am the police," said Renard. "I am the policeman in this village. Now you tell me who you are."

"Zaharia Lefort," said the boy.

"Lefort?" said Renard. "Are you related to Pierre Lefort?"

"Yes," said the boy. He suddenly looked very small sitting on the chair. "He is my father," he said, and began to cry. He turned his head so Renard would not see his tears. "They killed him," said the boy. "Did you know my father?"

"I knew him . . . only slightly," said Renard. "They killed him?"

"Did you put him in jail?" said the boy.

"Yes, I arrested him. He stole some things, so he had to go to jail. Who killed him?"

"When is Monsieur Morgon coming back?"

"He is away for a while. Who killed your father? Do you know?"

"No," said the boy. "I don't know. I didn't see anything. I don't know anything."

"Have you eaten?"

The boy had been eating whatever he could find in Louis's house, mostly canned goods. Whatever had been in the refrigerator had mostly spoiled. In fact, the boy had cleaned the refrigerator and had washed the dishes, which now stood in stacks by the sink.

"Monsieur Morgon is my friend," said Renard. "He will be very grateful that you have cleaned his house."

"Who made such a mess?" said the boy. "Was it Monsieur Morgon?"

"I think it was maybe the same people who killed your father. They were looking for something. That is why you are not safe here."

"But I have to stay and wait for Monsieur Morgon."

"I live nearby," said Renard. "My wife has made a nice supper. You can wait for Monsieur Morgon at my house." They walked down the hill to Renard's car. Renard carried the boy's bundle under one arm and rested the other arm lightly across the boy's thin shoulders. Zaharia wondered whether the police always put their arms on your shoulders to keep you from running. They drove the short distance to Renard's house.

"Isabelle, this is Zaharia Lefort," said Renard. "Zaharia, this is my wife, Isabelle." Zaharia looked at Isabelle then looked at the floor and murmured, "*Bonsoir, madame.*"

"*Bonsoir,* Zaharia," said Isabelle.

Isabelle put supper on the table, and she and Renard watched the boy devour a heaping plateful of food and then a second plateful. They made up Jean Marie's bed and carried Zaharia's things into the small bedroom. They showed him where the bathroom was and wished him a good night. When they got up the next morning, he was gone.

"He went straight back up to your house," said Renard to Louis the next day. They talked regularly now, from various phone booths, at prearranged times. "I knocked and he opened the door," said Renard, "like he lived there. 'I have to wait here for Monsieur Morgon,' he said. 'I do not want to miss him when he comes back,' he said. And that's where he is. He won't stay with us, but he can't stay there. It isn't safe.

"As best I can gather, he and Pierre fled Algeria on an oil tanker," said Renard. "They were in Marseille for a few days. His father gave him a list of people he could look up if he needed help, and your name was on the list. Pierre was killed in the hotel where they were staying."

"Do you have any idea who killed him?" Louis wondered.

"I think the boy saw them do it. He won't say so, but I'm guessing from some things he's said that the police were involved."

"He can't stay there," said Louis.

"There's more," said Renard. "He stole a police car in Lyon. They tried to arrest him, and he drove off in their car."

"He's a good driver," said Louis. "I remember that about him."

"He gave the police your name; he said you were his uncle and that he was coming to stay with you. They put your name in the computer, and guess what they found."

"How do you know all this?" Louis asked.

"I called Pénichon," said Renard. "He already knew about the boy. I told him the boy was here. Pénichon wanted him arrested, but I suggested he be left alone. That way he might lead us to you. Pénichon told me to leave the anti-terrorist tactics to the professionals, but I think he liked the idea. Listen, it could be a stroke of luck. If Pénichon and his higher-ups go for it, it could guarantee that security forces get involved."

Louis met Michael and Jennifer in Quimper in the park that ran along the river by the pottery works. They walked along the gravel paths under the plane trees. Leaves blew about in front of them, making odd scraping sounds. Up ahead a couple of gardeners tore dead plants from the flower beds and tossed them into a wooden cart.

"How have you been, Jennifer?" said Louis.

"I'm the same as I was, Dad. How should I be?"

"I want to ask a favor," said Louis, as though he had not heard her angry response.

"The answer is no," said Jennifer.

"Without hearing what it is?" said Louis.

"Yes."

"Fine," said Louis. "I'll accept that you won't do it. But I want to tell you what it is anyway."

"I don't want to hear it," said Jennifer.

"Listen to me, Jennifer," said Louis. His voice took on an edge that caused her to stop walking and turn to face him. "Be as angry as you want, Jennifer. See me as your enemy if that helps. But don't let your anger get in the way of your own well-being. Whatever harm I have done you, don't forget that I do not *mean* you harm. But there are those that do."

"Who was it that said that the road to hell is paved with good intentions?"

"Many people. And they were right about hell. But this is life, which is far more complicated and far less clear."

"You have all the answers, don't you, Dad?"

"All I've got is questions, Jennifer. But just listen to what I have to say."

"You think you can persuade me?" Jennifer said, as though she were daring him to try.

"No," said Louis. "I'm fairly sure I can't persuade you of anything. I don't know if you can even listen to facts right now. But I want you to hear them anyway. I want you to know where you stand. I want you to know what is going on and to what extent the outcome depends on you. Whatever wrong has been done you and whoever is to blame, it doesn't change reality one bit, it doesn't change what is."

"I'm all ears," said Jennifer. She stood with her eyes flashing and her arms folded across her chest. In that moment she reminded Louis of himself.

Louis told her about the boy Zaharia hiding out in his house in Saint Leon. "Some of the same people who are trying to kill me killed this boy's father. He saw them do it. He turned up at my house. He found his way there from Marseille. By himself. He's a plucky kid and a bright kid. And, from all appearances, a good kid. But he can't stay there, for his safety and for ours. He's an important witness to important and terrible crimes. I think he would be safest here in Quimper."

"And the favor is?"

"You keep him with you until this is all over."

"You must be crazy."

"It's possible, but I don't think so," said Louis.

"Why don't *you* keep him? He's *your* orphan. Why should I keep him?"

"He won't be safe with me. He will be safer with you. And you will be safer with him."

"And why not Michael?" She pointed her thumb in her brother's direction.

"Here is the ugly truth, Jennifer. You'll be decoys, you and the boy. His name is Zaharia."

"You make it sound more attractive all the time."

"Your apartment is larger than Michael's, isn't it? and better situated for escaping, if it comes to that."

"Escaping? From whom?"

"He is likely to be followed here by French special operations troops searching for me. They will see the two of you—you and Zaharia—as less dangerous than Michael or I would be."

"When will this all be over?" Jennifer said, suddenly sounding very tired. Her shoulders sagged, and she stared at the dead flowers heaped in the cart. "When, Dad?"

"Soon, I think. I can't promise anything, but I think it will be over soon."

"I'll think about it," she said, and turned and walked away.

"Thank you, Jennifer," said Louis, but she was already out of earshot.

XX

The garden at Louis's house was in disarray. The grass had not been cut in weeks, the hedges and shrubs had not been trimmed, and the vegetable garden was an overgrown jumble of dying vines, weeds, and collapsed, rotting greens. The tomato plants had pulled their stakes over, and the fruits had rotted on the ground. Only their dried-up, blackened skins were left. The melons had split open, and their flesh had been eaten away by insects and rodents. The rose by the front door—Pierre de Ronsard—had lost most of its leaves, and those few left on the vine were black.

Renard tried not to look at the mess as he knocked on the door. Zaharia peered through the window and then opened the door. "Zaharia," Renard said, "Monsieur Morgon is not coming back here, at least not yet. He can't come back right now. There are men waiting to hurt him. They say he is a terrorist. Do you know what a terrorist is? They say Monsieur Morgon is a terrorist."

"*Is* he a terrorist?" Zaharia wanted to know.

"No. No, he is not," said Renard. "He's in danger from the men who say he is a terrorist. Just as your father was. Your father knew something that it was dangerous for him to know. And Monsieur Morgon also knows something about these people that he should not know, something dangerous for him to know. Monsieur Morgon and I have made a plan to stop these men. But to make the plan work we need your help."

Zaharia's eyes widened, but he did not say anything.

"I am going to take you to see Monsieur Morgon . . ."

"You know where he is?"

"Yes, I do."

"Why didn't you tell me before?"

"Because if I had told you, you would have tried to go there, and that would have placed your life in danger and Monsieur Morgon's life too. You see, they could have followed you . . ."

"The police in Lyon tried to follow me, and they couldn't," said Zaharia.

"I know. But that's because you *knew* they were following you, and you could hide. This time you wouldn't have known that they were following you."

Zaharia considered this. "What is your plan?" he said.

"We're going to go see Monsieur Morgon. We'll be staying there for a while."

"Is it far?"

"It's not as far as Marseille," said Renard, "but it's not close by either. We'll drive there in my car."

"Is it a police car?"

"No, it's not. Listen, Zaharia: Monsieur Morgon and I need your help, but you have to trust me," said Renard. "Will you trust me?"

"Yes," said the boy.

"Good. Very good. Now, I want you to get all your things together. I'll come back for you in an hour, and we will drive to Monsieur Morgon. We'll be followed by some men in a car, but this time we *want* to be followed. The people following us will be on our side, but they don't know they are on our side, so we shouldn't let them know that we know we're being followed. I know it's a little confusing, but do you understand?"

"Yes, monsieur. I think so."

"Are you frightened, Zaharia?"

"Are the men following us police?"

"Yes, they are," said Renard. "But don't worry, Zaharia, they're good police. It will be fine."

"I'm not frightened," said Zaharia.

When Renard returned in an hour, he found the boy waiting on Louis's doorstep. The house was closed up. The shutters were latched shut and the door was fastened as well as it could be. Zaharia handed Renard the key. "You keep it," said Renard. "In a few hours you can give it to Monsieur Morgon yourself."

They drove down to the village, and Renard parked in front of his office. He went inside and called Pénichon. "We're about to leave," he said.

"Our people are in place," said Pénichon.

Renard stepped to the window. "Yes, I know," he said. "I see them."

"Really?" said Pénichon, sounding disappointed.

"It doesn't matter at this point, does it?" said Renard. "I just hope their skills will be up to the matter at hand."

"Don't worry about that," said Pénichon.

And, in fact, once they had left the village, the car shadowing them disappeared from view and did not reappear until they pulled up in Quimper in front of a tall yellow apartment building. The two men sitting inside the car pretended to look at a map as Renard walked the boy into the building. Zaharia looked at them and then at Renard. "That's them," Renard said under his breath. "Don't look at them again."

Renard walked Zaharia through the lobby and out the service entrance at the back of the building. He opened the heavy steel service door to the building across the alley, and they walked through the lobby of that building and out the front. "Why are we going through all these buildings?" Zaharia wanted to know.

"That way the men who followed us won't know which building we're actually in. They will think we're in the first building, which they will keep watching. But we'll actually be in a different building."

"Was that your plan?" Zaharia asked, his eyes wide.

"It was Monsieur Morgon's plan," said Renard. They waited until the traffic had passed, then crossed the street, and entered a stone apartment building with a bright blue door. They climbed three flights of stairs, walked to the end of the hall, and knocked.

Jennifer opened the door. "Hello, Zaharia," she said. "I'm Jennifer. Come in."

The boy looked from Jennifer to Renard and back again. "Jennifer is Monsieur Morgon's daughter," Renard explained. "You're going to stay with her for a while. And this is Monsieur Morgon. Do you remember him?" Jennifer stepped aside so Zaharia could see Louis standing in the center of the room.

"Hello, Zaharia," said Louis. "How are you? Do you remember me?"

"Yes," said Zaharia. Then he was silent.

For many days now this boy had been living a nightmare.

While it was certainly true that Pierre had been a thief and a rogue, he had loved the boy and had cared for him as best he knew how. Despite long absences, he had been the only father the boy had ever known.

When Louis had showed up in Algeria and Pierre had realized that his own life was in danger, his instinct, however misguided, had been to keep the boy with him and under his protection, and he had done so at a terrible risk to himself. The two had arrived in Marseille, where the boy had witnessed his father's assassination. He had been interviewed by the policeman who had killed his father. Then he had fled and had found his way alone across the entire country in search of a man he had seen only once. Louis Morgon—a name on a slip of paper. The man who was now standing in front of him.

The boy dropped his small bundle of clothes, stepped up to Louis, and threw his arms around the startled stranger. Zaharia buried his face in Louis's chest and wept. He wept for his lost father, he wept for his home in the Algerian desert, he wept for his mother and grandmother and for all the other people and places he imagined he would never see again. He wept from sadness for all that he had been through and from relief at having finally found his way to Monsieur Morgon.

Louis was startled by this sudden explosion of emotion and took a half step back, but the boy clung to him. Louis placed one hand on the back of the boy's head and patted it lightly. He thought he understood the boy's unhappiness. But a child's unhappiness has a way of turning into everybody else's unhappiness, and Louis quite unexpectedly found himself reliving his own misery and loss. He suddenly saw Solesme's face in front of him and folded the boy into his arms and held him tightly against his chest.

Startled and confused by this emotional scene, Renard stooped down, picked up the boy's small bundle, and put it on the couch. He cleared his throat. "You will sleep here, I think, Zaharia," he said. "Is that right, Jennifer? I think that is right." He cleared his throat again.

"Yes," said Jennifer. "I hope that is all right, Zaharia." She stepped toward the boy and put her hand lightly on his shoulder. "Are you hungry or thirsty?" she asked.

The boy released his hold on Louis. He wiped his eyes and looked down. "Oui, madame," he said.

"I had better go," said Renard. "I don't want them"—he gestured with his head toward the door—"to get suspicious." Renard left the apartment and crossed back through the adjacent buildings. The two policemen were sitting where he had left them. They continued watching the entrance to the tall yellow building as Renard drove away. Two hours later they were replaced by two other policemen.

The building was watched twenty-four hours a day. When Jennifer and the boy went out, they left by way of the yellow building. They shopped for groceries; they went to the bakery or the pastry shop; they took walks in the park. Sometimes they walked hand in hand. They were always followed. Michael came for a visit, and when he left, the policemen followed him. But he only led them back to his apartment.

Soon a new advertisement appeared in the *Herald Tribune* employment wanted section, and Louis responded. He wrote that Hugh Bowes was to come to Quimper and stay at the Grand Hôtel de Bretagne. He was to be unaccompanied. He should carry a cell phone with a particular number. Once Louis had assured himself that the situation was to his liking, he would send instructions as to exactly when and where they would meet.

Not surprisingly, Hugh declined to even consider coming to

Quimper without at least four companions, two of whom would stay with him throughout the entire meeting, and all of whom would be armed. Hugh's reaction was relayed to Louis by way of another advertisement, and Louis agreed to Hugh's amendment. Hugh could have four armed men, as he specified.

"What is he thinking?" the national security man, Phil, wondered. He stood with his hands deep in his pockets, peering down at the street from his window in the Old Executive Office Building.

"I would love to know," said Hugh.

"Sir," said Phil, "whatever he is thinking, *I* am thinking that the mouse has just let the cat through the door."

Hugh raised his eyebrows and looked at Phil. "Are you?"

"Mr. Secretary, you will have top men with you."

"I am certain of that," said Hugh.

"Do you have any idea how he got your cell phone number?"

"I cannot imagine," said Hugh. "You are sending snipers?"

"Absolutely. Three teams of two. They're arriving in Paris as we speak."

"Sanctioned by the French?"

Phil removed his glasses and polished them with his handkerchief.

"Good," said Hugh. "That is as it should be."

The Grand Hôtel de Bretagne is in a nineteenth-century chateau set in a walled park in the very center of Quimper. Originally built as the home of a wealthy industrialist, the building is not especially large as chateaux go. But it has a gorgeous aspect, and its symmetry is perfect. It is punctuated on its four corners by tall, slim towers, and three stories of windows run across its front and back.

The Bretagne's thirty-five sumptuous guest rooms are attended to by a highly trained staff of 150. There is an excellent kitchen, serving the finest *haute cuisine*. The dining room, with its floor-to-ceiling windows, looks out on a *potager* and an elaborate rose garden and is reserved, as the Bretagne's brochure notes, "for the exclusive use of the Hotel's cherished clients and their valued guests."

It was the first of November. The *potager* had been cleared and covered with straw except for a few last rows of winter greens. The tree roses had been pruned and wrapped for the winter in protective bundles of straw and burlap. A few late climbing roses remained in bloom beside the front entry.

Two black Mercedes limousines swept up the driveway, scattering gravel as they came. They crunched to a stop in front of the broad flagstone terrace. Footmen wearing black breeches and red jackets opened the doors of the first limousine and helped Hugh Bowes from the car and onto the waiting wheelchair. A footman pushed Hugh up the ramp, across the terrace, and through the lobby to the elevator. Accompanied by the desk manager, he was taken straight to his suite, which he pronounced more than satisfactory. "We're not here for a vacation," he said.

"No, sir," said the manager.

The occupants of the second limousine waved the footmen away. They gathered their own luggage, an assortment of strangely shaped bags and valises, and loaded them on the carts standing by for that purpose. They pushed the carts into the hotel and waited while one of their number retrieved their room keys.

Lou Coburn watched the footmen attending to Hugh's luggage and to his own. By the time he stepped to the desk, the clerk was waiting with his key.

"Nothing to sign?" Coburn asked.

"No sir. Nothing to sign. I hope everything is to your liking. Your party has the entire south wing reserved for your exclusive use." The clerk made an elegant motion in that direction. "Your meals will be served in the private dining room on the ground floor of that wing."

Of course everything was to Coburn's liking. How could it *not* be? Until a few days ago, he had been on the CIA's Osama bin Laden desk, and now he was on special assignment with former secretary of state Hugh Bowes staying at the Grand Hôtel de Bretagne. Had there ever been a greater or more unexpected stroke of pure, blessed luck?

Being assigned to the Osama desk had once been a career-making appointment, but not anymore. The trouble was, no one in the Administration wanted to hear the bad tidings the desk continually offered. It was nothing new, really: American friends and allies, like the Saudis and the Pakistanis, were still funneling money to bin Laden; bin Laden still had strong ties in England, France, Russia, Mexico; and still nobody knew where he was. Ever since the attacks on the World Trade Center and the Pentagon, the Osama bin Laden desk—which had long predicted something of that sort—had been the purveyor of only bad news, the messenger everyone wanted to shoot, and had thus gone from being a plum appointment to being known among the Agency's rank and file as "Siberia."

After being transferred there, Coburn had weighed his alternatives. There were private security jobs to be had in Afghanistan, Saudi Arabia, and Iraq, where he could make good money and remain in the trade, and he had been about to submit his resignation when Hugh Bowes had called. Hugh inquired after Coburn's health and well-being and expressed surprise that Coburn was thinking of a career change. "Are you dissatisfied with the course of your career?" he asked without apparent irony.

"Let's just say," Coburn said, "that I am considering my options."

Hugh paused for a moment. "Come see me this evening," he said. "Would you? I may have an interesting assignment for you."

Coburn was thinner than Hugh remembered. His eyes were narrow; his mouth was set. He appeared to have mostly recovered from his physical injuries, and he moved easily across the room, but something in him seemed changed. He winced slightly as he took a seat. "Broken ribs take a long time to heal," he said with a tight smile.

Hugh offered Coburn a drink. "Help yourself," said Hugh, gesturing toward the bottles standing on the bar. While Coburn was pouring himself a glass of whiskey, Hugh said that he would soon be meeting with the terrorist Louis Morgon.

Coburn took a sip from his drink. "So you know where he is?" Coburn asked lazily, as though the answer did not matter to him.

"We do," said Hugh, sipping from a frosty glass of water. "He's in France, in Brittany. The purpose of the meeting, which Morgon himself initiated, by the way, is to interrogate him about al Qaeda. He's almost certainly got useful intelligence, and he might well know something of their leadership structure. He might even be able to give us something useful on bin Laden himself.

"Admittedly, that is probably more than we should hope for. Nevertheless, we—meaning the Administration at the highest level—consider Morgon a sufficiently valuable resource to take a calculated risk. If we can persuade Morgon to give up what he's got, it might help turn the corner in the war on terror."

"And in the election," said Coburn.

Hugh shrugged and smiled. "That's not my concern, Coburn. Or yours." He paused. "Coburn," he said, looking the younger man in the eye, "I would like you with me on this . . . mission. There will be other security personnel, of course. But I would like you by my side."

"And why is that?" Coburn asked. How could he *not* wonder?

"You're right to ask," said Hugh. "It's because you have proved yourself competent at . . . what you do."

Coburn raised his eyebrows. Hugh waved his hand, as though he could chase Coburn's suspicions away like so many gnats. "Overconfidence was your principal shortcoming, Coburn. Wouldn't you agree? I believe your . . . recent experience has helped you rein in your overconfidence. Am I not correct in that belief?"

Coburn did not respond.

"More importantly," Hugh continued, "your experience with Morgon, knowing how he thinks, seeing how he works, will be very important. Invaluable, I should say. You know how easy it is to underestimate him. None of the others accompanying me will understand that as well as you."

Coburn looked to see whether Hugh was mocking him. "And what does Morgon get out of this?" he asked. "Why did he come forward all of a sudden?"

Hugh waved his hand again. "Witness protection or something of the sort."

"Something of the sort?" Coburn said.

"Think about it, Coburn. Though we didn't know exactly where he was, we had shut down his operation in Saint Leon. We killed some of his fellow terrorists. He was completely compromised for al Qaeda. He has become a liability for them, and they'll have no choice but to get rid of him. We offered him the chance to stop running. We're his best hope.

"Of course, whatever he has been 'offered,' . . . well, as you know, we simply don't make deals with terrorists. Ever. And, quite frankly, between you and me, if, in the course of our meeting with him, something were to go awry—say, he were to take some threatening action—and you were to have to kill him . . . well, I am quite certain that no one would be all that concerned about another dead terrorist. Would they? Especially one as cunning and lethal as Louis Morgon. Frankly, everyone would think whoever terminated him was a hero.

"Not that he *would* pull a gun." Hugh smiled. "Did you know that Morgon never carries a gun? Never. It's true. He absolutely refused to carry one when he was an agent in the field. And he certainly never would now. I mean, he marched right in on you without a gun, for goodness' sake. He used to say carrying a gun made it more likely that something would go wrong."

Hugh did not mention to Coburn his principal reason for inviting him to be part of the mission, which was Coburn's thirst for revenge. Coburn had been outsmarted and nearly killed by Louis Morgon. Hugh knew how that felt. He knew that Coburn's rage would transform him from a bodyguard into an assassin. "Maybe Louis will elect to meet in the Grand Hotel itself," said Hugh with a smile. "It would seem suicidal for him to do so. But wouldn't that be just like him, to walk straight into the lion's den?"

Hugh would demand the names of terrorists from Louis, and the dates of events, and Louis would deny knowing any names, or dates, or anything. Louis would deny being a terrorist at all. He would probably bring up old accusations against Hugh, or try to engage in philosophical discussions about right and wrong. Louis liked doing that sort of thing.

Or he might simply sit there being his maddening, inscrutable self. It did not matter what he did. It would be all too evident that he had nothing to trade, that he was a bad actor who had come forward in bad faith, that he was merely a malignant and deranged criminal who hated his country.

Whatever Louis chose to do would serve Hugh's purpose perfectly. Coburn would watch it all, hear it all, and feel his aching ribs with every breath he took. He would think of his ruined career and how Morgon, that pathetic son of a bitch standing right in front of him, was responsible. This traitor, this terrorist. "By the way, Coburn," said Hugh, "Jennifer is in France too. Did I mention that?" He took a sip of water. "And Michael, the son."

XXI

Hugh's breakfast arrived on a silver tray. The soft-boiled eggs were perfectly cooked, the croissant was buttery, the coffee was strong. He was not supposed to drink coffee, but this morning he allowed himself two cups. He shaved and dressed.

Jack Harney knocked on the door and let himself in. Harney, the Secret Service agent overseeing the operation, was a tall, beefy man, with round eyes and protruding ears, which gave him the look of an innocent farm boy. In fact, he had grown up in Elizabeth, New Jersey, the son of a policeman. At sixteen he had lied about his age and joined the Marines. After fifteen years he had left the Marines to join the Secret Service. He was a disciplined and competent agent and had risen through the ranks by dint of his hard work and devotion to the job. Hugh felt satisfied that he had in Harney a competent protector.

Harney's satellite phone rang. "It's the Oval Office, sir," he said, and passed the receiver to Hugh.

"Yes?" said Hugh. He listened. "That's right: tomorrow morning," he said. "Yes, November second, at eleven."

"Tomorrow then," said Phil in Washington. Hugh could hear the president's voice in the background. "And where is it to be?" said Phil. "Do you know where?"

"I'm to wait in my suite," said Hugh. "I'm supposed to get a call around ten. He'll let ten pass, of course. Just to try to shake things up a bit."

The president came on the line briefly to wish Hugh well, then he gave the phone back to Phil. "Sir, would you put Harney back on the line, please?"

"Yes, sir?" said Harney and listened. "No, sir. The French aren't giving anything away. I couldn't find out what they know, much less what they're planning. But I'm guessing they'll be nearby."

The negotiations had been long, but fruitless. The French had forbidden any American operation on French soil. They had insisted that law enforcement actions in France—and they saw the capture of a terrorist as a law enforcement issue—must be carried out by French forces. "We are fully equipped to deal with eventualities of this sort," an official from the justice ministry had said. "We have done so many times before. Terrorism is not something new to us in France. The 'war on terror' may be a sufficient excuse to make exceptions to the law in the United States, but it is not an excuse here. We have the safety of French citizens and the sovereign autonomy of France to consider."

"The president wants to proceed with or without the French," said Phil.

"Yes sir," said Harney.

"Check in with us in the morning when the call comes," said Phil.

"Yes, sir," said Harney. "And I'll call you when it's gone down." He hung up the phone. Not having the French on board was a minor inconvenience, but that was something for the diplomats to sort out.

"Since we don't know where or precisely when this will all be happening, Mr. Secretary, this will be more like a combat operation than a conventional Secret Service deployment." Hugh sat in a wingback chair in his sitting room and listened attentively. The heavy brocade window curtains were drawn. Military maps of the entire Finistère were spread out on the writing table and on the floor around it. "We are trained and experienced at improvisation, sir. You have nothing to worry about. As soon as the meet is called and the place is named, the advantage shifts from him to us, and we are in complete control."

Hugh smiled. "Thank you, Harney, for your assurances."

Harney had decided that he would accompany Hugh Bowes and Coburn to the meeting with Louis, acting as Hugh's second bodyguard. He would be in constant contact with his snipers by means of an earphone and a small microphone wired into the lapel of his jacket. He had already briefed Coburn on procedures and rules of engagement, and Coburn seemed prepared and competent, as far as Harney could tell.

Harney preferred working with Secret Service agents, and particularly those he had trained and oriented himself. He knew how they thought and what they were likely to do. Coburn seemed all right as far as he could tell; he had a clean record. But you never knew the whole story with these CIA types. Secretary Bowes had picked this guy; Harney did not know why. Still, the secretary trusted Coburn, and Harney would just have to be satisfied with that.

That night Hugh Bowes was awakened repeatedly by bad

dreams. Finally, as it was beginning to get light, he fell into a deep sleep. When he awoke two hours later, the brocade curtains had been pulled aside. It was a sunny day, but the wind was rocking the trees back and forth and causing shadows to dance on the gauze inner curtains, making crazy and disquieting shapes.

Hugh ordered breakfast, which arrived on a silver tray. There were two silver egg cups and a silver basket for the bread. The butter had been pressed into a small silver cup, the jam was in a silver pot, the tea—he had tea this morning—was in a glass sitting in a silver frame. He had not noticed all the silver yesterday. It made breakfast seem like a peculiar religious ritual, which made him uneasy.

There was a knock on the door, and Harney came into the room wearing a dark suit and tie. He was carrying a Kevlar vest for Hugh to put on under his jacket. "Everyone's ready and assembled, sir. When the call comes. The cars are out front."

The policemen keeping watch on the tall yellow building where they supposed Jennifer to be living saw the front door open and Jennifer and the boy emerge. They were followed by an older man. The policemen compared the man with the photo taped to the dashboard. "That's him," said the driver.

"But where did he come from?" said the other policeman.

Jennifer, Zaharia, and Louis walked to a car parked around the corner. They got in and drove off at a leisurely pace. Louis was driving. The policemen tried to follow at a discreet distance while Louis headed out of town toward the coast, but it seemed to them as though Louis slowed down whenever they got too far behind. After a while he turned off onto a small farm road that meandered through fields and pastures, and there was no way for the police to remain out of sight. They threaded their way between stone walls and hedgerows along narrow and perfectly unpredictable country lanes. They would round a bend and there would be Louis's car right in front of them, edging its way past a car coming in the opposite direction. For all intents and purposes, by choosing this route, Louis had made the French police into his personal security detail. The policeman who was not driving called Pénichon in Paris and gave him their GPS coordinates.

"He's with his daughter and the boy. He's taken a very odd route, but we're probably heading for the coast."

Penichon notified the special forces field commander in Quimper of Louis's whereabouts and direction, at which point the special forces troops ran from their barracks and climbed aboard a waiting truck. They sat in back on wooden benches facing one another. Each man's equipment was on the floor between his feet, and each held his automatic weapon at the ready between his knees. When they joined the chase, the special forces truck was no more than five minutes behind Louis and the French police, who now relayed their position and directions to the truck's driver. The truck quickly caught up with Louis and the police car.

At ten forty-five the telephone rang in Hugh Bowes's room. Hugh answered, and Harney picked up the extension.

"Hugh," said Louis.

"Hello, Louis." Hugh sounded friendly, as though a long lost friend had finally gotten in touch. "It's been many years, hasn't it?"

Louis paused. "Hugh," he said, "I gather your people are listening?"

"They are," said Hugh.

"Good. Then here are your instructions. From Quimper drive west on D 22 toward the village of Pen'noch just south of the Bay of Audierne." Louis could hear a map rattling in the background. "At the village of Kerkerat, just before reaching Pen'noch, turn northeast on C 115 and follow it for about five kilometers until you reach the parking area above the beach. Turn into the parking area and wait. Now please repeat the instructions back to me." Harney held out his notes so that Hugh could read from them.

"That is correct. Is your cell phone turned on?"

"It is," said Hugh.

Louis hung up. He dialed the number of Hugh's cell phone. "Keep this phone on," said Louis. "I will call you on it when you are there, which should be about forty-five minutes from now." Louis hung up.

Hugh's two limousines followed Louis's directions. Coburn drove the first car. Harney sat beside him, and Hugh sat alone in the back. "He's taking us to the beach, sir," said Harney, "because he wants us in the open so that he can see who we are, how many, and so on. It's likely he's not even there. Someone else will be watching. We'll probably be directed somewhere else from there. He wants to lead us around a little to unsettle us and throw us off."

Hugh hardly heard what Harney was saying. He watched the stone walls glide past, the strange, windswept landscape of flat fields and villages. There were not many trees, but those there were were short and permanently twisted and bent by the wind.

As Louis had promised, after forty-five minutes they reached the sandy parking area above the beach. There were no other cars. The parking area was surrounded by a rippling sea of grass as far as they could see to the north and south and down the face of the dunes to the beach below. You could see a few houses far to the north of the parking area, but Harney estimated they wcrc at least half a mile away.

The beach itself was enormous. It stretched into the far distance before disappearing into a silver haze. The great expanse of pale sand was interrupted only occasionally by the rounded shapes of ruined concrete bunkers which, from this vantage point, looked small and insubstantial. "The Germans built those," said Hugh, more to himself than to anyone else. "Against the invasion. It didn't make any difference. They were in the wrong place."

Looking out onto the beach beyond the bunkers all they saw was sand. It seemed such a great distance to the water's edge that you could not tell which was further, the ocean or the sky. On the horizon they could barely make out the tiny sails of pleasure boats, and the only sound to be heard was the wind blowing through the grass.

"Son of a bitch," said Coburn. "What are *they* doing here?" He had waded into the grass and was looking at the beach below. Harney joined him and saw that French special forces had set up two machine gun emplacements halfway down the dunes. At the same time, a half dozen of their men were trotting out toward the German bunker in front of them.

"Don't worry, Coburn," said Harney. "They're still on our side."

"They're here to keep us honest," said Hugh. At that moment his telephone rang.

"Yes?" he said. "Where? . . . All right." He hung up the phone. "We're to take one car, drive down the dune road"—he looked around—"right there, then drive out onto the beach toward the water's edge and park next to another car." Everyone looked up and down the beach, but there was no car to be seen. "He said we'd see him once we were on the beach." With Harney's assistance Hugh got back into the limousine. Harney got in front and Coburn drove.

As they started slowly down the sand track, Harney spoke into his microphone. "Everyone ready? Fire team one? . . . two? . . . three? Here we go then. Deploy." As the car descended, Harney could see his snipers fanning out along the top of the dunes. They carried boxes of ammunition and long-barreled weapons with telescopic sights. Harney recited instructions about rules of engagement, fields of fire, and particular signals they might need. He listened for their acknowledgments.

Hugh gazed out the window. He was not even thinking about Louis. He only marveled at the magnificent grandeur of this beach. He had never liked beaches. The sand was unpleasant and inconvenient. It got into everything. But this beach was different. He could see how you might love this beach. If Hugh had known more about it, he might have felt differently.

XXII

Along most coastlines of the world the tides rise and fall by one or two meters, gently marking the moon's gravitational pull. But there are a few spots around the planet where, owing to a confluence of deep ocean currents, a favorable rotation of the earth, and other geographical peculiarities, the tides can run to fifteen meters and more, and where they push and pull the water with such force and speed that the event, even for those who have watched it, defies imagination.

As the tide rushes out at the Bay of Fundy in Nova Scotia, which measures the world's highest tides—above sixteen meters—harbors are left empty and vast tracts of the ocean floor are laid bare. After approximately six and a half hours of rushing out, the tide turns. It moves back in with equal speed: up to eight knots (four meters a second), and the volume and the force of the moving water in some places equals that of all the rivers of the world combined.

Mont-Saint-Michel, the much visited citadel on the northern coast of Brittany, has a very different geography, but again the tides—the largest in Europe—are enormous. They can be nearly fifteen meters high. And here too a vast expanse of the ocean bottom is laid bare when the tide is out. Where there was water a few hours earlier, there are sand and mudflats extending fifteen kilometers out from shore. Because it is such a beguiling and apparently benign landscape, tourists are occasionally tempted, despite notices and warnings, to wander out onto the flats. They do so at their peril. Some drown in the returning water or in quicksand, which is in a different place after every tide. Or the fog arrives suddenly and, thinking they are headed for shore, they walk to the water.

The beach by Pen'noch where Louis and Hugh were set to meet is of course much less known than Mont-Saint-Michel, but its tides are comparable and they are no less treacherous. They run nearly as high, and the beach is vast and flat to the same deceptive effect. The low tide retreats far from shore. And when it returns, the return is sudden and rapid. Emile Zola once visited the beach at Pen'noch and wrote in a letter of the tide coming in *"à la vitesse d'un cheval au galop"*—at the speed of a galloping horse.

The locals know enough to avoid the tides by Pen'noch. And nowadays there are tide tables and notices posted in every hotel, in shops, in post offices, and on harbor bulletin boards so that visiting boaters may tie up properly and not later find their boats dangling from their moorings. There are signs at every point of beach access to warn of the dangers—the tides, the quicksand, and the fog—so that prudent walkers can travel safely across the beach. Except that Louis had removed the signs from around the parking area where Hugh and his entourage had just arrived.

The sand on the track down the dune was smooth going. The limousine rocked gently as they drove. At the bottom Coburn steered the car onto the beach and headed west. The sand was hard packed here too and gave only slightly under the tires. You could hear it splattering up inside the wheel wells. They drove easily and slowly away from the dunes and toward the water. The French forces who had taken up positions in front of one of the German bunkers watched them pass. The car continued slowly out toward the horizon.

Suddenly a small car appeared from behind a bunker down the beach and began driving on a course parallel to theirs. It drove at the same speed they were driving. It did not try to converge with their course, but continued straight ahead. After a while the car stopped. They had traveled far enough that the bunkers were but small dots on the horizon behind them.

"He's out of range of the snipers," said Harney. "And he can see anyone coming for miles. Not stupid." Coburn swung the limousine in a wide arc and drove toward the parked vehicle. As they approached he slowed down. He could see Louis in the driver's seat. No one else appeared to be in the car.

"It looks like he's alone," said Coburn.

"I doubt it," said Harney. "The car could be booby-trapped. Or someone could be in back. He'd be nuts to be alone."

"He's alone," said Hugh. And at that moment Louis got out of the car and walked toward them. He stood alone and exposed, twenty meters from any cover.

"He's nuts," said Harney. Neither Hugh nor Coburn said anything.

Louis stood and waited. The salt air filled his nostrils. The wind riffled through his hair. The sun hung pale to the south, and Louis turned to face it, all but ignoring the three men. He watched the sailboats darting gaily back and forth in the distance. He even closed his eyes for a moment while he waited for Hugh and his companions to assure themselves that it was safe to get out of their car.

Louis turned as three doors on the limousine opened at the same time. He watched the two younger men step out first. The front passenger stepped to the rear door and reached down to help Hugh. Hugh put his feet down on the sand and, with the passenger's help and by holding on to the door of the car, pulled himself upright. He steadied himself for a moment. Then all three men began walking toward Louis.

Louis did not know the passenger, but he recognized Coburn. He was not entirely surprised to see him. The three men moved slowly. The sand gave slightly under their feet, and Hugh held Harney's arm for support. They stopped when they were directly in front of Louis. Louis and the three men looked at one another in silence for a long moment.

"You've brought us a long distance, Louis," said Hugh finally. "You've caused a lot of trouble, and you've promised a great deal. I hope you intend to keep your promises."

"I promised to reveal everything I know about the inner workings of al Qaeda," said Louis. "Here is what I have." As he reached inside his jacket, both Harney and Coburn moved their hands to their jackets. Louis stopped and pulled his jacket open with two fingers to show that he was reaching for a piece of paper. The two men lowered their hands but kept their eyes on his hands. Louis withdrew the paper slowly and held it toward Hugh.

Hugh took the sheet of paper and looked at it. He turned it over. "There's nothing on this paper," he said, holding it toward Harney. "There's nothing on it," he said again. He sounded incredulous, then indignant. "It's blank. It was a trick to get us out here." He held the paper toward Coburn so that Coburn could see for himself the extent of Louis's treachery.

Hugh lifted his hand with the paper in it and after a moment threw the paper into the wind. The paper tumbled swiftly across the sand, turning end over end, growing smaller and smaller until it was out of sight.

"You knew, of course," said Louis finally, "that there wouldn't be anything on that paper. You knew that, Hugh. You know better than anyone that I have nothing to do with al Qaeda. You fabricated my terrorist history as a way of doing away with me. I simply made use of your fabrication to get you out here. Don't you feel even some slight obligation to explain to these men how you used and deceived them? Before we finish our business."

Harney's eyes narrowed, and he looked hard at Louis for a long second. Then he said to Coburn, "You hold him while I get Secretary Bowes back to shore."

Coburn was already reaching into his jacket, but Louis was faster. He pulled a large pistol—Coburn's pistol—from the back of his pants and pointed it at Coburn. "Leave it," said Louis. But Coburn continued drawing his pistol. Louis waited until he saw it, then he shot Coburn just below the left shoulder. Coburn was dead instantly. The impact of the bullet turned him around and he fell facedown, his eyes wide open, his mouth full of sand.

Harney and Hugh stood transfixed. "Into my car," Louis said. After a moment's hesitation the three men moved as one toward the little car. "Not you," he said to Harney when they got there. He patted Harney down and removed one pistol from inside his jacket and another from his calf. He removed Harney's earphone and microphone. "Stand right there," said Louis, "and keep your hands behind your head and your back to me. If you so much as look around, I will shoot you." Harney stood facing the sea, his fingers locked behind his neck, his elbows stretching up. Louis patted down Hugh, but he had no weapons.

Hugh got into the passenger's seat of Louis's car as Louis instructed, and Louis got in on the driver's side. From the dunes the sharpshooters with their powerful scopes could probably just see the car but not who was in it or where they sat. They would not have heard the shot at that distance, but they could probably make out Harney standing outside and Coburn lying in the sand. Now that Coburn was down and something had happened, the French and American troops would be advancing across the sand. Helicopters would be arriving soon.

"Now what?" said Hugh.

"A short wait," said Louis.

"For what?"

Louis did not answer. The two men sat in silence.

"You're finished, you know," said Hugh.

Louis looked at Hugh. "I know," he said. "And you're finished too."

"You're going to kill me?" said Hugh.

"Not exactly," said Louis. He was silent for a while longer. Then he cocked his head to one side and looked to the west. The sailboats were still zipping back and forth, their sails snapping and billowing in the wind. The sloop with the red sails looked like one of Jean Pierre's.

"Listen," said Louis. "Roll the window down and listen." Hugh looked puzzled, but he did as he was told. He heard a roaring sound. Harney too was leaning forward, listening and looking, trying to see what was making that noise.

"That will be the helicopters," said Hugh.

"Listen again," said Louis. Hugh cocked his head to the side. "It's the tide," said Louis.

Hugh still refused to understand. "Start the car," he ordered.

"We're staying," said Louis. Then they saw the water coming toward them, urgently pushed by lapping waves, advancing second by second, taking steady, relentless bites out of the sand. It was in front of them. It inched up the low rise on which the car sat. Then it was under them. Then it was past them, rushing toward the shore. Harney dropped his arms to his sides. He turned to face them, but Louis did not shoot him.

"Please," Harney said. "You can't do this. It's murder. Let him go. Let me save him. Don't you realize what you're doing, *who* this is?"

"Oh, yes," said Louis. "I know who this is. And if you make it back to Washington, you will know too. There's a large packet of evidence on its way there. *Everyone* will know who this is." Hugh could only stare in disbelief at the water that was everywhere.

In the end, of course, Louis was wrong. After all, what good purpose would have been served by revealing Hugh Bowes's crimes to the general public? It would only have undermined the faith of the American people in their government. Instead, Hugh's death would be announced as a tragic accident, and he would be celebrated as an American hero.

It is not entirely accurate to say that the sand here is flat or that it rises toward the shore. The sand is *generally* flat and it *generally* rises. But in the three or more kilometers Harney had to cover if he was going to reach the dunes, the surface undulated. True, the undulations were scarcely noticeable. It was a matter of centimeters here and there. But the water found the undulations like a swift animal instinctively seeking out the low ground. Harney stood on slightly elevated, still dry sand, while the limousine a short distance away stood in water up to its hubcaps. Harney could look toward the shore and see where the water was pooling, where it was forming rivulets and pushing ahead, and where the water had not yet arrived. But even as he watched, the nearest islands of sand collapsed and disappeared into the rising tide.

Harney started running. He lost his shoes almost immediately in a patch of soft sand that sucked first one then the other from his feet. But he was a strong and determined runner. He tried to read the water, to see where the slightly shallower water might be, and at first he was successful. He lifted his legs, getting his feet out of the water in order to run faster. The tide was with him, pushing at the back of his legs, which gave him courage.

Harney shed his jacket and his vest and his holster as he ran. For a while he kept pace with the tide. It did not seem to be getting ahead of him. Then he suddenly found himself in a place where the sand dipped slightly downward. It was only a matter of fifteen centimeters, six inches maybe, but the water was to his knees. Then it got deeper still.

Harney was not running now. He had to fight to move forward, swinging his arms and hurling his body forward. His breath came in gasps. He did not think he could go on, but he kept on anyway. Then he was suddenly in shallower water again, and he ran again for all he was worth. Then it sloped downward again. And so it went for what seemed an eternity. The closer he got to the dunes, the more the sand undulated. He reached a deeper pool. The water was roaring and swirling about.

When Harney was finally met by the French special forces, he was half swimming and half wading. The soldiers caught him up in their arms, and the water surged around them as they pulled him to shore, where he collapsed. They had called for amphibious vehicles, but no one had been prepared for this and so they were still waiting.

After watching the water, transfixed, for he did not know how long, Hugh Bowes opened the car door. Harney was gone. The limousine off a slight distance was sitting at an odd angle, the water halfway up its side. Hugh could see that Louis was not going to stop him. He stepped out into the water. He closed the door. The water was not very deep where he stood, but he was weak and the force and movement of it knocked his feet from under him. He fell, cracking his head on the car's fender and landing on his back. He lay there stunned for a moment, then rolled onto his side with difficulty and got to his hands and knees. He stood up as best he could and staggered about, trying to find his footing. "The helicopters!" he shouted, but there were no helicopters.

He took a few hesitant steps toward the distant shore and fell again, pulled over again by the currents and the unreliable bottom. He stood up again. He fell again and stood up again, fell and stood up. After Hugh had fallen a few more times, Louis could see that, although he was moving toward shore, he was also moving into deeper water. Each time he fell, he remained down longer before he got up again. Now his face went into the water, and he came up gasping and spitting. The water was too deep where he found himself for him to rest on his hands and knees, and he splashed and flailed about until he somehow managed to stand. Louis could see that Hugh was exhausted.

Louis could not hear Hugh's sobs above the roar of the water, but he could see his mouth opening and closing, his lips peeled back from his teeth, his wide-open eyes looking about wildly as he struggled to keep his head out of the rising tide, to stand against the powerful surge. Louis had imagined that he could watch Hugh die without feeling either sorrow or guilt, but in the moment that Coburn had pitched forward onto the sand, everything had changed. Now he saw what he had engineered reflected in Hugh's desperate fight to remain alive, in the terror on his face.

Louis tried to distract himself so the inevitable would come more quickly. *If the water rises ten meters in six hours, that's, let's see: one and a half meters an hour. That's five feet an hour. That's a foot every twelve minutes. The water's been here maybe fifteen minutes?* Louis looked at his watch. *Maybe twenty. In less than half an hour the car will be gone. I will be gone. It will be over.* In fact, the water was rising faster than that. But even twenty minutes was a long time to die this way.

The sea was coming into the car through the floorboards. Louis felt the force of the tide pushing against the car, rocking it. He felt the car list to the left as the wheels sank into the softening sand. He remembered standing on the beach once at the water's edge—where had it been? Florida?—and letting the water cut the sand out from under his bare feet. That was long ago. How old had he been? Twelve maybe. He had tottered unsteadily until he had fallen over, laughing. Red and white umbrellas were flapping along the beach. A skywriter was spelling out something. N . . . I . . . V . . .

When Louis tried to get out of the car he could not open his door. The water swept against it, holding it closed. When he finally got the door open, the water pulled it open the rest of the way, nearly tearing it from its hinges. The water rushed through the car, pushed against his chest, and held him pressed in his seat. Louis managed to get out but was almost immediately swept off his feet. He did not see Hugh. *Where is Hugh?*

The intention to kill another human is a terrible thing, however it comes about, and for whatever reasons. When a victim protects himself by killing his assailant, in effect, the two trade places: the victim becomes the killer and the killer becomes the victim. Louis finally saw Hugh and for a moment wanted to go help him. But go how? And help him how?

How did Hugh keep standing? And why? Louis held himself upright against the car door and watched Hugh flounder about. Hugh fell over once more, and this time he did not stand up. He was gone.

Why don't the helicopters come? But they did not come. They never came. Maybe there were no helicopters. Louis took a step away from the car and suddenly he was in deep water. There was no ground beneath him. He grabbed at the car door and pulled himself back to the car.

Louis had of course known all along that he would go to prison if he were not shot down there on the beach and if he survived the tide. Now he had taken two lives. *It has come to this,* he thought. He released his grip on the car door once again. *It has to end here. It wasn't a struggle between good and evil. It never was. It was a struggle between manipulation and treachery.* Louis felt himself being pulled away from the car, swept along wherever the ocean wanted to carry him. He could still see the top of his car, although the Mercedes was gone. He tried to stand, but he could not get his feet down, and when he finally did, there was no bottom. He was in deep water. *Hugh is gone. Coburn is gone. The water is cold.*

Soon Louis did not feel the cold anymore. He did not struggle. The weight of his clothes pulled him down. Everything was silent. The water filled his mouth and burned his nose and throat. The salt burned his eyes. He tried to keep them open, but the darkness of the water frightened him, as though he were peering into eternity. It hurt his soul, so he closed his eyes. *Sophistry. Self-serving sophistry.*

XXIII

Louis was lying on his back on the hard bottom of a small boat. The waves slapping the sides of the boat banged in his head. He opened his eyes and saw the rigging clattering unbearably against the wooden mast above him. The half-furled red spinnaker flapped in the wind. The boat shuddered and the engine roared. The boat's maker, Jean Pierre Lamarche, peered down into his face. "He is coming to," said Jean Pierre.

"Is Hugh gone?" said Louis.

"You crazy bastard," said Renard. Louis turned his head slightly. The policeman sat in the stern. His hair was wet, and he was wrapped in a blanket. Louis was wrapped in a blanket too, and his nose and throat burned. The diesel fumes made him sick to his stomach, and Jean Pierre held his head while he retched and vomited over the side.

They made for the harbor at Pen'noch. The dock where they tied up was filled with French police and special forces, but the Americans were nowhere to be seen. When Louis was loaded into an ambulance, a police guard got in with him.

A guard remained with him the entire time he was in the hospital. After three days he was transferred to a prison hospital. Louis was signed in and deposited in a ward with green walls and high, barred windows. He lay in one of five narrow beds. The occupants of the other four beds watched him nervously. After all, he was the only murderer among them.

When Louis had recovered his health sufficiently, he was transferred to the regular prison population to await trial. This prison was a bleak concrete compound of flat buildings with slits for windows, surrounded by high fences topped with razor wire. Louis shared a cell with another murderer. The man, who had been in prison for twenty years for strangling his wife, peered at Louis through thick glasses. "I am André," he said. "You are welcome to read my books."

Louis was visited in prison by Mâitre Jean François Cohen, a criminal lawyer he had engaged for his defense. Maître Cohen sat across a gray steel table and shuffled through numerous files. He showed Louis various papers, asking if this were his signature or whether he had been somewhere on that particular date.

"I doubt that the case will ever come to trial," said Maître Cohen. "The matter is extremely delicate. For the French and for the Americans. And while your documentation is not entirely unambiguous, it raises enough questions to be compelling and, I might add, quite damning toward the Americans. Especially the Americans. No one will be very eager to have you talking to the press about the things you have witnessed."

"I have no intention of talking to the press," said Louis.

"That," said Maître Cohen, looking at Louis sternly and raising his index finger in admonition, "is something you should absolutely keep to yourself."

Louis was allowed visitors once a week. Michael and Jennifer often came together, and sometimes they brought Zaharia with them. One day Michael announced that he was going home. "I think it is safe," he said. "What do you think?"

"I'm sure it's fine," said Louis. "You should go home, Michael. Be with Rosita. Get on with your lives. You've been away far too long. Jennifer, you should go home too."

"I know I should," said Jennifer. She did not tell him that she was reluctant to leave. She flew home with Michael. And Sarah and Rosita were waiting for them at the airport, where they all had a tearful reunion.

Zaharia was required to remain in France a while longer. He stayed with the Renards in Saint Leon until the investigation into the deaths of the American citizens Randall Sziemanski, also known as Lou Coburn, and Huge Bowes was completed. Then he was sent home to Algeria to live with his grandmother, Camille Lefort.

Despite the fact that neither body was ever recovered, despite the substantial dossier of evidence against the two deceased, and contrary to the assurances of Maître Cohen, the United States Department of Justice petitioned France to extradite Louis Morgon to the United States to stand trial for murder. An American assistant attorney general had taken a strong interest in the case and saw the stern prosecution of Louis Morgon as an effective deterrent in the war on terror.

The French government had no intention of extraditing Louis, particularly while they had several investigations of their own going on. The boy Zaharia, for instance, had been able to identify one of the Marseille policemen he had seen murder his father. In exchange for leniency, the policeman implicated the other men involved, other policemen, but also civilians who turned out not to be terrorists at all but street thugs who had been, by every indication, in the employ of some other nation's clandestine service. The American CIA was strongly suspected.

Pénichon's investigation of Renard's activities, while it exposed highly irregular and unauthorized behavior on Renard's part, turned up nothing of a criminal nature. Renard received a letter of reprimand and a stern warning to confine his attentions to village affairs. Pénichon also investigated Louis's visit to Algeria and concluded that the trip had apparently been made to discover connections between the burglar Pierre Lefort and the deceased Hugh Bowes. As far as Pénichon was able to determine, it had never been Morgon's plan to conduct or participate in any terroristic activities. In the end, Renard had to admit that Pénichon was a far more competent investigator than he would have expected.

The evidence surrounding Hugh Bowes's malfeasance and the terroristic kidnapping of Louis's daughter by Sziemanski was more than sufficient to persuade the French investigators that the murder of the two Americans had been committed in self-defense. "It is better, then," declared the presiding justice minister, "better for *everyone* concerned, including the Americans, that the case be closed."

The Americans did not like being told by the French whom they should and should not prosecute, but after some discussion in Washington about the Louis Morgon case, it was quickly seen to be, in the larger scheme of things, not only a fairly insignificant case, but also one with sufficiently inconvenient facts that it should be allowed to disappear into the government's secret archives as quickly as possible. In fact, by the time this decision was reached, the president and his cabinet had already turned their attention to other, more urgent and more important matters.

A burial ceremony with full military honors was held for Hugh Bowes, the former secretary of state, at Arlington National Cemetery. An empty casket was lowered into the ground while dignitaries from around the world stood with bowed heads. The grave, on a hillside just to the north of the Kennedy graves, was marked by a simple white stone with Hugh's name and dates, along with the dates of his tenure as secretary of state, and the motto, *his* motto: *To Serve Is Everything*.

The president declared a national day of mourning and delivered a stirring eulogy during the memorial service at the National Cathedral. "Hugh Bowes was a force for light and good in the world," he said. "Long after he had left office, he remained a tireless worker for peace and justice. We will not soon see his like again." The flags on all official buildings were lowered to half-staff.

In early February, on the day marking the end of Louis's third month in prison, he was escorted to the warden's office. "Monsieur Morgon," said the warden with great ceremony, as though Louis were being awarded an honorary university degree, "you are free to go."

As Louis stepped from the front gate of the prison with a small package of his belongings, Renard dropped his cigarette to the ground and crushed it beneath his foot. The men shook hands solemnly, and Renard took the package and carried it to the car. As they drove, Louis watched in wonderment as the landscape passed by in its infinite variety. The birds scattered and darted in random patterns. Every tree was surprising in some way. None looked like the one before it or the next one down the road. No vista resembled any other. "I had already forgotten," he said, "how abundant and endless and different things are. The worst thing about prison is how quickly everything becomes the same."

At home Louis repaired the damaged door once again. He

cleaned the house and put everything back in order, even better order than it had been in before. He took a long time to alphabetize all his books by author, something he had never done before. When that was finished, he turned his attention to the ruined garden and the neglected roses. He pulled up the previous year's vines and weeds and turned the soil. He used old egg cartons in which to start seeds in his kitchen window—lettuce, beets, tomatoes, basil—and checked each morning to see whether anything had sprouted. Once the tiny, tender plants began to push their way up through the dark soil, he nursed them as though his life depended on it. And in some sense perhaps it did.

One day his friend Jean Pierre Lamarche arrived from Pen'noch for a visit. The two men took walks through the countryside and sat together on Louis's terrace. But, in spite of their affection for one another, they could not find much to say to bridge the awkwardness between them. Jean Pierre was friends with Louis Bertrand, but he did not quite know Louis Morgon. Louis apologized for his deception, as he had apologized to Samad earlier, and Jean Pierre waved off his apology as Samad had. It was not betrayal Jean Pierre felt, so much as confusion. It would sort itself out, he said.

Even Louis and Renard's visits were awkward. They spoke of ordinary things, as they always had, of their children, of food, of police work. But there were certain things they wanted to talk about that they did not. Louis seemed to the policeman to be living somewhere else. His melancholy had turned to sorrow, which seemed a far different and more difficult and serious thing.

Louis had always liked to talk about his painting, which had always annoyed the policeman, since he did not understand the first thing about it and so could only listen in dumb silence. Now, however, for the sake of conversation and friendship

Renard ventured to ask, "So what are you painting? What are you working on?" Louis waved aside his inquiry. "I'm not painting," he said, and Renard feared it might be true.

Jennifer called from Virginia. She described how the clinic had been neglected during her absence and had fallen on hard times. "Nobody cared about it as much as I did," she said, "or knew how to keep it going. No one knew how to raise money. No one kept after the volunteers—the doctors and nurses. We just had to close our doors." She paused. "But I got it started once, and I can do it again," she said.

"I know you can, Jenny," said Louis. "I'm sure you can, and it's worth doing. It's important. It was a great thing, and it will be again," he said. Maybe if she could restart the clinic, he could restart . . . what?

"What about you, Dad?" she said.

"Me? I don't know. I'm sorting things out."

Michael called too. "I might try to show some of my drawings," said Michael. "Like you suggested."

"They're good drawings, Michael. You should show them."

"Maybe I will."

"How is Rosita?" said Louis.

"She moved out. My being away for so long. We're talking."

"That's good. That's important. Keep talking."

"But, how are you, Dad?"

Michael sent Louis a drawing he had made on assignment for a science magazine of a microscopic sea creature. The creature was blue and had six legs and numerous toes. It was meticulously rendered in India ink and watercolor and had a compelling sense of reality about it. "This thing actually exists," said Michael. "I worked from slides." Louis framed the drawing and hung it on the wall just inside the front door.

Louis had always cherished his solitude, but lately it had turned into loneliness. And one blustery day when he felt particularly alone, he picked up the phone and dialed Sarah's number without quite knowing what he was doing. He wanted to apologize, of course, for the trouble he had caused, and to learn how she had fared throughout the entire ordeal. But he also had other reasons that he could not quite fathom. He listened to the phone ring without having any sense of what he would say if she answered.

Sarah was polite but not especially friendly. She appreciated his concern, she said. She told him briefly how she had left Washington, as he had suggested, but had only gone as far as Pittsburgh. "I stayed with my sister for a while. They could have found me if they had wanted to," she said. "Anyway, it's over. When I think of it, it seems like a terrible nightmare." Her voice softened then. "I can't imagine how it must have been for you."

"Like a terrible nightmare," said Louis. He paused for a long time. "It was awful," he said finally. "In a way it still is."

"But now it's over," said Sarah.

"Yes," said Louis. "You know? I think it is." It sounded to Sarah as though this were the first time he had allowed himself to think such a thing.

"Jenny told me that your friend died. Solesme? Was that her name? I'm sorry to hear that."

"Thank you," said Louis. He felt the conversation drifting away from him, but Sarah was not quite ready for it to end.

"How is that young boy," she said, "the one Jenny told me about? Jenny seems very fond of him."

"Zaharia," said Louis. "Yes. I think he and Jenny developed quite an attachment. I don't know how he's doing. I haven't heard anything. After all the interviews and depositions, he was sent back to Algeria to live with his grandmother. I hope he is all right . . ." Then after a moment: "I'm sure he's all right. He is . . . a remarkable boy."

"That's what Jenny said."

"His father was a brute," said Louis, suddenly wanting to talk. "At least as far as I could tell. He was a thief and a thug. I don't know much about the mother except that she was out of the picture. Anyway, the boy was poor. He hadn't spent much time in school and had very little contact with the outside world, as far as I could tell. Then, without warning, he was torn from his home in the Algerian desert and brought to France. He saw his father killed by the police—"

"My god," said Sarah.

"I know," said Louis. "It really is unimaginable. Then he found his way across the entire country by himself. And finally . . . he was caught right in the middle of everything. Thanks to me." Louis lapsed into silence again.

Sarah waited. Just when she thought he would not say anything more, he said, "And yet he's this positive kid, sweet and trusting and generous. How can that be? How does that even *happen*?"

"Do you think you'll see him again?" Sarah said.

Louis hesitated. "I don't know. If he comes to France. Someday, maybe. I would like to."

"Why don't you go see him?" she said.

"I couldn't."

"Why not? Go to Algeria. You always said how much you loved Algeria."

"I can't do that. You don't understand. His grandmother blames me for her son's death. I would have to at least, I don't know . . . I can't do that . . ."

The jonquils had sent up their first flower stalks, but they looked as though they regretted having done so. Louis was raking the leaves away from the flower beds by the front door so that the sun could warm them better. He heard someone coming up the drive and turned to see the little yellow mail truck cresting the hill. Ghislaine Bidon cranked down the window and handed him his mail.

Louis propped the rake under his arm and leafed through the brochures and envelopes while she turned around and disappeared back down the hill. There was an envelope bearing an Algerian stamp and addressed, in careful block letters, to Monsieur Louis Morgon. Louis tucked the other mail into his pocket and tore open the envelope.

Cher Monsieur Morgon,

I hope you are very well. I am living with my grandmother. I am doing very well. I am going to school, and I am learning many things. I am learning to speak and write French correctly. My grandmother says I must learn French. She is right. This is so I can return to France one day. When I go, I want to visit you. And also Monsieur and Madame Renard. Tell them hello for me.

How is Jennifer? I hope she is well. And I hope Michael is well too. Are they back in the United States? I found Washington on the map. I will also visit them there one day. Would you please send me Jennifer's address, so I can write to her? Thank you.

Do you plan to visit Algeria someday soon? If you do, I hope you will come see me. I would like that very much.

With sincerest respect and regards, your friend,
Zaharia Lefort

Louis carried the letter into the house, laid it on the table, and read it again. He returned to the yard and worked on the leaves some more, but after a while he laid the rake aside and went inside. He found his phone diary and dialed the telephone.

"Hello?" he said. "Is this the Hôtel dc Boufa? . . . May I speak with Samad al Nhouri? . . . Tell him it is Louis Morgon.

"Samad, my friend, it is Louis Morgon . . . In France . . . Yes, it is a very good connection. As though you were next door . . . I am fine, thank you, and I hope you are well? . . . I am glad to hear it. And Moamar and the rest of your family? . . . That is very good . . . Yes, they are fine too; I spoke to them only a few days ago.

"Yes, it did . . . No, it did not turn out as I had hoped it would. But . . . I am fine, and it is over . . . Yes, it is over. Thank you. And thank you and Moamar for everything you did to help me. I will always be grateful to you both.

"Yes, it makes an amazing story for your collection. I will tell you everything when I see you . . . Yes, Samad, I am calling to reserve a room at the Boufa, if . . . Yes . . . number six, if it is available . . ."